THE FRIDAY NIGHT CLUB

THE
FRIDAY NIGHT CLUB

Sofia Lundberg

Alyson Richman

M.J. Rose

BERKLEY
NEW YORK

BERKLEY
An imprint of Penguin Random House LLC
penguinrandomhouse.com

Copyright © 2023 by Sofia Lundberg, Alyson Richman, and M.J. Rose
Readers Guide copyright © 2023 by Penguin Random House LLC
Penguin Random House supports copyright. Copyright fuels creativity, encourages
diverse voices, promotes free speech, and creates a vibrant culture. Thank you for
buying an authorized edition of this book and for complying with copyright laws by
not reproducing, scanning, or distributing any part of it in any form without
permission. You are supporting writers and allowing Penguin Random House to
continue to publish books for every reader.

BERKLEY and the BERKLEY & B colophon are registered trademarks of
Penguin Random House LLC.

Library of Congress Cataloging-in-Publication Data

Names: Lundberg, Sofia, 1974- author. | Richman, Alyson, author. |
Rose, M.J., 1953- author.
Title: The Friday Night Club / Sofia Lundberg, Alyson Richman, M.J. Rose.
Description: First edition. | New York : Berkley, 2023.
Identifiers: LCCN 2022037546 (print) | LCCN 2022037547 (ebook) |
ISBN 9780593200490 (trade paperback) | ISBN 9780593200506 (ebook)
Subjects: LCSH: Klint, Hilma af, 1862-1944—Fiction. | Women
painters—Sweden—Fiction. | Art museum curators—Fiction. |
Art—Exhibitions—Fiction. | LCGFT: Biographical fiction. | Novels.
Classification: LCC PT9877.22.U535 F75 2023 (print) |
LCC PT9877.22.U535 (ebook) | DDC 839.73/8—dc23/eng/20220920
LC record available at https://lccn.loc.gov/2022037546
LC ebook record available at https://lccn.loc.gov/2022037547

First Edition: May 2023

Printed in the United States of America
1st Printing

Book design by Kristin del Rosario
Title page art: Abstract shapes © Aestro Studio / Shutterstock.com

To all the artists of today and yesterday
who have persevered . . .

Life is a farce if a person does not serve truth.

—HILMA AF KLINT

THE FRIDAY NIGHT CLUB

Anna lifted the last letter to the flame and watched as the delicate paper curled and disintegrated, the words evaporating into ash. She had spent the past several hours reading each of the letters, remembering every detail, every moment, that had been written. As the ebb and flow of their correspondence pulled her back in time, she felt the weight of her now old body fall away and the aches and pains of age disappear as her heart was once again filled with the memories of her youth with Hilma.

Even with their hair white and their skin feathered with lines, the two maintained the distinct auras they had since they were young. Hilma exuded a palpable physical strength, while Anna appeared more ethereal, like breath or water—a color you couldn't quite detect but could still feel around you. Years of fragile health and bouts with asthma had made her refrain from any form of physical exertion, but her mind and spirit were as determined as her friend's; they just worked in a different way.

Only that afternoon, Hilma had instructed Anna to burn their old letters, while she continued to pack up her paintings and place into the wooden boxes all her sketchbooks and notebooks from the meetings from the Friday Night Club decades before.

The place in Munsö was large enough to store everything, just to Hilma's liking. Anna had built the structure on land granted to her by a family with close ties to her own, thus ensuring her friend had the space and stability to paint without worry. Hilma had crafted a studio with high ceilings and tall windows, creating an artistic vault filled with towering canvases saturated with bright constellations of halos and stars. It was almost as though her friend had climbed a ladder to the sky and pulled down all of the mysteries perched above, painting them with a kaleidoscope of colors so others could have a keyhole to gaze into the heavens.

The property near Lake Mälaren had always been a refuge for both Hilma and Anna. Windswept in the autumn as the leaves tumbled from the birch and oak trees, the air fragrant with pine needles and juniper berries. In the summer, the countryside became alight with meadows of red poppies, bluebells, and wild daisies. They both had always drawn sustenance from nature, the vicissitudes of the seasons, and a landscape's ability to magically transform from verdant green to snowy white.

The month before, Anna had made a personal vow to savor as much beauty outside as she could. Old age had settled firmly in her bones, and she was unsure how many journeys to the island remained for her. The midsummer light afforded little darkness, and Hilma, neglecting to monitor the time on the grandfather clock, typically worked past midnight, as only then did the sky grow dim. So every morning, Anna set out for an early walk as her friend slept in for a few short hours.

The island welcomed Anna as it stirred from its brief nocturnal slumber. The bees hummed in the morning glories, the butterflies took flight, and blackbirds and white gulls filled the breeze with song. As Anna approached the lake, she took off her sandals and left them behind in the grass. She then pulled her long skirt up to her knees and began to slowly wade into the water, rejoicing at the cold sensation on her skin. These daily rituals restored her and helped her to feel like a young girl again, despite her being trapped in a body that was now nearly seventy-four years old.

She had always loved the water, for it felt like a natural extension of her spirit. Perhaps that was why her friendship with Hilma had survived so long. If Anna was like water, her friend was fire. But she had learned to soften her friend's temper over time, often sacrificing her own feelings because, above all else, she wanted Hilma to always create.

The past few weeks with Hilma had been particularly intense and full of challenges. Hilma's focus had been all-consuming, and she had no time for lunch breaks or walks to search for strawberries, despite Anna's invitations.

The year before, as her seventieth birthday approached, Hilma had made the decision that all of her twelve hundred paintings and one hundred twenty-five notebooks would be sealed away for future generations, not to be opened until twenty years after her death. On their pages, those notebooks had detailed so much life, so many visions. They were written not only in Hilma's hand but also by the other women in the spiritual and artistic group she and Anna had joined nearly forty years earlier, which they affectionately referred to as "De Fem" or "The Five."

After they graduated from the Royal Academy of Fine Arts in Stockholm, Hilma and Anna spent several years pushing their artistic boundaries beyond simple landscape paintings and portraits. Their desire to reach for more than what their peers at school aspired to defined them. After all, their friendship had been founded on a mutual disdain for convention. Anna was fortunate her widowed mother never pushed her to marry, but rather encouraged her and her sister to pursue their own individual paths. And Hilma had been so strong-willed. No one, not even her high-ranking naval officer father, could sway her from what she believed to be her true calling: her art.

And how lucky the two of them felt when they joined forces with the others—Cornelia, Mathilda, and Sigrid. Like Hilma and Anna, these three women were brimming with curiosity and a desire to transcend the everyday norms of their existence.

For forty years, the women maintained their friendship, and it was still hard for Anna to believe that she and Hilma were the only surviving members of their special club, as Mathilda, Cornelia, and Sigrid were all now dead. Some days when the two of them opened the windows of the studio, the crisp lake air seemed to carry the spirit of one of the three. The pages in Hilma's journals would rustle, or a painting would occasionally tip over. Only the other day, a white dove had nested itself outside as Hilma labored, and Anna studied it intently. "I think Cornelia has come to visit us today," she announced before looking back at her friend, who was slowly and methodically packing things away. She never told Hilma when she felt Mathilda's presence. It was always when the sky turned cloudy and the mice scampered beneath the floorboards, an unwanted rhythm intruding upon their peace and quiet.

But this evening, it was only the two of them in the atelier. Hilma and she had nearly completed their final preparations. After she nailed the second-to-last crate shut, Hilma had looked up and stared at Anna, a smile slowly forming at her lips. Her white hair suddenly became gold in front of Anna's eyes, and the arctic blue eyes filled with life. Restored before her, like the black-and-white lines of a coloring book suddenly ablaze with color, her friend beamed with determination.

"I'm nearly done, Anna. Go back and finish with the letters, the diaries too."

Anna paused. "It's our whole lives, Hilma. It's not as easy as that." She looked down at her palms. Some of the ash had come off on her fingers, and part of her didn't want to ever remove those dark smudges.

"I will be judged by my work and nothing else," Hilma answered firmly.

There was a time that Anna might have been able to change her friend's mind, or at least start a dialogue and have the possibility of influence. But that period had long since vanished. There was no arguing with Hilma now. The past was behind them, and Anna recognized that she needed to align herself with Hilma's vision, imagining a future in which the crated paintings and notebooks would one day be able to speak for themselves.

Anna did as she was instructed. Hovering over the kindling, created from dry twigs she had collected from the garden, she took the last letter and read it slowly, but this time aloud. Articulating each word like a benediction she wanted to seal in her heart forever.

She lit the flame, letter upon letter disintegrating into a feather of smoke.

She then opened one of Hilma's leather-bound diaries, and a single photograph slid out. It was not one of just Anna and Hilma but of all five women together. Anna held it above the fire. The faces of her friends glowed as the paper softened and bent from the heat. She realized that this she would never be able to burn, despite Hilma's wishes. Instead, Anna slipped it inside her apron pocket, and then laid the remaining diaries on top of the burning embers.

After everything was reduced to ash, she bent down and scooped some of the dark powder into an envelope and took it to give to Hilma.

"Here," she uttered quietly. "Tuck it someplace safe so it can rest among all the other sacred things."

Hilma accepted the envelope and set it inside the last of the boxes. Anna turned away just as she heard the sound of the hammer striking the last nail on the crate.

They walked outside, exiting the studio together. Hilma shut the large doors and looped a chain through their handles, locking them shut, then extended an open palm to Anna.

"Come, my old friend." She beckoned, and Anna felt her long fingers pulled into Hilma's. The warmth of Hilma's skin moved through her body like much-needed medicine.

They walked quietly toward the steeple, two small figures shuttering the past behind them. Anna placed her free hand over her apron pocket, carrying the three others with her as she believed they rightfully deserved.

CHAPTER ONE

EBEN

Present Day
New York City

People say that a curator builds bridges between an artist and the public. As a bridge builder, I have always tried not to place my own limits on a show but rather to let the artist's oeuvre dictate. If that displays a lack of imagination on my part, I can accept it. I am a man who is all too aware of how dangerous an imagination can be. I am, though, fascinated by its power and have organized my life in such a way that I can study it. So, in retrospect, I shouldn't have been surprised when the strength of one particular artist's creativity disorganized my life and changed its trajectory completely.

It began in Stockholm, Sweden, more than two years ago on a snowy Friday night. Lost and very cold, I was cursing myself for venturing out of my hotel without checking the weather and taking a map. But it hadn't been snowing when I'd started, and I had planned to venture only across the street.

The Grand Hôtel, one of Europe's grande dame accommodations, was situated on the waterfront. Stockholm was often called the Venice of the North. At first, I'd stood on the esplanade, looking at the large chunks of ice floating downstream like irregular jigsaw-puzzle pieces, and then, suddenly adventurous, walked a bit farther. Having reached the Strömbron, I crossed the causeway and, on the other side, proceeded into Gamla Stan, the Old Town, originally built in the late 1200s.

Feeling like I'd stepped back in time, I wandered, charmed by the pastel-colored buildings and narrow cobblestoned streets. The snow began quickly and then became heavy. I knew I should head back, but I wasn't sure which way to go. As I came to the conclusion I had just made a big circle, I became aware of a woman heading toward me.

As she passed underneath a streetlamp, what I first noticed was the flash of hair the color of champagne. Next was the triangular-shaped face with its sharp nose and wide, almond-shaped eyes. Eyes that widened to almost impossible proportions upon her noticing me.

Blythe Larkin didn't try to hug me when she reached me. Or hold out her hand for a shake. When it struck me, in that confusing moment, that she wasn't even smiling, a wave of sadness crashed over me.

Earlier, at the opening reception of the conference, everyone had been talking about how it was particularly cold out even for Stockholm. But Blythe was wearing only a thin coat. It occurred to me that I should take off my heavier one and put it around her shoulders. Then I reminded myself that she wasn't someone I needed to take care of anymore. In fact, she had never needed taking care of.

I wasn't expecting to see her that night, but for years I had known it was possible I would run into her again. There are certain inevitabilities. The chance that two people close in age working in the same small field might at some point attend the same museum opening, gallery show, biennial, or symposium, is anything but a mystical alignment of the stars.

"Eben Elliot," Blythe said, treating my name like a whole thought.

"Aren't you cold?"

"A little." She laughed as she always had at my non sequiturs, and the sound threatened to send me reeling into memories. "I didn't know it was going to snow."

"Neither did I," I said.

"What are you doing here—" I started to ask, and then realized I knew the answer. "Of course, you must be here for the conference. Except I didn't see you today at the opening reception."

"I missed it. A delay at home."

Home? I didn't know if that was still London and found the thought disturbing.

"But now you're here." I sounded like an idiot, but in my defense, I hadn't seen her in eight years and was stymied.

"I am." She nodded. "I'm giving a talk, on the subject of my new book."

I hadn't read through the schedule. I wasn't even supposed to attend this symposium. "Yes, congratulations. You've already had two books published, haven't you?"

Why was I asking as if I didn't know? Both of her books were in the gift shop at the museum where I worked. Whenever I walked through, her name on the covers would leap out at me like neon.

"Where are you headed?" she asked, gesturing to the street.

"I was trying to get back to the hotel, but I came—"

"Came out without a map?" she interrupted with a knowing look.

It is annoying, endearing, and embarrassing to have an old lover remind you of how little you have changed.

"So it seems."

"You're staying at the conference hotel?"

I nodded.

"Me too. I was heading back. Come on." She pointed in the opposite direction to where I'd been about to turn.

I had a sudden flash of a giant Louise Bourgeois sculpture that had recently gone off at auction at Sotheby's. A bronze spider the size of a large living room. Ironic that Blythe, who was not even five foot three and quite slender, would remind me of a twelve-foot-high arachnid. It was because Blythe wove webs too. As sticky and silky as the ones spiders spun. How could such tiny creatures make traps so much larger and stronger than they themselves were?

We crossed a large square bordered by medieval buildings with a frosted fountain in its center. Falling snow cast the whole scene in cobalt.

"It looks a bit like a Eugène Fredrik Jansson painting."

When I didn't respond, she explained. "He was a late

nineteenth-century Swedish landscape painter. Probably best known for his nighttime land- and cityscapes dominated by shades of blue."

"I'm not as well educated as I should be about Swedish painters," I said, thinking I should spend some time rectifying that while I was here.

"So, what were you doing tonight? Just out walking?" she asked.

Clearly it was a question, but she asked it as if she knew the answer already. Which she probably did—something else about me that she remembered.

When I travel, I usually spend the first day and night walking. Partly to get the feel of the city I'm in. Partly to deal with jet lag. And partly propelled by curiosity about whether there is anywhere in this world that might feel like home.

My tiny corner of Manhattan, where I have always lived and now also work, is the only place I have ever felt truly comfortable. I'm not sure why. It could certainly be because I was born and raised there. Blood from my childhood scrapes had seeped into those sidewalks. I experienced my first kiss on our brownstone steps. My mother's memorial service was held at a temple only a few blocks away.

But it's also possible I can't envisage being comfortable anywhere else because of my truly impaired imagination. I've always envied artists and writers whose minds can take off on flights of fancy . . . Marc Chagall, René Magritte, Dalí . . . Gabriel García Márquez, Carlos Castaneda, Isabel Allende. . . . In fact, I've envied just about every goddamn writer of fiction.

Every painter, sculptor, and draftsman who can pick up their tool of choice and create a simulacrum of the world. I can't.

"I didn't see your name on the list of attendees," Blythe said as we exited the square and headed down Köpmangatan Street.

So she'd searched the registration roster for me?

"I wasn't scheduled to come. A colleague at the Guggenheim had a family emergency. I took her place."

The topic of the conference was diversity—a serious topic to all collectors, art historians, museum directors, and curators. There was no question that the art world had favored white men for centuries, and there was an effort underway to examine and rectify the practice. I had been glad Dr. Perlstein, my supervisor, had tapped me to attend in Audrey Titus's place. I had a personal connection to the topic. My mother had been a sculptor prior to her untimely death when I was two years old. Her work had been brash and brazen, and I, and several scholars I'd talked to, had always believed she would have received much more recognition despite her truncated life had she been a man.

"So running into each other now isn't that surreal. We would have run into each other one way or another," she said.

I turned to look at her. She was facing ahead, so I couldn't see her eyes, but I guessed there was mirth in the deep green depths. We did know each other well. Too well, maybe.

In the past, when she talked to me about the universe showing us a path, or fate having a hand in an event, I tended to mock her. There is enough mystery in the workings of the world without trying to find more, I used to muse. Now I couldn't help myself and invited more of the past into the present. "Nope, not a Hecate moment."

Blythe had coined the phrase, attaching the name of the Greek goddess of magic to what I called coincidences but what she felt were incidents guided by fate or kismet. She wasn't formally religious, nor did she believe in witches and wizards, but Blythe was a very spiritual woman in touch with the metaphysical world. We'd met during our first semester of graduate school at the Courtauld Institute of Art. I was writing my thesis on the use of holes in Constantin Brancusi's and Henry Moore's sculpture, and she was doing hers on artists who claimed their art was guided by spirits.

"You actually said that without any irony," Blythe said, sounding a bit surprised.

I didn't blame her for being taken aback. I'd been a real prick about Blythe's beliefs, and I'd always believed my cynicism had led to our split.

"I've had a while to reflect. It has been a long time."

She nodded. "That it has, Eben."

Did she sound wistful? Sullen? Merely pensive? I couldn't tell how she felt. Hell, I didn't even know how I felt. We had been together, inseparable, and very much in love for our two years at Courtauld. Then, just a week before graduation, Blythe ended our relationship. I returned to New York. Blythe remained in London. We had not seen each other, or been in touch, since.

"You said you didn't notice my name on the list of attendees. . . ."

"Is that a question? You haven't gotten any better at finishing your sentences, Eben, have you?"

I had a bad habit of assuming people would know where my conversations were headed. It was a result of my ability to second-guess what other people were going to say. Although I'd never been able to do that with Blythe. She never took the path I expected. She wasn't easy to read. She saw things I didn't in paintings. Had ideas that had never occurred to me. No one had ever surprised me as much as Blythe. And being surprised left me shaken and off-kilter. After our breakup, I tried to console myself that at least I wouldn't have to feel that way anymore.

"So, why were you looking for my name on the list of attendees?" I asked.

She took a breath as if deciding how to answer. "I always look."

If she'd wanted me to ask why, it wouldn't be the first time one of us disappointed the other.

We'd reached the causeway and crossed it. We were quiet the rest of the way back to the Grand. When we arrived, two men were standing outside, smoking. I didn't know either of them, but they both knew Blythe and greeted her warmly. She introduced us. One was a Spanish historian from the Prado, the other a French journalist. They were going in to have a drink at the bar and invited us to join them.

Blythe accepted the invitation, but I declined. I didn't want to sit in a hotel bar with two strangers and Blythe, who was nearly a stranger to me now.

"Perhaps you'd like to join us in the morning, though?" the

Frenchman said. "We're going to the Moderna Museet for a private showing. Not something you should miss; I'm sure we could get you an invitation."

The Moderna was one of Europe's leading museums of modern and contemporary art. I had met the curator earlier that day at the symposium, and she had asked me to attend.

"I was already invited; yes, I'm planning on it." Had I said that so Blythe would know I was as much a part of the inner circle as she and her friends were? I was ashamed of myself and hoped she hadn't noticed. I stole a glance over and saw her eyes were alight. She'd caught it. Of course she had. She'd always teased me about my ridiculous need to prove my standing.

"Perfect, then," the Frenchman said. "We'll see you in the morning."

I bade good night to the two men and turned to Blythe.

"Will you be coming to the Moderna as well?" I asked.

"Yes, I wouldn't miss it," she answered. There was a half smile on her lips, an expression that suddenly brought me back years.

If the two other men hadn't been standing there, I might have said something else, but what with the jet lag and the strangeness of seeing her and that damn look in her eyes, I chose not to.

"Well then, it was good running into you. I'll see you tomorrow."

"Good night, Eben."

Had her voice softened when she'd said my name? I wasn't sure. I put her and the question out of my mind and went upstairs to my room. The thing was, she didn't stay out of my mind. I might not have slept well at all if not for that little pill that I washed down with a tall glass of water.

. . . . .

The next morning, I met the others at the front of the hotel, where a bus was waiting to take our group to the museum. On board, I looked for Blythe. When the bus took off without her, I couldn't pretend I wasn't disappointed.

We arrived on Skeppsholmen just a few minutes later, and pulled up in front of a low-rise redbrick building that had once been a navy drill hall. Inside, I immediately saw Blythe was already there, talking to the Moderna's curator. From her red cheeks and windblown hair, I realized she must have walked.

Once all of us were assembled, the curator came over, greeted us, and took us on a tour of what was considered the world's finest collection of artists from the region, including work by Gösta Adrian-Nilsson, Ivan Aguéli, Vera Nilsson, Sven Erixson, Nils Dardel, Siri Derkert, Björn Lövin, and Marie-Louise Ekman.

"And now for our most recent addition—a room with several paintings done by the great artist Hilma af Klint. We are very proud that we will finally have this permanent display of some of her paintings," the curator said as she ushered us into the next gallery.

"Do you remember her?"

Blythe had not been near me during the rest of our tour, but somehow we'd wound up next to each other.

"No," I said.

She looked disappointed.

We entered a large room with twenty-foot ceilings. Giant paintings filled the space with color. I looked from one cryptic canvas to the next. These paintings were lush, fresh, and exciting. Beautiful compositions in oranges, pinks, reds, yellows, light blues, and lavenders. Each painting a world unto itself but all speaking the same symbolic language suggesting flowers, seeds, wombs, vaginas, embryos, moons, suns, and stars.

Now I vaguely did remember Hilma af Klint. She was one of the artists mentioned in Blythe's thesis, and as such she was a figure on the periphery of my worst memory. My difficulty with the woo-woo aspects of Blythe's research had been a serious problem for us and one of the factors that led to our breakup. The area where we disagreed most bitterly. She believed in all sorts of esoteric concepts. And I—well, the only faith I have is in not having faith.

The curator's voice brought me back to the present.

"Their Friday night séances began in 1896. And in the winter of 1906, Hilma af Klint took up the spirit's specific challenge and for the next nine years devoted herself to what she called *Paintings for the Temple*, some of which you see here. The entire oeuvre included over one hundred ninety-three paintings in various sizes. Hilma's overarching idea was to convey the knowledge of how *all is one*. She wanted to show what is beyond the visible dualistic world. The temple to which the title of her series refers didn't relate to an actual building at first. But in time it did, and her sketches for the temple show a spiral-shaped edifice that mirrored the many spirals in her paintings. She eventually tried but failed to get the temple built with the help of Rudolf Steiner. Today, I think of it mostly as a metaphor for spiritual evolution."

As I listened, I looked from one canvas to the next. And then I noticed the dozens of spirals in the abstract designs. A specific shape I knew as well as my own name. The helicoid Hilma af Klint had painted over and over was the same shape as the central design of the museum where I had been working for the last seven years, the Guggenheim Museum in New York City.

"Excuse me," I said when the curator stopped speaking.

"Yes, Mr. Elliot?"

"Did you say she called them *Paintings for the Temple*?" I put the emphasis on the last word.

"Yes, exactly."

Across from me, I saw Blythe nod imperceptibly, acknowledging that I'd stumbled on exactly what she'd known I'd see.

In 1943, when the Guggenheim's first director, Hilla Rebay, wrote to Frank Lloyd Wright asking him to design the museum, she described what she envisioned as a place that would be a "temple to the spirit." Her exact words.

How was it that a virtually unknown female artist in Sweden painted these for a spiral-shaped temple full of art thirty years before Frank Lloyd Wright ever put pencil to paper to design a spiral-shaped temple full of art?

At some point, Blythe had come to stand beside me again.

This time I caught a whiff of her scent that I remembered from so long ago.

"Now *this* is a Hecate moment," she whispered.

. . . . .

After spending far more time walking around the Hilma af Klint exhibit that day in Stockholm, Blythe and I left the Moderna Museet together and walked back to the conference hotel.

"So, what did you think of all that? Of the spirals in Hilma's work and her desire to build a temple to house her paintings and the similarity of her imagined temple to the Guggenheim?" she asked.

"It was striking."

"And the paintings?"

"Intricate, complicated, and brilliant. I'm especially interested in what the curator said about all this work being hidden away in a time capsule for decades."

"It was very sad that she knew no one would appreciate her work in her own time. One of the tragedies of her life," Blythe said. "Of the lives of so many women artists."

"I'm actually shocked about the dates. She started in this vein of drawing in 1896?"

Blythe nodded.

"And then began the temple paintings in 1906?"

"Yes."

"So she actually predated Kandinsky, Kazimir Malevich, Piet Mondrian, and František Kupka by years and hasn't gotten any credit for that?"

"Yes." Blythe smiled. "One of the things I'll be talking about this afternoon. The fact that now many of us believe that Kandinsky was influenced by her. We know he was in Stockholm in the early 1900s. At that point, Hilma was at the center of the art world, with her studio above one of the most important galleries. Kandinsky would have surely seen her paintings in those years before his style changed and he had his breakthrough. When you look at his oeuvre with this knowledge, you can see how many elements his paintings have in common with Hilma's. Yet she precedes him and the rest of them. She exemplifies the fate of so many women, people of different cultures, and outsiders."

We stopped on the bridge to watch the waterway's traffic.

"I'm still trying to process that she was already creating these highly sophisticated non-objective paintings by 1906, and all of the books credit Kandinsky and cite 1910 or later with the start of the movement. There's been so little conversation about her. Why is that?" I asked.

"For one, because she stopped showing her paintings to anyone outside of De Fem by the early 1920s. No one understood what she was trying to convey, and she decided to keep them private until the world caught up with her. So determined was she to protect her creativity, she stipulated in her will that the archive of her work be sealed until twenty years after her death. As a result, nothing was even seen till the end of the 1960s. At that point, her nephew and beneficiary offered her legacy to the Moderna, but she was unknown and they weren't interested. He subsequently formed the Hilma af Klint Foundation and has worked diligently to introduce his aunt's work to the art world, but it has been slow going. She's had few international showings. In the States, she's been included in only one group show, at the Los Angeles County Museum of Art in 1986—*The Spiritual in Art*. Outside of Sweden, she really hasn't landed on anyone's radar."

"Except yours. She's one of the artists you wrote your thesis about."

Blythe nodded.

I took a deep breath.

The boat we'd been observing was crossing the river, and I watched it push apart floating pieces of ice. We started walking again. I could see the hotel ahead.

"Well, here we are back where we started . . . or ended, rather," Blythe said in a voice tinged with sadness.

I looked down at her hands by her side and without thought reached over and took her right hand in mine. She turned to look at me. For a moment, neither of us said anything. There was a gulf between us as wide as the river we were crossing. Years of being apart. Of each living lives the other knew nothing about. But there was something else there as well. The thing between us that had never changed. I'd felt it the evening before and felt it again now.

"It was good running into you," she said.

"Yes, it was."

"And . . ." She hesitated. "Maybe we can talk more. Later. Tonight?"

"Yes."

"I . . ." She hesitated again.

"What is it?"

"I had wondered what it would be like to see you again. I didn't think it would be like this."

"Like what, Blythe?"

She leaned toward me, reached up, and kissed me.

I hadn't expected that. Not one bit.

At first her lips were cold and then they weren't. My hands, of their own accord, found her hips and pulled her toward me. The snow had started falling again; it was freezing, but we stood there pressed up to each other, relearning a landscape that we had once known so well.

Gently, she pulled away. Her lips were a little bruised; her eyes were soft.

"I'm sorry, I didn't—" she said.

"No, please, the last thing I want you to do is apologize."

"I can't believe I did that. I had only intended to ask you if we could talk."

"And we can."

We reached the hotel, and Blythe disentangled her hand from mine. I didn't know what she'd been thinking as we'd walked those last few yards. I'd been thinking that I'd forgotten how silken her skin felt and how many hours we'd spent touching in those years we'd been together. I'd never gotten enough of her, and she'd acted as if she felt the same. Until she didn't anymore.

We walked up to the hotel. Those of our colleagues who'd also been at the museum were just getting off the bus. One called out to Blythe that he wanted to ask her a question. We waited. He wanted to know more about Hilma af Klint and her séances. As she answered, others from the group gathered to listen until there was a small crowd out on the sidewalk.

It seemed everyone knew about her expertise on Hilma af Klint but me.

"Forgive me," she finally said to everyone. "I have to go over my notes for my lecture this afternoon."

She broke away and headed inside. I followed her. "Do you really need to go over your notes, or do you have time for coffee?" I asked.

Her eyes, her beautiful eyes, searched mine, and for a few seconds she didn't answer. I have never been much of a romantic. I've never read poetry. I find sappy movies and pop music that prattles on endlessly about loss annoying. I don't like picnics or celebrate Valentine's Day. But Blythe was an incurable romantic and often she would write out bits of poems and leave them for me. During those two years we were together, I'd been moved, despite myself, by some of them. And now, standing in the busy entranceway of the hotel, I remembered a line of a poem she'd read to me once.

"Had we but world enough and time, this coyness, lady, were no crime. . . ."

Hearing it, Blythe smiled. Despite all the people around us and the cacophony in the lobby, it was as if we'd slipped back into the easy intimacy we'd once shared.

And then her demeanor changed. Suddenly, she looked apprehensive.

"Are you nervous about your lecture?"

She gave a short laugh. "No. I teach a lecture class to over two hundred students. This will be easy-peasy."

"Easy-peasy." Now I laughed. I hadn't heard anyone use that expression in years.

Yet another conference goer approached us. This time it was to talk to me, and Blythe used the interruption to excuse herself, saying she really did need to go over her notes.

I wished her luck and returned to the conversation with my colleague. Afterward, I went to the hotel restaurant to have some coffee and try to sort out the mess in my addled brain. While I waited for my order, I took out my phone and found a text from Daphne. It was brief, as her texts usually were.

> **How is the conference? Landed an A-list client today—very busy here. Have an event March 29—you free? Check in tomorrow?**

I felt a sudden peculiar emptiness and then disappointment. There was nothing wrong with the message. Daphne Thorne and I had been seeing each other for three months. I had gotten used to her shorthand. So why was I reacting like that?

On paper, so much about Daphne was right. She'd grown up in Manhattan as well, so we shared a lot of the same cultural references. She owned her own wealth management firm and so was educated about the arts. She was coolly chic and cultured in a New York way. She was independent, which I liked. She took being self-sufficient very seriously and claimed no relationship would ever define her. I appreciated all that and enjoyed her acerbic sense of humor. We seemed to fit well together without complications.

So why was I feeling like something was wrong?

We'd first met at the museum. One of her clients, Branford

Jones, had a long-term goal of sitting on the board of a New York museum. As a first step, Daphne had suggested he fund shows at several museums and see which one he found most compatible. After contacting our corporate sponsorship department and finding out what we had coming up, she suggested he look into co-funding the Helen Frankenthaler show we were planning.

My supervisor asked me to make the presentation as the show's associate curator. Jones was interested, and over the next few weeks we had several meetings. Once he'd signed on and all the sponsorship details were worked out, he and his wife threw a party to celebrate our collaboration. Daphne and I wound up leaving at the same time. It was raining heavily when we got downstairs, and she offered to drop me off, since she had a car picking her up. I accepted the offer rather than getting soaked while waiting for a cab, and I hopped in.

"I never mix business with pleasure," she said. "But now that the business part is over, do you want to go for a nightcap?"

"It would be my pleasure," I said.

She laughed. We began sleeping together that night.

It was that simple.

As I reread her text, it suddenly felt a little too simple. That was Daphne. No questions about what I'd been doing or recriminations about why I hadn't yet contacted her. Just taking care of business. Still, being with a woman who was so much like me was much easier, I reminded myself as I took a sip of the strong black coffee.

Easier than what? I wondered. Who was I comparing her to? As if I didn't know.

· · · · ·

Blythe's lecture started at one p.m. She'd taken the title from a famous 1971 essay—"Why Have There Been No Great Woman Artists?," written by Linda Nochlin. The piece had made waves when it was published and still does.

I took a seat in the second row. I watched Blythe's face as I listened to her give her impassioned speech.

She'd been twenty-four when we'd met, our first year at Courtauld. Three years my junior. She'd come to graduate school straight from getting her undergraduate degree at the Sorbonne—her father was French, her mother British. I'd taken another route and, after Yale, had gone to work at Gagosian Art Gallery in New York. A few years later, when I realized I wasn't going to get where I wanted with my career without at least a master's degree, I enrolled at Courtauld.

As I watched Blythe at the podium, I thought that she seemed not to have aged at all in the last eight years. Nor had she altered her eclectic style. Her blond hair still fell in Pre-Raphaelite waves down to her shoulders, and her eyes were still rimmed in smudged kohl. She wore a half dozen amulets and talismans hanging from silver chains around her neck. And she still had wrapped round her wrists the same black-and-red silk cords with evil eyes, hamsas, and little Buddha charms.

She was wearing big silver hoop earrings, an emerald green poet's blouse, and a long skirt in a green a few shades darker.

Blythe always looked as if she'd studied centuries of styles, borrowing and winnowing them down to create a unique look.

I tried my best to concentrate on what Blythe was saying. But I managed only a few minutes before I was thinking of those heady days in London when we fell for each other, harder than I'd ever fallen for anyone before. Or since, I had to admit, if I was honest with myself. Which I tried to be.

And now here we were in a hotel in Stockholm. Away from all of our obligations, and maybe we could— And then it struck me that I knew nothing about her life now. Was she married? Did she have a family? What was wrong with me? Blythe was giving an erudite lecture on an important subject I should have been paying attention to, and instead, I was remembering the feel of her hair and the shine of her skin after we'd made love.

What was the pull between us? Why hadn't it dissipated and disappeared in all these years? This woman had walked out on me with practically no explanation, certainly not one that made sense. It left me embarrassingly bereft, and all these years later I was still fantasizing about her.

The greater fool I. I focused. Blythe was speaking about Hilma af Klint.

"This woman, whom we now see as one of Sweden's greatest painters, was a mystic. An artist who claimed to have received messages from spirits who set her on the course to creating some of the most powerful and original non-objective paintings we have ever seen. And yet in her lifetime—even today—she was dismissed by many for being a *crazy woman*, a *kook*. Do we look at Rothko that way? He was deeply involved in the spiritual world. What of Delacroix, who believed angels helped him paint?"

The af Klints we'd seen that morning in the museum flashed on the screen behind Blythe. And there were those spirals again, pulling me in. They were one of nature's most fascinating forms, imbued with symbolic meanings through the centuries. A form that had inspired artists from Leonardo da Vinci to architects like Frank Lloyd Wright.

"She was a mystery during her lifetime and still is today. She left over one hundred twenty-five detailed notebooks that are rich with information and at the same time leave so many unanswered questions. On its own, the temple she envisioned is a curiosity. . . ."

The slide behind Blythe was replaced by one showing a rough drawing of the structure that af Klint had sketched—so like the building where I worked, to which hundreds of thousands of art lovers came every year to walk its ramp and study its offerings.

Blythe finished her talk and was greeted by applause. She walked off the stage and immediately was surrounded by enough of a crowd that I stayed away. I knew we had plans to see each other later.

But that never happened.

At the end of the day, finished attending panels and lectures, I went up to my room, called the hotel operator, and asked to be connected to Blythe's room. But I was told that she had checked out. The depth of my shock and disappointment surprised me. She had vanished from my life before. Why wouldn't she do it again? I chalked it up to nostalgia and threw myself into the conference for the next two days. I then went home, leaving behind my stirred-up memories and dreams of a reunion.

. . . . .

Stockholm, October 14, 1896

My dear Anna,

Please forgive the lateness of this letter, but I needed Mathilda to confirm the exact details for the meeting of the Edelweiss Society. I'm happy to report that one of the members has offered us the use of her wonderful garden house! You and Hilma are most welcome to join us at six o'clock.

I will be waiting for you two ten minutes prior to the start of the meeting at the corner of Karlavägen and Grev Turegatan.

I realize that Hilma was disappointed by the last meeting, but I do hope you can convince her to give the society another chance . . . especially since Mathilda will also be there, and she tells me a special guest will be in attendance too.

Please know how much I admire both you and Hilma. It brightens my heart to have the three of us reconnect after such a long absence, for which I am entirely to blame. I so look forward to seeing the two of you again tomorrow evening.

With great affection,
Cornelia

· · · · ·

CHAPTER TWO

Friday Night, No. 1
October 16, 1896
Stockholm

Anna would never forget that afternoon when she first saw Hilma standing outside the entrance to Slöjdskolan, the traditional art school they both attended in their adolescent years. Hilma was just shy of seventeen years old at the time. Anna had just turned nineteen. But the memory of that first sight of her friend as a young painter still burned inside her. Hilma had a petite stature but seemed far taller than she actually was. Lean and radiant as a sunflower, she stood out amid a sea of colorless faces. With her wide-open eyes and luminescent skin, she appeared to be lit from within.

Hilma was clasping an austere-looking paint box, which from afar looked like a wooden suitcase. Had it not been for a crowd of art students congregating outside the school's stone steps, one would have thought Hilma was set to go on a long journey. Her chin lifted and her gaze rose above the crowd, as though she'd set her sights on something glorious in the distance.

Anna liked to think that Hilma was instinctively searching for her that day. She was running late and had to rush toward the entrance just as the other students had begun to go inside the building. Yet Hilma had remained outside, a solitary figure on the top step, regal in stature, as though she were enthroned. That image of her cherished friend would always be pressed in her mind, for it exemplified her: a woman who knew her gifts transcended the ordinary, an artist whose deep sense of purpose raised her toward the clouds.

Middle age, however, had now snuck up on the two women. Hilma had continued to paint with all-consuming commitment to her artistic calling, even refusing a marriage proposal from a strong-willed and ardent doctor who had become fascinated by her intense personality and sharp tongue, but her male peers' resistance to granting her acceptance frustrated her deeply.

They'd agreed to attend a meeting that night of the Edelweiss Society, a group formed to promote spiritual awakening. A former classmate, Cornelia Cederberg, also attended with her older sister. Anna arrived at Hilma's studio on Hamngatan and found her friend staring at her easel. The table arranged at the center of the room was cluttered with sheets of paper; an open tin of pastels had spilled over on one of the sketch pads, and a half-eaten brown apple lay carelessly abandoned on a stool. In the corner, a scientific journal, smudged with yellow fingerprints, had been tossed on the floor.

And yet the room bloomed with the sights and scents of

creativity. The fragrance of turpentine floated through the air, and an amber-colored flask filled with linseed oil stood next to a wooden palette dotted with creamy mounds of paint.

On Hilma's easel was a watercolor painting of a cluster of autumn roses. Anna loved the fact that even in the chaos of her surroundings, Hilma could still create something as beautiful and ethereal as a vase of delicate blooms.

Anna stepped closer to the still life and extended her finger toward the thick parchment.

"The paper-thin skins of the petals remind me of the Venetian lanterns we loved during our trip to Italy." Her mind went back there, if only for a moment. "Remember how the light came through the deep red paper?"

Hilma nodded, though the gesture was more an acknowledgment of the comparison's being correct than of the sentimental memory behind it.

Her face was tired, her eyes baggy from lack of sleep. Now that she was in her mid-thirties, the fatigue from the long hours of painting was difficult to mask. She pointed to the vase, and frustration washed over her. "The flowers are now wilted, and I won't have them tomorrow to paint."

"At least you captured them at their peak," Anna said.

"I want to redo them," Hilma complained.

"I will buy you fresh ones in the morning—how's that? But we have to get going, or we'll be late for tonight's meeting."

Hilma ignored her. She dabbed her brush in water and began to apply a few more fiery brushstrokes to her watercolor study.

Anna stood back and began leafing through the magazines

on Hilma's worktable. Her friend had an insatiable appetite for knowledge, whether it was of the mysteries of the stars or the ever-evolving theories about atoms. Anna picked up the latest copy of the *Dagens Nyheter*, and a letter slipped from its pages.

> *My darling Hilma, why do you still torment me? . . . I must see you! It is most unfair that you reduce me to such childish pleas and tantrums when all I want is a chance to talk. . . .*

She instantly recognized the handwriting. How long would this Dr. Hellström torment her friend with his persistent and ridiculous advances? Didn't he realize that Hilma would never accept his marriage proposals? Anna slipped the letter back inside and silently fumed.

"I really don't want to go out. . . . I want to stay and work," Hilma complained as she continued to add small brushstrokes to the watercolor. "These meetings at the Edelweiss Society have been a terrible disappointment."

Anna sighed and tried to put her irritation about the letter behind her. But it weighed deeply. She and Hilma had always promised to share everything with each other.

"I think it will be different tonight." Anna's voice was now hopeful. "Please come and give it one more try. . . . Maybe you'll hear from your sister this time. . . ."

Hilma shook her head, then looked at Anna with glassy, impatient eyes. "I've attended countless séances in the sixteen years since Hermina passed. I've been to nearly every spiritualist meeting in Stockholm, opening my heart and mind to the possibility of another realm where departed souls continue to exist. But she's never relayed any message to me." Her face fell. "What if there really is nothing more after we die?"

Anna studied her friend standing by her easel, her hair streaked with paint, her fingers callused from gripping a brush for hours.

"Our art will remain," she answered. She pointed to the canvas that Hilma had been painting. "You cannot call that nothing."

Hilma took a rag from her pocket and twisted it around her hand. Then dabbed her brow.

"Fine. I'll go." She stepped closer to her friend. "But only because you're insisting."

"Good." Anna smiled, and it gave her a small sense of victory to know she'd been able to convince her. "But now we must hurry—Cornelia will be waiting for us."

"Cornelia? That girl hasn't picked up a paintbrush in over fifteen years! I have little hope for her now that she's nearly forty!"

"Maybe she'll hear something tonight that will motivate her to return to her art," Anna offered optimistically.

Hilma didn't answer. They had both known Cornelia for as long as they'd known each other. A few years older than they were, she was in her last year at the Slöjdskolan when Anna and Hilma enrolled. Although Cornelia hadn't continued her artistic training at the Royal Academy like they had, Anna would never deny that she was gifted. She remembered how Cornelia had once done an oil study of a goldfinch where every tiny feather on the bird's breast was clearly visible. Even Hilma had been impressed as she peered over the luminous canvas. Cornelia had once been as fine a painter as either of them, quieter than Hilma, definitely less original, but certainly talented. It saddened Anna that life had somehow dried out their friend's brush prematurely.

Hilma rolled her eyes. "And is Cornelia the one who made that dress for you?"

She pointed to the violet skirt and bodice that Anna had chosen to wear to the Edelweiss meeting. It was sewn from a bolt of exotic imported fabric, and the neat lines and expert tailoring accentuated Anna's slim physique.

"Forget what I'm wearing, Hilma. We need to get you dressed in something presentable. You can't wear that smock when you meet the others."

"This is all I have," she admitted. Hilma unbuttoned her smock to reveal a white blouse dotted with coffee stains and a long black skirt dusty with streaks of blue pastel chalk.

"Maybe you can borrow something from Alma or Charlotta?" Anna searched the room to see if either of the two women with whom Hilma shared her studio had left anything behind.

"Those two? The only things you'll find on the wall hooks are two black suits, matching hats, and silk cravats. They were dressing up in men's clothing and smoking cigars last night while I tried to paint!"

Anna walked over to the corner and touched the wool sleeve of one of the jackets, appraised the narrow shoulders and hand-stitched lapels, then looked at her friend in her stained clothes.

"I have an idea," she said, a smile curled at her lips, "but you'll need to get undressed."

• • • • •

Anna and Hilma were already twenty minutes late. Cornelia stood waiting for her two friends to arrive. She had been nervous all day, hopeful that the Edelweiss meeting would not disappoint.

For years, Cornelia had admired Hilma and Anna for having the courage to apply to the Royal Academy, but her friendship with Hilma, whose hard shell she found intimidating, had always been a bit strained.

"Without more fortitude," Hilma once told her on the steps of the Slöjdskolan, "you'll never survive as an artist. As women, we have to fight harder for everything." She puffed out her chest. "From our very first breath, we're forced to overcome the disappointment that we weren't born a son."

Cornelia had understood this deeply. Her brother had been the light in her parents' eyes, and when he died, he took something irreplaceably meaningful with him. What was it? Hope, perhaps? Even if her sister, Mathilda, was widely respected among her peers in her field as a spiritualist and writer, her achievements were unfairly diminished because she was not a man. Cornelia wasn't even sure if her parents had ever realized all that her elder sister had accomplished, except for marrying. And Cornelia hadn't managed to do even that.

She sighed, and then squinted as she saw Anna strolling down the street toward the meetinghouse with a young gentleman pulled tightly to her side.

"Good evening; sorry we're a little late!" Anna cried out.

Cornelia was so pleased to see her friend dressed in the violet silk dress she had created for her that she no longer minded that she had kept her waiting. Watching the material move from opacity to iridescence as Anna walked along the leaf-strewn brick path brought a smile to her face. But while she recognized her childhood friend, the identity of the man who now locked arms with her was a mystery.

"It took us a little longer than expected," Anna said in apology as they stepped closer. "Hopefully, we can still help you set up inside." She let go of the young man's arm.

Cornelia focused on the gentleman as he lifted his chin and revealed his face to her. She knew at once those glacial blue eyes that penetrated with their intense gaze.

"Hilma?" Cornelia leaned in closer. "Is that you?"

A thin smile curled at Hilma's lips.

She lifted a single finger in front of her mouth, as if to signal to Cornelia that she shouldn't say another word.

"Keep her secret for tonight," Anna whispered.

Cornelia stepped back and considered Hilma for a moment. Would she have suspected anything had she not recognized her former classmate's distinctly colored eyes or her fierce look? She studied the face that peeked out from beneath the hat and the thin wisps of brown hair that had been tucked behind her ears. With her breasts camouflaged beneath the suit jacket, and her thin neck wrapped in a thick silk cravat, Hilma certainly didn't come across as the pinnacle of masculinity. Even so, Cornelia believed she could surely pass for a young man.

"I will," she answered, but inside, her heart raced with a nervous energy. Masquerading as a man in public was not a harmless prank. Should she be discovered, not only would Hilma's reputation be jeopardized, but Anna's and Cornelia's would be as well, merely by association.

"I won't say a word," she promised as they walked toward the building. Once they entered, however, Cornelia found it hard to hide her worry. She doubted the others in the group would actually suspect anything. But her sister, Mathilda, had been born with a sixth sense, and Cornelia wondered if she would see right through Hilma's disguise.

She eyed her sister in the far corner of the room. Mathilda appeared to be trapped in conversation with Carl von Bergen, the writer.

Hilma stood next to Anna, adjusted her tie, and grew emboldened. A mischievous grin emerged on her face.

"You mentioned a special guest was coming tonight. Do you know who?" Hilma asked.

"Mathilda wouldn't reveal his name, but he's supposed to be quite famous. . . ." Cornelia turned and saw her sister had escaped from the tedium of von Bergen's clutches and was now approaching them. "I know little else . . . but we can certainly ask her for more details."

Hilma's eyes beamed. She had longed to meet Mathilda, the famous editor of *Efteråt*, the esteemed spiritualist magazine. Broad shouldered and dressed completely in black, except for a small silver brooch with a white edelweiss flower inside, Mathilda exuded a strong masculine presence that rivaled Hilma's, even when Hilma wore her male attire.

Cornelia reached for her sister's hand. "You remember Anna. . . ." She gestured toward her friend.

"Ah, yes, of course. A colleague of yours from art school."

"It's a pleasure to see you again," Anna said politely.

Mathilda's eyes now fell on Hilma. Her gaze narrowed as she studied this fellow in front of her.

"And this is . . ." Cornelia's voice faltered. She knew Mathilda would discern any dishonesty in her voice.

"This person needs no introduction," Mathilda stated plainly, sidestepping the danger of Hilma's arriving in disguise. Her patience had already been tested by her conversation with von Bergen. She had not seen Hilma in many years, but her identity was still clear to her. Mathilda refused to play the fool.

"The three of you should find seats as soon as possible. We have two special guests arriving tonight. One is a man you'll recognize from the papers, for he is as outspoken in his politics as he is in his fiction. The other is a woman whom I've heard has strong spiritual powers. Her name is Sigrid, and I'm quite eager to meet her."

· · · · ·

"Please, please . . ." Von Bergen was now ordering everyone around him to bring in any extra seating they could find. "We need more chairs! Someone should go outside and fetch the garden furniture."

"Why don't you come help me get them, young man?" he asked, pointing to Hilma. "We'll leave the ladies to set up the ones that are already inside."

Cornelia watched to see how her friend would react. If Hilma answered, her natural female-sounding voice would certainly betray her.

"My cousin had a bad accident this summer," Anna quickly interjected. "Sadly, he fell off a horse, and the injury was quite severe." She patted Hilma gently on the back. "He's been mute ever since."

"Mute? How terrible! He can't speak a single word?"

"No," Anna lied. "He can't take off his hat either, because the wound on top of his head is far too unsightly. It would pain my cousin to reveal it to anyone."

"Oh my," von Bergen sympathized. He leaned forward, closer to the three women, and Cornelia thought she smelled the faint trace of alcohol on the writer's breath. "He is rather small for a man," he mumbled. "He's certainly had a rough time of it, hasn't he?"

"Indeed. It's been very difficult for him and our whole family." Her eyes lowered. "I told my aunt that I'd bring him tonight because we thought maybe the spirits would inform us when his voice might come back."

"I see. . . . That makes sense. Let's hope they do! Well, never mind, I'll go get the chairs myself."

Hilma shook her head in defiance.

"Well, if you insist," replied von Bergen. He gestured for Hilma to follow.

· · · · ·

The garden house, offered to them for the night by one of the founding members, had been transformed. While the room was sparsely furnished, the vaulted stucco ceiling and large cabinet toward the rear made it the perfect place for the make-shift altar. Two beeswax candles had been placed at either side of a wooden crucifix. With great tenderness, a small blue vase with a posy of edelweiss flowers had been arranged for added atmosphere.

Cornelia, her heart still heavy from the weight of her sister's disapproval, watched as Hilma and von Bergen hauled chairs in from the outside and arranged them in four neat rows.

"Too bad you can't take off your hat, young man," von Bergen said kindly. "It's getting awfully hot in here now."

Hilma smiled.

"We should probably all sit down," Cornelia suggested to her friends. "Mathilda mentioned that a special guest is coming tonight."

"He's actually a friend of mine!" von Bergen interrupted. "You can't let your sister take all the credit." He winked. "Aren't you impressed I've managed to get such an illustrious figure to join us?" He turned to Mathilda.

She made no effort to hide her displeasure. "We are all equals here," Mathilda muttered before sitting down.

As everyone began to settle in anticipation of the meeting, a tall woman entered the room. Her long brown hair was parted down the middle and coiled behind her ears. Her shoulders were strong and sturdy. A large cross dangled between her breasts. She walked solemnly toward one of the unoccupied rows in the back and sat down.

Cornelia and Anna both turned their heads to gaze at her. "She reminds me of Joan of Arc," Anna whispered.

44

Hilma nodded in agreement. The heat had intensified within the small crowded space, and Hilma's face flushed a bright shade of crimson beneath her hat.

·····

With all of the seats now occupied, Huldine Beamish, the founder of the Edelweiss Society, stood at the front of the altar clutching her Bible, her silver hair pulled tightly behind her ears.

"Let us begin," Huldine commanded. The group began to repeat a series of mantras before entering into a period of meditation. After several minutes, silence enveloped them.

Then without warning came a loud sound. The doors flung open, and a gust of wind whipped through the room, bringing with it a tumble of leaves.

All of the members turned their heads toward the back of the hall, only to see the latest guest stumble over the threshold.

"Well, what do you know?" A devilish-looking man, sporting a half-tied bright red-and-white polka-dotted foulard, burst into the room. "All these solemn and serious people are waiting here just for me?"

Cornelia raised her hand to her mouth when she saw who it was. The man needed no introduction; he was August Strindberg, the famous author and playwright. His image appeared regularly in the newspapers, just as Mathilda had hinted. Not just in the critics' corners, where his dramatic works were considered a revolt against all social conventions, but in the society pages as well. It was well-known gossip around town that he had a weakness for the ladies. Recently, he had also begun to dabble in what he believed was another form of uncharted knowledge, mysticism and the occult.

"August, what a pleasure to see you," von Bergen's voice boomed as he leaped up from his seat.

Strindberg teetered as he walked toward his friend. The air became thicker with the smell of alcohol that trailed him. He stopped suddenly, as if something else had caught his interest. He turned around and barged in between the seats, pushing past people who had to turn to make room for him. He pointed at several women.

"Too fat."

"Too ugly."

"Too short."

As he stumbled over the chairs, each woman's face transformed from placid politeness to shock and revulsion.

"You look pretty," he said, pointing to Hilma. "Too bad you're a boy."

When he reached the front of the room, he paused and bowed so deeply that his forehead actually brushed up against Huldine's chest. She recoiled.

"Let us begin," she repeated, trying to regain her composure. Resembling a frustrated schoolteacher, Huldine motioned for everyone to settle down.

"I don't want to speak to the spirits unless I have one of these beauties at my side!" August announced, and sat down. His speech was so slurred, the others could barely understand it. Abruptly, he pulled out a flask of absinthe, took a deep swig, and then reached out to pull Anna onto his lap.

Hilma leaped up. "Let go of her," she said sternly. She used all her strength to make him release Anna, but in the scuffle, Hilma's hat tumbled to the floor, and her long brown hair came spilling out.

"Ah, I knew you were too comely to be a man!" Strindberg cried out as he lay splayed on the floor, his red-and-white polka-dotted cravat now covering his face.

"Come on, then, continue with your spiritualism, don't mind me," he tittered, hiccupping loudly.

His vulgar behavior had already caused several members of the group, both women and men, to get up and leave. August clutched at the air as though he were trying to catch them in a net.

"Where are you going? We have the spirits to talk to. Come back!" he shouted in desperation, holding out his arms.

Suddenly, the tall woman with the crucifix necklace stood up and leaned over him.

"I have five children, Mr. Strindberg, and never in my life have I seen such bad behavior! You should be deeply ashamed of yourself. Deeply!" Her voice boomed through the entire hall.

"I left my family to come here tonight," she continued. "I wanted to have an evening of spiritual awakening, and you have ruined it for me. You made it a spectacle." Her eyes bore into him. "A circus of the lowest kind."

"Well, you're sure a feisty one, aren't you? You might look like a nun . . . but five children?" Strindberg pulled himself off the ground and clumsily tried to retie his cravat. "Your husband must find that mouth on you to be a bit of an aphrodisiac!"

"Sigrid, we apologize," Huldine pleaded. "I would never have invited you if I thought . . ."

"Yes," Mathilda agreed.

Huldine glared angrily at von Bergen, who eventually got to his feet and took August firmly by the arm, leading him away.

Silence settled over the room once again.

"Please understand that this kind of thing hardly ever happens," Mathilda explained. "What a shameless man. He may well be a prominent writer, but he has no place here. Please, give the Edelweiss Society another chance."

Sigrid shook her head. "No, I don't think this is right for me. I'll never receive any messages here. There's far too much disharmony."

She gathered up her skirt in her hand and left.

Stockholm, October 17, 1896

Dear Sigrid Hedman,

My sincere apologies for the events last evening. It was so awful that I lack the words to describe it. For certain, Strindberg went far beyond normal behavior. A great shock that an admired and famous author could ever act in such a way! I assure you, this has never happened before, and I do hope that he will keep his sad excuse for a person secluded away until he can manage to stay sober.

I regret that this has happened at your first meeting with the Edelweiss Society. As you know, I've been wanting you to attend for so long. I've been hearing rumors about your spiritual ability for many years now, and I do think that we can create something magical together.

My sister, Cornelia, has arranged for a private meeting this Friday with two other very interesting women—Anna Cassel and Hilma af Klint. They are both artists, trained at the Royal Academy, who seek greater understanding of the spiritual realm. We would all be delighted if you could find the time to come.

It will take place at our apartment on Kammakargatan at seven o'clock. In connection with the meeting, I would love to tell you more about my work with Efteråt. Maybe you can even write a piece for the magazine, about your personal experiences.

I do hope to see you there.

Sincerely,
Mathilda Nilsson

· · · · ·

CHAPTER THREE

Friday Night, No. 2
October 23, 1896
Stockholm

For Sigrid, the decision to accept Mathilda's invitation was not a difficult one. Despite the lack of professionalism she had found at the Edelweiss Society, she still longed to pursue something for herself after years of devoting her time to her five children. They had finally reached an age at which they didn't need her as much as before. Just reading Mathilda's letter, Sigrid knew she was sincere. An evening with a group of five women sounded perfect, and Sigrid instantly imagined a more harmonious gathering, worthy of a second try.

The meeting had snuck up on her after a busy week. She planned to take a long walk beforehand to clear her mind after a chaotic dinner with her teenagers. Sigrid had selfishly decided to serve supper early, but no one was hungry, and the youngest, Kerstin, got into a fight with her brother over who got to use the spare bicycle with their friends.

"Behave," she said to them sternly. But they didn't listen and continued to bicker between themselves. "Please try to settle all of this before your father comes home." Sigrid couldn't wait to leave for the night; she pulled her Bible off the table and shut the door.

As she stepped into the street, the cool air offered her some much-needed relief.

Her mind had been brimming with curiosity about that artist, Hilma af Klint. It wasn't just that she'd been bold enough to dress like a man, although that certainly made her unique. Sigrid was far more intrigued by the strange mix of colors that radiated from her, an intense halo of yellow, with rings of blue and a flash of pink. She had never seen someone exude a prism of colors like that before.

Sigrid had possessed her gift for seeing the auras of other people since she was in grade school, beginning when she noticed a halo of orange around her teacher, Mrs. Andersson. When she mentioned to her friend that their teacher should really have a name that captured the rays of sunshine that floated off her skin, her schoolmate looked at her like she had lost her mind. Sigrid couldn't believe that no one else could see the colors that flashed so vividly before her.

From that moment on, she kept her gift a secret, never revealing it to anyone. She didn't want others to know she was different. What if they thought she was insane and sent her to an asylum, putting her away for a lifetime? No, she knew she had to be careful. Folke, her son, had the same ability. Sigrid had realized it when he was very young but had given him strict instructions to keep quiet about it.

Sigrid held her woolen skirt firmly in one hand, lifting it lightly so the hem wouldn't drag along the cobblestones that were slick with rain. She walked in the middle of the street, crisscrossing between the piles of horse manure and the puddles. She strolled leisurely in the direction of Kammakargatan, past the beautiful Saint Johannes Church where she could hear the notes from the organ floating in the air. It was as if someone were playing just for her on this special day.

She flushed with anticipation. She might not be as talented as the other women in the group, but she truly saw the world in color. She wanted to read the auras of more than just Hilma tonight, for every person had their own shade. As for her loving husband, Ernst, his color was always red. The warm embrace of love.

* * * * *

With only an hour before the other women arrived, Mathilda slipped into the privacy of her bedroom to prepare her focus. Like so much of the apartment, the room was filled with exotic objects Anders had brought back from his travels at sea: the black-and-gold ginger jar from the Far East, the embroidered tapestries from India, and the blue-and-green peacock feathers from New Guinea that she had glued by hand around the edge of her oval dressing mirror.

Her husband always returned from his journeys with something to delight and inspire her. Theirs had always been a unique and unconventional marriage. While his job as a sea captain sometimes required him to be away for weeks or months at a time, it enabled Mathilda to have the freedom and space to focus on her own work. Mathilda had no need for a ship; her visions had the power to transport her anywhere.

"When I travel, I try to see the world through your eyes. To appreciate the wisdom and history that come from these foreign places and the people who inhabit them." His words had made her feel that he understood her more than any other person in this world.

He did not care that she was neither feminine nor delicate, the qualities that most men sought when they meant to take a wife. He loved her strength, her curiosity, and her intellect. He did not mind that she had no interest in frivolity, unlike her sister, Cornelia, who could spend hours caressing a bolt of silk and imagining the different ways she could transform it into a dress or a set of curtains. In fact, Mathilda's favorite gift had been the wooden humidor Anders had purchased for her in South America. Inside were four hand-rolled cigars. She lifted the cover and pulled one out, inhaling the rich scent of tobacco leaves, and slipped it into the pocket of her vest.

. . . . .

With so little time until the guests arrived, the space for the séance still needed to be arranged. Where was Cornelia when she needed her? Mathilda felt herself growing impatient.

"Cornelia!" she shouted. "The other women will all be arriving shortly, and I will not be embarrassed again. After the Edelweiss debacle, I want everything to run smoothly."

There was no reply. Mathilda stomped off to find her.

"Did you hear me?" She found Cornelia hunched in the corner of her room, a set of paints splayed out in front of her.

She grasped a thin sable brush, and a garland of green flowers now circled the top of a teapot.

"You're painting now?" Mathilda cried out. "When there is so much else to do?"

Cornelia looked up. A line of green paint streaked her lip from when she had absentmindedly placed the brush in her mouth.

"I'm sorry, the time must have slipped away from me. . . ."

Mathilda let out an exasperated sigh. Her sister's room was filled with so many things she herself could never appreciate. One corner was crowded with wooden rings used for her embroidery; another corner brimmed with paper and paints. The desk was stacked with fabric and colorful ribbons, which Cornelia used to make her frivolous dresses.

"I have had clients all day coming into the office, sharing their stories with me. I have written the cover article for the latest *Efterât* edition and have already begun working on my next column." Mathilda's frustration was apparent. "You lose yourself too easily in these crafts, and you never complete anything."

She stepped farther into Cornelia's room and picked up a piece of embroidery. "This cushion, for example . . . You worked on it obsessively for a week but then just moved on to something else. These materials cost money, you know."

Cornelia put down the teapot she was holding, got up, and untied her apron.

"I bought the materials with my own money—money I earned from the animal studies I did for the veterinary institute." She paused. "I do work."

"That may be, but you don't pay a single krona for your upkeep here. You act like a housewife, but without a household of your own. Wasting your future."

Mathilda shook her head.

"I'm grateful for everything you and Anders do for me. For letting me stay here," Cornelia said.

"Good. But you need to start using your talents too. It's now too late for you to get married, so you'll have to start behaving like an intellectual, not a housewife. You have so many artistic qualities. That school saw it all those years ago, and I still see it."

"I'm not like Anna and Hilma."

"Why not? You were all admitted to the same school, three women in a male environment, against all odds. But it seems that Anna and Hilma make the most of their talents, while you spend your time alone in here, messing about with all kinds of rubbish! Porcelain and cushions. It's nonsense. Nonsense. It still frustrates me that you never applied to the Royal Academy. . . . I told you that you should."

"I will take on more commissions, paint more canvases. . . . That will bring in some money." Cornelia's eyes were welling up, and her voice was weak.

"You need to find one thing that you love and stick with it. That's the only way you'll succeed . . . and not flit away on all of these distractions." Mathilda's hands moved toward a new bolt of fabric she had not noticed before.

Although she did not have a weakness for beautiful things, the color of the fabric entranced her. Pale blue silk, so smooth when she ran her palm over it. It felt like liquid sky.

"Another new purchase, Cornelia?"

Mathilda could hardly help herself; she knew it must have cost a fortune. She picked it up to examine it more closely. Once again, her sister's judgment bewildered her.

"Please don't touch that one," Cornelia cried out.

But before Mathilda could put the fabric back in place, a handwritten note slipped out from one of the silken folds and floated to the ground.

My darling C. I see your eyes in all things blue; I want to experience this fabric rippling like the ocean when we dance. Create something beautiful with it. K.

"K!" Mathilda's voice rose in disbelief. "Who is K?"

"It's . . . an . . ." Cornelia didn't know what to say. Her cheeks were scarlet.

Mathilda lifted her hands in exasperation. "I am now completely at a loss for words. A love affair with a man who buys you silks . . . I only hope he is not married."

Cornelia's face blanched.

"The women will be here any minute, and I have no energy to discuss any of this further. I must regain my composure so the spirits will talk through me."

Cornelia knew there was no use trying to explain, so she kept quiet. Mathilda had seen through her veil.

· · · · ·

The grandfather clock rang and signaled that the time of the meeting had arrived. Mathilda's office glowed with candlelight as each woman was led inside. The first to come to the apartment were Hilma and Anna. No longer in male attire, Hilma

57

wore an elegant black dress, her flaxen hair pulled back into a tight chignon.

Eager to put her confrontation with her sister behind her for the evening, Mathilda greeted Hilma warmly.

"I see you left your brother at home. . . . I will miss seeing his hat."

"Ah, but he still lives inside me. . . ." Hilma took a fist to her breast. Her answer was meant to be coy, but it pleased Mathilda, and she smiled.

"We all have male and female sides within us. I'm happy you weren't just attempting a silly folly the last time."

"Not at all," Hilma said, her voice returning to a more serious tone. "I'm here because I've always sought higher knowledge."

"So you've attended séances in the past, then?"

"My sister died nearly twenty years ago from pneumonia, and I've been trying to find a way to communicate with her ever since."

"The dead are all around us; we just need to find a way to give them a voice," Mathilda sympathized.

"Yes, it's one of the reasons we came to the Edelweiss meeting," Anna added. "As artists, we must be open to all the forces around us. We are at a crucial moment in history, when science is revealing new wonders. So we must continue to search for more wisdom wherever we can find it. Right, Hilma?" She looked over at her friend knowingly. For years, Hilma had shared with her books written by well-known Theosophists such as Helena Blavatsky who believed only a thin veil separated us from the spiritual realm and that reincarnation continued until absolute consciousness was achieved. "In the mean-time, I brought you both this. . . . It's a small gift to show our gratitude for your hosting tonight."

Anna held out a black leather notebook with a gold-tooled border around the edges. "I thought this might be useful to write down what we experience." Anna extended the notebook in the direction of both women, but Cornelia reached out to take it first.

"Oh, how kind! Thank you," she said, brightening. "This will be so helpful to have handy!"

Another voice emerged. Sigrid stood at the room's threshold. Her brown hair was braided just as it had been the week before, in a coil behind her head. She clutched a Bible.

"I'm sorry I am late," she apologized. "It is not an easy task to get five children to eat their dinner early and not fight over the littlest thing. . . ."

Her oval face, pale against her austere black dress, was without expression.

"We all can only imagine. . . . Please come in. . . ." Mathilda made a welcoming gesture with her hand toward the interior of the room. The first thing that greeted the women was a make-shift altar she kept in the corner of her office. Draped in a white tablecloth, the pedestal was decorated with a crucifix, a small statue of the Virgin Mary, a golden triangle, and two burning taper candles.

"Oh, how lovely," Sigrid remarked. "I feel a special energy here, as though we were creating our own secret church." She looked over at the triangle and smiled. "You even have the sign of the Holy Trinity. How wonderful."

"Yes, I hoped to create a feeling of unity here tonight after the disharmony we experienced at Edelweiss. Stockholm is full of spiritual dilettantes, men and women trying to access the other side with mediums who are more like circus leaders asking for a sum of money for a good show. This evening, I wanted to show respect for all the spirits in the universe," Mathilda answered as she assessed her altar with an air of satisfaction.

"So no money will be exchanged tonight, then? Hilma asked. "In the past when we attended a séance, Anna and I've had to pay a fee to the host." She pursed her lips. "It did always leave a rather bitter aftertaste in my mouth."

"Oh, my sister would never dream of that!" Cornelia cut in.

"I am not a charlatan," Mathilda clarified. "I believe we are all equals here. We are five women seeking wisdom." She cleared her throat. "One doesn't charge money for that."

"Love and knowledge," Anna added, "should always be free."

· · · · ·

The candlelight enveloped the newly formed group and shadows flickered over their faces.

"Let's cleanse the air in the room before we begin," Mathilda suggested. For several minutes the women had been exchanging pleasantries among themselves.

But now Mathilda tried to corral them back to the reason they had all come together.

"We must start to sharpen our intention for this evening's gathering," she announced as she walked toward her cabinet and pulled out a cluster of dried sage leaves tied together with string. She lifted it to her nose and inhaled its aroma, then passed it around. "Let this clear your passages," she told them.

Each one of them took the sachet and breathed its fragrance in, before returning it to her for safekeeping.

"It is important we each pay respect to the spiritual masters who will guide us tonight." Mathilda pointed to the altar.

"Do any of you have any questions?" she asked the four women.

Sigrid did not answer, but instead stepped toward the altar and lifted a single finger toward the porcelain Virgin.

"I wonder if I might lead tonight," she asked. Her tone was surprisingly matter-of-fact.

Mathilda arched an eyebrow, clearly taken aback. "I am sorry if you didn't understand the intention of tonight's meeting, but I will be the one channeling."

"I see," Sigrid answered flatly. She walked back toward the group. "It's only that I am seeing a fireball of orange color suddenly flash inside the room. I thought perhaps it was a sign that I should be the one to reach toward it."

"Well, let us pull that globe of energy into our hearts and use it to forge a connection among all five of us in this room," Mathilda answered, trying to sound upbeat.

"Yes," Cornelia agreed. "That sounds like the right path for tonight's gathering."

"We should begin now that dusk is upon us," Mathilda advised.

"Please find your seats at the table."

"As you've been searching for your sister, Hilma, please take the chair that has a bowl of water in front of it. If you see any movement during the séance, you must tell us at once."

"Am I the only one to look down at the bowl?"

"Yes," Mathilda answered firmly.

"I can sit next to her," Anna offered.

Mathilda nodded.

Anna moved toward the table, inhaling a heady aroma in the air that was different from the fragrance of sage. The smell reached deep into her nostrils. How very peculiar, she thought. Warm globes of light filled the room, yet nothing was on fire. But strangely, she detected the scent of smoke.

"Hilma, remember that you must tell us if you observe even the slightest movement in the water."

"Yes, I understand."

"Good. Except for Anna and Hilma, we must all close our eyes and hold hands," Mathilda instructed. "Please, may the spirits offer us their wisdom and guidance," she intoned, her eyes closed and her head lowered. "Honor us with your presence. . . . Reward us with your gifts of knowledge." Then she said to the others, "Please repeat after me. *Nåd och ljus, Nåd och ljus . . .*" "Grace and light," the women chanted in unison.

Five voices merged into one.

Nothing happened for several seconds. Mathilda looked over at Hilma, whose head was bowed, her gaze firmly fixated on the bowl of water. Long fingers of light flickered across Sigrid's face; her expression was twisted in intense concentration.

"Please, great spirits of grace and wisdom, guide us with your knowledge. Show us a sign that you hear our voices on this blessed night."

The women continued with locked hands, their grips moistened by perspiration and determination. The room swelled with energy and breath.

"Spirits, let us know you are with us. Show us there is a reason we five have all joined hands tonight as one . . . ," Mathilda intoned. She pursed her lips and began to hum. Her body rocked from side to side and then jolted back in her chair with great force.

Suddenly, the candle in front of Sigrid burned higher into the air. The dimly lit room flared with light. And most unexpectedly, the flame caught the edge of one of the dry palm leaves, and it began to burn.

And at the same time, the water in the bowl rippled with tiny waves. "It's moving!" Hilma cried out. "The water . . . it's moving!"

Sigrid's eyes flashed open.

In response to this dramatic sequence of events, Anna jumped up, grabbed the bowl of water, and threw it over the leaf, extinguishing the small fire.

All five women witnessed a thin feather of smoke coming from the water-soaked leaf.

Mathilda remained slouched for several seconds before returning to her body. A thin line of perspiration ran down from one of her temples. She gathered herself and then slowly stood up. She looked over to Sigrid, noticing that the fire had come from the candle in front of her chair.

"Ladies, this has been a most remarkable response. We have been visited by the two elements of earth—fire and water."

Hilma looked up, her face awash in wonder. While she had hoped to get a message from her sister, she could not deny the power of what she had just witnessed.

"We must meet every Friday from now on," Mathilda announced. "The spirits are with us."

CHAPTER FOUR

·····

EBEN

Present Day
New York City

My walk to work takes only five minutes. It's a little more than four blocks from the brownstone where I live to the museum. I walk out my door, turn right on Ninety-Third, turn left at the corner onto Fifth Avenue, and then head downtown. You don't see the Guggenheim until you hit the corner of Eighty-Ninth Street. The structure comes upon you like a surprise.

New York is a city of boxes. Narrow or tall, taking up a full city block or nestled in between other brownstones, all the buildings are rectangles of one size or another. But Frank Lloyd Wright built a cream-colored spiral to house the art collection of Solomon R. Guggenheim. It's a short building in a city of skyscrapers, with space all around it, and that, too, is unusual in Manhattan. Air rights are valuable. But spatial elegance is even more sought after. The museum is a work of art itself. Which of course is what its detractors have been criticizing it for since it was unveiled in 1959 shortly after its architect passed away. "Architecture for architecture's sake" was one of the kindest things said about it.

It's not a building without controversy. Some call it a giant snail that crawled out of Central Park. Others say it looks like a spaceship that landed on the avenue. An inverted oatmeal dish. A hot cross bun. A washing machine. The director and writer Woody Allen famously called it a giant lavatory basin. Jackie Onassis concurred.

But I agreed with what the architecture critic Paul Goldberger said about it: "I think the legacy of this building is in the message that architecture does not have to lie down and play dead in front of art. That there are other ways to show art than in a neutral space. That an architect can do something that's powerful in itself and that enhances the experience of looking at art."

I think of the Guggenheim as a town in itself. You come into the lobby, which functions as a town square. Check your coat, get your ticket, or head for the café. When you're ready to engage with the art, you walk up the ramp, which rises like a gently sloping hillside, and go around and around, walking from floor to floor, interacting with the amazing artwork.

It's not like every other museum. Or any other museum. The Guggenheim, like its founder, like its architect, breaks with tradition. With reality. There are no vertical lines and no horizons. It allows you to daydream. It gives you the opportunity to look at things differently. And if your eyes tire and your brain needs a break, you can turn away from the artwork and look down over the ramp to the lobby beneath you, or look up at the skylight, or across to see other art lovers as they make their way up and down and around.

For me, my walk to the Guggenheim every morning never gets old. And I'm grateful that I'm Dr. Perlstein's associate curator, because her office is still in the Fifth Avenue building. Because the Guggenheim now has branches in other cities in other countries, the foundation has outgrown the office space at the Wright building. Most employees have offices downtown, at Liberty Plaza, in one of its glass towers. But because Dr. Perlstein is the director for special collections and senior curator, she needs to be on-site.

That Monday morning in July, four months after my trip to Stockholm, we had our weekly eleven o'clock curators' meeting. Twenty of us in the conference room, some coming from downtown. Dr. Perlstein thought it was important to have the meetings in situ, discussing the art where the art would be seen.

We were all on time, but she was ten minutes late, which was very unusual for her. When she did arrive, she was flustered, which was also unusual. And then she broke protocol. Usually we talk about current exhibits and attendance first, but Dr. Perlstein announced that we had a problem with a show that was scheduled for the coming year.

"I've been on the phone all morning to straighten this out—but it looks like we have an emergency. We have to cancel the Lucian Freud exhibit scheduled for October."

There were audible gasps and groans. Preparing and planning an exhibit for the main rotunda of the museum takes anywhere from three to five years. We'd started planning this one in 2014.

Dr. Perlstein explained in brief what had happened. It didn't matter why the exhibit was being canceled. We had a huge problem on our hands. A giant hole in our schedule with less than sixteen months to replace it with another exhibition, fund it, and create a catalog for it. An almost unheard-of timetable.

"I tried to rearrange one of the 2018 shows, but the works are all spoken for. The most logical thing for us to do is to come up with an exhibit based on our holdings. It's a safe plan and requires the least funding—but we already have three house shows scheduled between now and the fall of 2018, and we can't afford to have a slow season."

Dr. Perlstein ran through what the Metropolitan, the Museum of Modern Art, the Brooklyn Museum, and the Whitney had on the books for the same period. All of the exhibitions were compelling. Each of them difficult to compete with. Which was why we had Lucian Freud slotted against them. In a museum-rich city like New York, each institution fights to come up with concepts to draw in the crowds. It's not so much that we are trying to steal attendance away from any other show as it is that we're attempting to ensure we're one of the must-see stops on every art lover's itinerary.

As various curators offered ideas, I pulled out my notebook and read through my last few months of notes. In the process of visiting museums, exploring art galleries, finding articles, and discovering and reading books on new or forgotten artists, I often jotted down ideas for potential shows.

Based on some of my scribbles and sketches, I threw out a few ideas. Nothing caught anyone's attention. I continued searching back through the pages—through June, May, April.

And then I got to March and my notes on Hilma af Klint.

As soon as I saw her name, I knew I'd hit on a real possibility. I could picture those paintings in our museum with a clarity that surprised me. They belonged here. In a building that was almost identical to the one that this artist had envisioned years before Hilla Rebay and Solomon Guggenheim began talking about what their own temple to the spirit would look like.

I read what I'd written.

Artist or mystic?
Non-objective 1906. Before Kandinsky.
Paintings for the Temple vs. Temple to the Spirit.

"I have a thought," I said. "And this one is really possible because all the artwork involved is owned by a foundation or on display in just one museum." I had everyone's attention.

One of the most difficult aspects of putting on a major exhibit is borrowing the various works of art from different museums, collectors, and foundations around the world. A rotunda show could mean one hundred or more lending agreements and pieces that had to be shipped back and forth.

"Who is it, Eben?" Dr. Perlstein asked.

"A retrospective of Hilma af Klint's work."

There was almost no reaction except from Dr. Perlstein and Audrey Titus, who both were nodding. I guessed the rest of the people in the room had to search their memories to even place the name.

"I should have thought of her. Great choice, Eben. I've been fascinated by her for years," Audrey said. She was one of our most senior curators, and the one who'd had the family emergency that prevented her from attending the symposium in Stockholm.

"I'm embarrassed to admit this," Henry Green said. He had been with the Guggenheim for over fifteen years and was an expert on twentieth-century photography. "I don't know who she is. Hilma af Klimt—related to Gustav Klimt?"

There were a few murmurs of agreement from around the table.

"Not Klimt," I said. "K-L-I-N-T. An obscure Swedish artist who hid her work away for decades."

"Interesting, interesting choice, Eben. What's your thinking?" Dr. Perlstein asked.

"Art history has overlooked her, so we'd be the first to turn the spotlight on her outside of Sweden. She was a radical visionary whose work shows a drastic stylistic break from her predecessors years before Kandinsky and Mondrian even thought of non-objective painting. She broke new ground and gets no credit for it. That's the most important reason. And then there's the fact that no museum in the world is more perfect to do it than us. Hilma af Klint created over one hundred paintings to be displayed in a temple she designed. I saw her sketch. Her temple is a spiral almost identical to ours. Except it was drawn more than twenty years before Rebay and Guggenheim ever approached Frank Lloyd Wright. She even included a spiral symbol in numerous paintings." I surprised myself a little by my passion. I hadn't thought about Hilma af Klint since returning from my trip, months before.

"Well, that is totally fascinating," Dr. Perlstein said. "I knew about her, but I've never studied her work. I'd love to see that sketch of her temple."

For a moment, I thought of Blythe and her Hecate moments. I hadn't spoken to her since Stockholm. She'd have loved to be in this room right now.

"You implied the work will be fairly uncomplicated to borrow?" Audrey asked.

"Her paintings and drawings aren't scattered around the world," I said. "Almost a hundred percent of her work is owned by the Hilma af Klint Foundation, which is run by her great-nephew, with just a few pieces on loan to the Moderna Museet. Everything we need is in Stockholm. If those two institutions agree to lend us what we want, we'll be home free."

"The #MeToo angle is really timely," Cecily Mann added. At twenty-three, she was our youngest assistant and often talked in hashtags. Although her habit could be slightly annoying, she kept us abreast of the most current issues and topics trending in social media. "This could put us at the forefront of the art canon's feminist expansion."

"Building on that is that Hilma was also a mystic," Audrey explained to those of us around the table. "She was heavily involved with a group of four other women who engaged in regular séances in order to communicate with spirits to guide them with their work. They were connected to Theosophy if I remember correctly." She turned to me. "How much of the group and their spiritualism would figure into the show?"

"It's an interesting footnote," I said. "Not the theme. What's important are her paintings. The ones I saw were monumental and way ahead of her time."

"Which is why the spiritualism angle works," Audrey persisted.

"I think it's the wrong direction to take," I said.

"Why is that, Eben?" Dr. Perlstein asked.

"It will overshadow her paintings. You know how people will seize on it. What is so original and fascinating about Hilma af Klint is her radical innovation—what she did with color and size and abstractions before anyone anywhere else."

"And that's exactly why the mysticism matters," Audrey countered. "She claimed the spirits moved her hand. That they told her what to do. She had insight beyond logic. She had a deep and abiding faith in her spiritual beliefs, and that allowed her to create magnificence," Audrey said with great passion. "Interest in psychic phenomena and the occult is high these days."

I couldn't help moaning, which earned me a rebuking glance from Dr. Perlstein. Another bad habit of mine.

I looked at Audrey. "Sorry."

She lifted her eyebrows and shrugged.

"Do you have anything useful to add to Audrey's comment on the metaphysical aspect, Eben?" Dr. Perlstein asked.

"I do. If we go that route, I am very concerned people will see Hilma as a mystic first. As a kook. Even a witch. They're going to miss the importance of her place in the modern art movement. And that is the one aspect that shouldn't be down-played."

Dr. Perlstein interrupted. "Before we break out the boxing gloves, let's see if this show is even a possibility. I have to say I hope it is, because I have faith that the argument you two are having is exactly the kind of controversy that would get us a lot of attention and bring people in."

"Faith," Audrey said, echoing one of my least favorite words. "That has to be one of the show's themes. Faith in her talent, in the messages the spirits gave her, and in her decision to put her paintings away for the future."

*   *   *   *   *

Walking out of the museum an hour later to meet a gallery owner whom I had lunch plans with was not as pleasant an experience as walking in that morning.

As I approached the exit, Stan Bigelow, a fifty-something guard who had been working at the museum longer than I had, shook his head. "There's a mob out there, Eben. You might want to go out through the basement and the back. Though they might be there too."

I stepped up to the glass door and peered out. As far as I could see, in front of the museum, to the right, and to the left, protestors were lying down on the pavement. As if playing dead.

"What the hell?" I turned back to Stan.

"It's the Forrest Family Trust issue."

"So they've finally landed on our doorstep?"

"It appears they have."

The entire arts community knew about Forrest Family Trust protests. At the Guggenheim, we knew we'd be targeted sooner or later. Clearly our time had come.

The Forrest Family owned a giant pharmaceutical company that manufactured, among other things, a pain medication that was responsible for hundreds of thousands of deaths due to addiction. The family was being sued for billions of dollars for misleading marketing of the drug since it had first been approved in the mid-1990s. The problem for so many art institutions was that Forrest Family members were rabid art patrons and in the last thirty years had donated huge sums of money to build new wings and fund exhibitions.

In recent months, a prominent painter and radical, Iris Vestry, had started an advocacy organization to shame museums and universities into refusing funding and removing all signage bearing the Forrest name. Over a hundred well-known artists had joined her group, called De-Forrest Now, and staged sit-ins and demonstrations like the one that had just formed outside the Guggenheim.

I could see at least two dozen protesters lying behind the sawhorses that had been set up to allow an unfettered entrance to and exit from our front door to the sidewalk and down the street. Others stood close to the barriers and handed out what appeared to be dollar bills to museumgoers.

"It looks pretty peaceful," I said to Stan.

"About as peaceful as a horror movie," he replied. "They call it a 'die-in.' And those bills are fake dollars labeled 'blood money' and soaked in what I assume is red paint but looks like real blood."

I didn't feel like retracing my steps and going out the back exit. It would make me late.

"I'll brave it," I said, and Stan opened the door for me.

When I reached the protesters, one on my right offered me an ersatz dollar bill, which I took.

"De-Forrest the Guggenheim. Demand action," she said.

As I walked toward the sidewalk, which was littered with more of the fake money, I examined what I was holding.

It was a photocopied dollar that seemed like a perfect replica of our currency, except *Big Pharma States of America* was printed where it should have read *The United States of America*. The ersatz bill also featured *400,000 Dead* instead of a serial number. Where the treasury secretary's name should have been was the forged, I assumed, signature of Nathan Forrest, the head of the family dynasty. The family name was also used in various ways on the bill.

On the flip side, which was also smeared with what looked like blood, our museum was replicated in the left spot where a luminary should have been. I assumed the group changed that image depending on the institution they were protesting in front of that week.

All in all, it was a powerful and extremely well-done articulation of our currency. And I wouldn't have expected less from Iris Vestry. The museum had included her in a 2012 show of art activists. Her mentor had been one of the Guerilla Girls, a group of feminist activist artists who first surfaced in 1985, dedicated to exposing gender and ethnic bias in art, politics, film, and pop culture. Always wearing gorilla masks in public, they had staged hundreds of protests since they formed, and their outrageous visuals had brought an enormous amount of attention to their causes. Sadly, though, there was still so far to go with the imbalances they focused on.

Returning from my lunch, I found a message from Dr. Perlstein to come see her, and so I made my way up the staircase. Our offices were on the top two floors of the six-story rectangle that had been designed by the firm of Gwathmey Siegel and built in 1992. The new building afforded the museum four additional exhibition galleries, used mostly for our permanent collection, as well as two floors devoted to offices.

Dr. Perlstein looked up when I entered. Her office was painted white with cobalt blue accents. Her desk was at one end of the room, situated in front of overcrowded bookshelves. An aluminum table with six matching chairs was at the other end, in front of more overcrowded bookshelves. A large window took up the north wall. The updated version of old paned windows—five over five—looked out on Eighty-Ninth Street.

"Did you just come back from lunch?" Dr. Perlstein asked. I nodded.

"Is it any better out there?" she asked.

"The protesters? No. If anything, there are more of them now than when I went out."

"This is a nightmare for the board. I don't like the situation any more than Iris Vestry does. What the Forrests have done as a business is despicable. And I don't have any argument that going forward no institution should benefit from their largesse. But it's a very complicated struggle to figure out what to do about money we've all already taken and used to build wings, libraries, and galleries."

She took off her oversize square glasses and rubbed between her eyes. "Back to the business at hand. I think you'll be pleased to know I've already made some serious headway with the Hilma af Klint idea you had this morning. I know the director of the Moderna personally and called her. She agreed to lend us the paintings and immediately put me in touch with the Hilma af Klint Foundation. Miraculously, I got through to them right way, and they agreed as well. It's almost as if it were fated."

I winced.

She hesitated. "What is it, Eben? You don't look happy."

"I most certainly am."

"Then why your reaction?"

"The part about fate. Sorry, I can already feel the woo-woo aspects of this getting out of hand."

"I think you are too worried about that. We can manage it. A group of five women holding séances isn't exactly a coven of witches slaughtering animals and drinking their blood at midnight in front of an altar made of nude men. Do you agree?"

"Well, that was specific." I laughed.

She did, too, and then said, "Okay, then. Let's get to work. I think we can just pull this off, but I'm going to need you working at superhuman levels to get the catalog done and help with the sponsorship packages."

I nodded, hoping that was all she was going to say about the catalog. We both knew she was referring to a period last year when I'd screwed up and almost been fired. Over the summer, my father had had a mild heart attack. That in itself wasn't the problem. What was, was that his second wife, whom I'd never gotten along with, was trying to turn him against me and take control of his business as well as his health management.

It wasn't that I wanted control, but I was close to my father, and his new marriage was getting between us, and I didn't want that to happen. When I flew down to Florida to see to things, I turned over my workload to another associate curator without informing my supervisor. As it turned out, the associate screwed up a major essay and annoyed an important author so much, the author pulled out.

When I returned from my trip, Dr. Perlstein let me know that I'd made a serious error in judgment. For a few days, I thought I might lose my job, but in the end, given the nature of my father's situation, she just gave me a stern warning that I couldn't take it upon myself to decide how to handle every decision.

It wasn't the first time she'd talked to me about my tendency to act alone. My independence was a serious flaw—not necessarily in life, but certainly in the collaborative atmosphere of a museum.

"I'm very excited about this show, Eben," Dr. Perlstein said. "I think the female aspect, the hidden legacy, the devoted artist who was shunned by the male art establishment while moved and directed by mystical influences, seems so right for today. Our biggest challenge is going to be finding funding. That and lining up the right historians for the catalog within the time frame. Why don't you put together a rough schedule, a list of themes and titles for the show, and ideas for essays you think we should try for. Let's get all that done by the end of the week."

Three days to do a job that normally would take a month. But this wasn't a typical situation.

I was still in Dr. Perlstein's office when her assistant came to the door. The police, who had been on duty outside the museum all day because of the demonstration, had arrested one of the protesters, and all hell had broken loose downstairs. Dr. Perlstein sighed and shifted gears to deal with her newest problem, and I returned to my office.

I pulled up a calendar on my computer and for the next hour filled in various boxes with dates we'd need to meet to make everything happen by October 2018. And then I rearranged them. And then I rearranged them again. Finally satisfied, I emailed the document to Dr. Perlstein as a suggested schedule. My next effort—by far the most important one to me—was to come up with the theme for the show, since that would also dictate the direction of the catalog.

Sitting in my office isn't how I think best. Walking or swimming is.

Most mornings I swim at Asphalt Green, a magnificent art deco asphalt plant erected in 1941 that was reconfigured into a sports center in 1993. My usual weekday time is seven a.m., and I try to stick to that on weekends so I get there before it's too crowded. But I'd missed that morning and decided to try my luck in the afternoon.

I put my phone in my pocket and left the building, this time doing what Stan had suggested earlier that day and leaving through the basement to avoid the melee in front. I didn't want to be distracted by the protest.

I was lucky to score a lane after only a five-minute wait. I was surprised to see a kid, only about seven or eight, doing laps next to me. She looked like a baby seal in her navy suit and with her navy cap tight on her head, and the technique of her breast-stroke was among the best I'd ever seen anyone—let alone a child—do.

It usually takes only five or ten laps for my mind to slip into a meditative state where I'm not aware of who's around me or the noise or people coming or going. But the little girl's surprising form and speed distracted me.

As always, I swam for forty-five minutes. She was still going when I got out. While I toweled off, I watched her glide through the water. I can take or leave ballet or modern dance, but swimmers mesmerize me.

"She's very good, isn't she?" a man in his fifties, I guessed, with a slight accent said to me. Wearing jeans and a chambray shirt and leather driving shoes, he was the epitome of casual elegance.

I noticed the old-fashioned stopwatch he was holding—at the ready to end its gentle ticking as soon as the child stopped.

"She is excellent." I nodded to the stopwatch. "Is she in training?"

"Her mother is debating that. We're not sure if it's really good for Willa to do something so competitive when she's still so young. Her mother wants her to have a childhood with as little stress as possible. And I agree . . ." He shrugged. "But Willa wants it so badly that we're entertaining it."

The child pulled up at the edge of the pool. "Hey, Pop, how did I do?" she asked breathlessly.

He checked her time.

"Two minutes faster."

She fist-pumped the air and swam to the ladder. By the time she was out of the pool, her father had a big white-and-blue-striped towel open. She ran into it. He wrapped her up, hugging her. When he let her go, she pulled off her bathing cap and shook loose a headful of blond curls.

"Amazing job, Willa," her father said.

"It was," I added. "I couldn't help but notice you swimming next to me, and you did really great."

She was a little shy but gave me a gentle smile. "Thanks."

"Have a great day," I said to both of them, and headed off to the changing rooms.

During my swim, I'd thought about the paintings I'd seen in Stockholm and what I'd learned from the Moderna curator and Blythe's lecture on Hilma af Klint. I realized that to come up with the right angle for the catalog I needed to immerse mysef in what had been written. And that meant hours of homework. Which meant canceling my evening plans.

On my walk back to the museum, I pulled my phone out of my pocket and called Daphne. We were supposed to go to a cocktail party hosted by one of her clients, then have dinner afterward. I knew she'd be fine with me not going. My relationship with her was as easy as ever, and easy worked for me. I'd known the opposite once. And I suddenly remembered the sound of Blythe laughing and saying "easy-peasy" to me in Stockholm. God, the two of us had been anything but.

Daphne's voice came over the line—her recorded voice. I left a message and hung up, not wanting to dwell on the fact that I was relieved I'd gotten voice mail. I just wasn't in the mood to chat. I wanted to get back to Hilma af Klint and the exhibit.

Looking back, I realized that was when I got the first glimmer of the idea. I remembered one of the interesting things that Blythe had told me about Hilma and that Audrey had alluded to earlier that morning. Because af Klint had been rebuffed and ignored by her contemporaries in the art world, she'd decided to protect herself and her ability to create by not showing her work at all. She'd even made provisions for the paintings and drawings to be hidden away and not shown until at least two decades after her death. She believed that her work would be understood only in a distant future. So sure was she of that eventual acceptance, she had spent years cataloging and numbering more than a thousand pieces.

I spent the rest of the afternoon back at the office doing research. There were no biographies of her written in English—only one in Swedish—and only a handful of articles. Just before it was time to leave, I went to the Guggenheim library and tracked down the catalog from the 1986 LACMA show that included Hilma and borrowed it for the night.

I walked home, book in hand, thinking about Hilma. Upstairs, I poured some vodka into a glass, cut a lime and added that and some ice, and took the drink into the living room. I pulled out the catalog and, sitting with my feet up on the coffee table, read the essay about Hilma af Klint first and then went back and read the others. Including the one written by Blythe Larkin.

When there was nothing left in the glass but the lime wedge,

I put down the book and looked at the mantelpiece clock, surprised at how much time had passed.

As I rose and went to open the window, my eyes rested on my mother's last piece of sculpture. I had several of her finished works on display in my home. One in the library/dining room, another in the foyer. My father had some in Florida. A dozen had been sold to private collections, and a few were in minor museums.

My mother had been a twenty-six-year-old up-and-coming sculptor when she met my father. She carved in marble, focusing on non-objective shapes—circles, infinity symbols, and squares—and piercing them all with holes of various sizes, inside of which she placed intricate figures built out of clay and cast in bronze. The people, small and almost doll-like, inside of the large abstract shapes looked like creatures exploring distant planets. They were searchers, wanderers, pilgrims. I'd always wanted to know more about them and had scoured the notebooks my mother had left behind. But there were no words in any of them. Only endless sketches of the large forms and the small characters. Each work was titled simply—*Circle, No. 5*; *Square, No. 8*. My father had told me he'd asked her once why she didn't give them more interesting names, and she'd said she wanted people to title them themselves. That what someone else saw in her work was even more important than what she did.

Her last, unfinished piece, the one I kept in front of the window in my living room, was a four-foot-tall white marble infinity loop. Three-quarters of it—the top toward the middle of the bottom loop—had been polished to a high satin, smooth to the touch, but the lower half was still rough. You could see my mother's chisel marks.

Inside the lower half of the top loop, she'd placed her small people. Each a different shade of golden bronze. A baby crawling and a toddler standing, reaching up for something. It was one of the very few pieces that she had given a proper name. *Tomorrow, No. 1.* I knew its name because I'd found the sketches for it in one of her notebooks. From the drawing, I knew the baby/toddler was me at different ages.

Hilma af Klint left notebooks, too, I thought as I walked past my mother's sculpture. The essay I'd just read had included many quotes from them, including one in which she decreed all her works should be kept hidden away until twenty years after her death.

I knew many artists think about the future and plan for what will happen to their work. Some even obsess about how they will be viewed through the lens of history and about the lasting impact of their oeuvre. They cling to the idea that long after they are gone, people who view what they have created will be gifted with a look inside their soul and that their art will remain relevant. But what of the artists who aren't even slightly relevant in their own time? Do they have only the future? Was Hilma protecting herself from more rejection by hiding her work away, or was she truly prophetic?

Did she know she was painting for generations yet to come who would appreciate and understand her efforts? Was she painting for the future?

·····

Dear Hilma,

I have been struggling since our last Friday night meeting to work on my own paintings. I know you will understand this frustration more than anyone. For days now, I've been trying to finish a small landscape, to render the quiet solitude I feel when I am surrounded by the golden oaks and birch trees up north. But the colors have become too muddy, and the canvas has not yet mirrored what's in my mind's eye. I know my concentration has been affected by Lotten's illness. Some days she is so tired and her complexion so pale that she looks as though she is only steps away from heaven. The pain in seeing her suffer is almost too great for me, and I often wish I, not she, were the one born with the weak heart, so I would be spared seeing her in such a fragile condition.

I realize you comprehend this anguish, that there isn't a day that goes by when you don't think of your darling sister, Hermina. I had been hoping that Mathilda would channel a message from her during our last session, but perhaps it will come in the near future. We must strengthen our bonds as a group in the meantime. I yearn to be connected with a group of spiritually minded souls who seek answers like we do to life's many mysteries. The other day, I was struck by the memory of you at our island residence, when we went to collect wildflowers in the fields beyond the lake. . . . Do you remember that afternoon when you held the red poppy in your hand and began to pluck the petals away from the middle because you wanted to see how the fibers attached to the center, and how the center connected them to the stem? Even then you wanted to learn how nature fitted all of its intricate pieces together. You made me infinitely more curious about the world, Hilma, and I'll be forever grateful that you've made my life so rich. I cannot wait to see what we learn with our new group. I hope our hearts and minds will be filled with more knowledge, more wisdom, and a deeper sense of what our legacies should be in the short time we have on this earth.

It will be good to see you again this Friday at Blanch's gallery before the meeting. I feel like it's been far too long since we last walked through there together and gazed at the paintings. How wonderful it will be as a prelude to another séance.

Always,
Your Anna

CHAPTER FIVE

• • • • •

Friday Night, No. 3
October 30, 1896
Stockholm

Anna clutched her cape closer to her chest and pitched her umbrella in the direction of the wind. She had to hurry to meet Hilma.

As the sheets of rain continued to fall, Anna muttered under her breath about the absurdity of heading out in weather as inclement as this. After her initial excitement to see the new exhibit, the rain had put a damper on things, and then Lotten had her first good day in weeks. She had even felt well enough to leave her bed and play a few of her favorite pieces on her beloved piano. Part of Anna thought she should spend the afternoon with her sister. But the recent discovery of Hellström's letter to Hilma had unnerved her. She worried that her friend might invite that wretched doctor to go in her place. It was hard to forget how Hilma had once described his having an irrepressible and insatiable hunger for her.

"He's like a wolf," she confided. "He gets as much satisfaction from the hunt as he does from the catch." Hilma's eyes sparkled, and she threw her head back and laughed. Anna knew her friend deeply enjoyed keeping him hungry for her, that she drew power from his desire.

"I'll never actually marry him, Anna," Hilma had promised her time and time again.

But her old flame never seemed to completely vanish from their lives. Months, even years, would pass, but somehow Hellström would always reappear, a persistent dark shadow Anna longed to erase.

· · · · ·

Blanch's café and art gallery in the Kungsträdgården remained one of Hilma and Anna's favorite places in Stockholm, and it was located conveniently on the ground floor of Hilma's building. The elegant vaulted space, with the carved plaster walls and Belle Epoque flourishes, presented an arena of intriguing contrasts. Blanch, the handsome and stylish founder, had been hailed as a genius by some, using his clever eye to juxtapose the classically ornamental setting with the work of rising avant-garde artists of the day. The end result was a fashionable destination within Stockholm's city center that offered a glimpse at impressionistic paintings that many Swedes had never seen before, and in an environment that welcomed them with ease and comfort. Not to mention a flute of champagne.

Anna would never forget the moment she stepped into Blanch's for the first time, when she and Hilma were young art students. Against the soft light of chandeliers and plush carpets, she had been swept away by seeing so many artists and writers whom she had only heard of in passing. She spotted Hanna Hirsch and Georg Pauli huddled in a corner, their heads tilted in conversation. Jenny Nystrom, the popular folk illustrator, mingled with the elegant painter Eva Bonnier, who had just returned from her sojourn abroad.

Hilma had sniffed at a canvas she spotted by one of their classmates, Anders Zorn.

"He thinks he's a meteorite." She scowled. "Propelled faster above everyone else." She had walked quickly past all of Anders's entries that afternoon, not giving them a second of her attention.

But then something magical happened. Both she and Hilma had instinctively paused at the same painting, each of them completely captivated by the sight of a wholly unique canvas by a French artist named Claude Monet who was also included in the exhibit.

He had painted a seascape at sunset, the rocky, jagged cliffs of Normandy set against a vibrant orange-and-apricot-colored sky. His palette seemed to glow against the dark wall of Blanch's salon.

"It's like it possesses its own illumination," Anna had whispered in awe.

Hilma had inched closer and peered to examine the texture of Monet's brushstrokes.

"You can feel the energy lifting off the canvas," she declared, amazed. "It's as if he captured the very essence of the sunset—the splendor of it, not just all of its colors."

Anna had loved every moment of the exhibit, for it had indicated a new progression of painting beyond the stodgy atmosphere of the academy within which she and Hilma lived each day. Gone were the dark, oppressive backgrounds, and the somber faces illuminated by a sheath of light, that so many Dutch and Scandinavian masters had done for centuries. Here, on the walls of Blanch's salon, were paintings that looked like they had been painted outside in the sunshine, the way Hilma and she had loved to do during their summer holiday on the archipelago islands. The pastel-colored canvases were filled with a warmth and a sense of creative urgency that thrilled her.

Anna appreciated seeing how many Swedish artists were experimenting in the French impressionist style. Hilma, however, refused to give them any credit.

"If a Swede comes back from France and then paints like a Frenchman, what does that make them?" Hilma questioned. "A visionary or just a copycat?"

Anna became quiet. Her friend had posed an interesting question, and Anna was unsure of the answer.

"Wouldn't it be something," Hilma said, filling the silence between them, "if a Frenchman came to Sweden and took something back from us!" She tossed her head back. "Now, that I'd certainly like to see. . . ."

. . . . .

Hilma and Anna had now been to countless openings since that first one nearly a decade earlier. Anna was hopeful the exhibit this afternoon would exhilarate them, especially before they joined the others for their weekly Friday night séance.

"I was beginning to worry you wouldn't come." Hilma

leaned in and kissed Anna on both cheeks. "I'm glad you did despite the terrible weather."

Anna unbuckled her cloak and shook out her umbrella, then handed them to the young woman checking coats. Anna quickly glanced at the copy of *Dagens Nyheter* tucked underneath her friend's arm.

"Oh, Hilma, what are you reading now?" Anna asked, pointing to the newspaper. "Another article about X-rays?"

Hilma laughed. "No, actually the splitting of atoms . . ."

Anna shook her head. "You're obsessed with all this science. I'm beginning to wonder, are you a painter or a physicist?"

"Can't I be both? I don't understand how anyone would not read all they can about these latest discoveries. It helps us understand how everything is intertwined." She snapped a finger to the newspaper headline. "Aren't we all atoms, swirling around in the universe? We can come together and be one. Or we can exist individually. Science is a metaphor for life . . . for the universe."

Anna sighed. "Your mind never stops, does it?"

"No, it doesn't." Hilma fixed her eyes on Anna, her lips turning upward like those of a mischievous cat. "And that is why I wanted you to see one painting in particular. . . ." She slid her arm through Anna's and pressed herself close. "To be an artist means to always be curious." She planted a little kiss on Anna's shoulder. "And to always be searching for connections . . . Who knows, with the recent development in X-rays, wouldn't it be wonderful if there was a way to *see* the spirits among us?"

As they walked into the main hall of Blanch's salon, Anna felt hot beneath the wool of her dress. It pleased her to see that Hilma was wearing the green velvet scarf she'd bought for her during their grand tour in Italy nearly a decade before. During many subsequent winter nights, when the snow piled high on the windowsills outside her Floragatan apartment, Anna's heart felt like it was stoking a fire whenever she remembered all they had done together there.

She cherished the memories, especially as her life over the past few months had grown stifling due to Lotten's poor health. She felt young again every time she thought of that trip. It was her secret candy, one she could unwrap and savor when she was by herself. And it never failed to make Anna feel alive. Confined to working in a small area of her bedroom, she yearned for the coming summer months, when she could paint outside again and not have to open her window to soften the fumes of linseed oil and turpentine, which she knew were not good for her lungs or her sister's.

While she hadn't been granted the use of an art studio from the Swedish Art Association like Hilma had, Anna hadn't advocated for herself either. She just didn't have the same ambition that Hilma possessed. This had always been one of the main differences between them.

Hilma was always searching for something, whereas Anna found herself more satisfied by life. Was this a sign of complacency on her part? Anna wasn't sure, but what she did know was that she had always been easily contented, whereas her friend seemed to find a source of creativity in her discontent.

The new exhibit this evening, however, energized Hilma. With every canvas she passed, the flush in her cheeks intensified.

"Look at this." Hilma beckoned, pointing to a wood-block print of two swans. She and Hilma shared an affinity for the large-winged bird. Both of them had painted black-and-white versions of it, which had since become a motif between them.

"He's made the neck too short," Hilma critiqued, shaking her head. "You'd think Blanch could do better than exhibit something as amateurish as this."

Anna sensed that Hilma had been hoping for Blanch to invite her to hang some of her artwork on the walls of his salon, but the offer had never arrived.

"Maybe Mathilda will be able to reach deeper with the spirits tonight and give us more answers," Anna said optimistically. "All of us want more guidance on our true path and clarity about what our legacy will be. Neither of us is getting any younger, after all."

"Says who?" Hilma laughed. She thrust her shoulders back and puffed out her chest. "Thirty-four is hardly ancient, my friend."

Anna reached out and touched the green velvet scarf. "I must ask Cornelia to make you something new to wrap around your throat. This one is getting too worn."

Hilma shrugged, unfazed by the missing threads on the scarf's tasseled edge.

Anna had made the comment hoping that Hilma would say something nostalgic about the scarf. But as many times as she wished her friend would reveal a bit of sentimentality, she only found herself disappointed. One thing was undeniable about Hilma: she hated to look backward.

· · · · ·

In a dark room, bathed in candlelight, Anna and Hilma found Mathilda enthroned in a wicker rocking chair, a large notebook lying open on her lap.

"Come sit down," she said as she lifted her head from her written pages. "The other women will be joining us in a moment." Mathilda gestured with her hand like a sultan toward the four empty chairs.

"I have written something today for my magazine that I want to share with you all," she said solemnly. "I think it will help lead us to a place of important meditation."

Hilma pulled off her scarf and inhaled the scent of incense from the room.

"Is that frankincense?" She sniffed the air.

Mathilda nodded and leaned back in her chair. "Yes. I like to burn it to clear my head. Anders brought the oil back from his last trip to the West Indies." She inhaled deeply. "These small rituals of purification are essential when trying to enter other realms. That's why I wanted you all to breathe in a little of it before our meeting."

Hilma turned toward the small votive with the burning oil. The scent enlivened her senses. When she opened her eyes, the other women were pulling over chairs to sit beside her.

Sigrid smiled in her dark, somber clothes. Cornelia was dressed in a mystical color, a pale blue silk that mirrored the sky.

" 'The other day I had a vision that was so real, it was as if the spirits were speaking directly through me. . . .' " Anna watched as Mathilda began reading aloud from her diary.

" 'I was led to a room with a wooden cabinet that was adorned with a plank in the shape of a triangle. Coming from this triangle was a strong white light—an energy—that stretched toward me, penetrating my entire body. In that moment, I was flooded with warmth, a sense that I was being used as a vessel to contain the power of spirits traveled from far beyond. Although no words were uttered, I was filled with a sense of purpose. As I stepped closer, I opened my arms and surrendered fully to it, embracing it with my heart, my mind, and my complete entity. It was then that a sense of weightlessness came over me, and my body felt as though it were lifting toward the heavens. . . .' "

Mathilda stopped reading and opened her eyes toward the group. "I wanted to share that with you because I felt this was an important message that was meant to guide us."

"The fact that you felt this white light means something. . . ." Sigrid's eyes flickered because she knew exactly what Mathilda had felt when she experienced that warmth. "It represents new beginnings and entering a new, pure path in life."

"Yes," Mathilda agreed. "And that is why I thought we should begin our Friday meeting meditating upon this vision." She closed the book and scanned the faces of the four women in front of her. All of them were captivated by her words.

"We are now De Fem. 'The Five.' And this number has great significance. In the Bible, it is the number of human creation. God has created us with five fingers, five toes." Mathilda lifted her hands up and spread her fingers toward the group. She paused. "But there is even more meaning to this number. The mystics believe there are five elements to the universe: earth, air, fire, water and 'quintessence,' which translates as 'the spirit.' It is the most powerful element of all.

"As we embark on a journey that will bring us new wisdom and higher learning, we five must come together as a whole. I realize we each want to hear from the other side. That you, Hilma, yearn to communicate with your dear sister, Hermina. That you, Anna, want to believe there is a world that is even more beautiful than the one we live in now." She sucked in the fragrant air and exhaled. "All of us also seek guidance on how to best use our natural gifts, whether it be through art or spiritual channeling, a talent I know Sigrid shares with me.

"But . . . we must be patient." Her voice grew louder. "We must believe that with each Friday that we come together, we'll discover one more piece of the larger universe."

Cornelia let out a nervous little laugh.

"Our curiosity is not enough." Mathilda eyed her sister sternly. "We must temper our desire to learn too quickly. Important knowledge is revealed slowly. We must listen and wait for the mysteries to be revealed to us in good time."

She placed her fingertips together and formed the shape of a triangle, allowing it to hover just above her heart.

"Sigrid, please light the candles at the altar. Cornelia, be prepared to start your drawings. Let's close our eyes and begin."

From Mathilda's mouth emerged a sound, a single tone filling the room and forcing everyone to sink into meditation. She stopped briefly to catch her breath, but then continued the sound. It made them rock gently from side to side, as if they were dancing. Cornelia's back bent over the sketchbook as she let her hand move in the direction the spirits pointed. Her head followed every move her hand made, as if she were drawing in a trance. Circle upon circle appeared.

Stockholm, January 15, 1901

My dearest Anna,

Have you read Mathilda's latest column in Efteråt? It's all about reincarnation, and it's wonderful! I read the section about the woman who believed she was a gladiator in ancient Rome, and I was riveted. Mathilda writes that our most intuitive desires are based on knowledge from experiences in our past lives. So that the reason a housewife in Småland might have an inexplicable desire to collect ancient swords is because her spirit still remembers the need to protect herself in battle.

I cannot help but think of the powerful forces inside me that have always made me feel different. How many times did Mother tell me that I must accept my fate and realize certain doors will remain closed to me because I am a woman? But I cannot accept it, Anna! For my own discomfort runs even deeper. I can confide only in you that I do not see myself as purely female. Yes, there are parts of me that are undeniably a woman, but inside me rages a male force. This inner conflict makes me feel like a tempest! I believe in God. I believe he has put me in this body to harvest more wisdom and to challenge me, but the daily struggles are a weighty burden to bear. The unfairness of having spent my entire creative life fighting to have the same opportunities as our male peers without any success is a bitter pill to swallow.

I have to question it . . . and yet, the constant battling has gotten me nowhere. I have not had any of my paintings selected for exhibition? I have not been able to get a gallerist to represent me?

And while, yes, I've been one of the few females to get a studio through the Royal Art Society, time and time again I'm rebuffed for opportunities I see being given to less-talented artists like Ludwig and Fredrick! It makes my blood boil, Anna!

When I read Mathilda's words, they make me think in a past life we were a happy couple. You were my beautiful female companion who knew how to steward my restless warrior ways. That is the explanation I have created to understand why I feel comfortable with you more than any other. I hope when I see you this Friday for our next séance, we hear from the other side that this suspicion I have inside me is not a silly fantasy, but rather an undeniable truth. It will give me hope that these restless seeds inside me are not irritants, but rather the remnants I believe them to be, ones of a former life.

Yours always,
Hilma

. . . . .

CHAPTER SIX

Friday Night, No. 182
January 18, 1901
Stockholm

She wouldn't have immediately recognized him had he not approached her. Lars Hellström must have been waiting on that park bench in the Kungsträdgården near Hilma's studio for some time, despite the cold.

The oak trees that bordered the park were white and heavy with snow. As Anna walked beneath the canopy of frozen branches, a man in a heavy wool coat and hat suddenly appeared, creating a long shadow in front of her.

"Anna Cassel?" His voice sounded slippery, shifting in the way Hilma had once described mercury to her.

She stared at him. "What do *you* want?" Just the sight of him caused her stomach to twist into knots.

His face had aged considerably since she had last seen him. Long trenches of wrinkles lined his forehead, and his eyes seemed cloudy. He had spent years trying to convince Hilma to marry him, and it was clear her constant rejections of him had transformed him into a wretched, bitter version of his younger self.

"I've been watching all of you. . . ." His breath puffed in the cold air.

Anna straightened her shoulders and lifted her chin, staring directly into his eyes. He smelled like he had been drinking.

"And I know where you're off to now, Miss Cassel. . . ."

"Really? And where is that?"

"One of your unnatural sapphic meetings . . ."

"I have no idea what you're talking about. Please step away." She gestured with her hand for him to move from her path.

"I know what the five of you have gotten up to for the past few years," he spat. "It's most unnatural, and, more importantly"—he leaned in closer to her, whispering through his teeth—*"it's against the law."*

A sick, nervous feeling rushed through Anna, but she forced herself not to show him how much he had upset her. She had learned early in her childhood that when an animal is about to attack, the best defense is to show no fear.

"Aren't you a doctor?" Anna narrowed her eyes. "Don't you have better things to do than to be drinking in the King's Garden? I should think you'd be better off someplace warm, rather than waiting outside in the cold to confront me."

He grunted. "Your friend used me; you know that? That woman is sly as a fox! She had me buy her painting supplies . . . and purchase all these expensive science books from Germany," he hissed. "She's going to use you too—just you wait!"

"I doubt that very much. Our friendship is pure," Anna muttered as she quickened her step and hurried toward Hilma's studio. The séance was starting at six o'clock, and she was already late.

• • • • •

The door to the studio was ajar, and the sound of the other women's voices was a welcome relief to her ears. Eager to put the confrontation with Lars behind her, Anna stepped inside.

Candles glowed from the windowsills, and the canvases of Hilma's studio mates, Alma and Charlotta, were stacked against a wall, along with their three easels.

Hilma's divan was pushed into a corner, and every inch of wall was covered with her paintings. Vibrant watercolors, in a palette of blue marine and marigold yellow, hung from a clothesline. The image reminded Anna of beads on a necklace, each shape like an iridescent stone harvested from the sea. So much of her recent work had been inspired by the automatic drawings that Cornelia made during their weekly séances. It was as if she had started to see the world in a different way. And it warmed Anna's heart to see how her two artistic friends were building upon each other's ideas, particularly Cornelia, who had recently come into her own.

Anna caught sight of a smaller canvas, tucked into another corner and propped up against a painting of two swans, one black and one white, their beaks touching. From a quick glance, one might have thought it was a portrait of a middle-aged gentleman. But as Anna peered closer, she saw Hilma had been working on a self-portrait; she had rendered herself as a man.

• • • • •

"Anna!" Hilma rushed over to greet her. "Thank goodness, you've finally come. I was beginning to worry. But I'm relieved you're here now . . . so we can begin soon."

She allowed herself to relax in the warmth of her friend's embrace. As this evening's hostess, Hilma looked especially regal in the long white smock that covered her black dress. Her ash-blond hair was loose, almost wild. It reminded Anna of the Renaissance paintings they had admired on their trip to Italy together. She smiled at her friend, forcing back the terrible image of Hellström confronting her. If he had been waiting in the cold to threaten her, she could only imagine how many times he had likely done the same to Hilma. She found it mystifying that this man could not get over a broken engagement that happened years before. But then, Anna knew how unusual Hilma was. He obviously saw her as a rare species he wanted to possess.

"Are you certain everything is all right?" You look like you've seen a ghost. . . ."

Anna felt her words get caught in her throat. She knew it wasn't the right time to inform Hilma that Lars had been stalking around her studio.

"Well, if you have seen a ghost, my friend, I think that's a good sign!" Hilma's voice lifted. "Mathilda seems especially inspired this evening. I wasn't the only person impressed by her latest article. She's heard similar responses from dozens of readers. Reincarnation is on everyone's mind. . . . She hopes it's a sign we'll hear from the other side tonight."

"We have all been yearning for a breakthrough," Anna answered, still distracted.

Hilma squinted at her friend. "You aren't typically the restless one in the group. Are you sure nothing's the matter?"

Again, Anna evaded her questions. "I'm sorry . . . yes . . . I'm just as anxious as everyone else to make more progress."

Sigrid left her conversation with Cornelia and stepped toward them. Dressed in her somber dark clothes, she wore a second necklace nestled beside her crucifix. She touched the cameo with her hand. "This belonged to my grandmother, and I thought tonight her spirit might visit us." She smiled optimistically. "We were so close, and she was a progressive thinker too. She believed that heaven was not a place in the sky . . . but rather in the air that surrounds us." Sigrid's eyes lit up. "I think I received my own spiritual gifts from her . . . for she used to say, 'When we take a breath, we pull in the wisdom from those who've passed before us.'" She inhaled, her breast expanding beneath the cloth of her dress.

"She sounds like she possessed great knowledge," Hilma agreed. "I can understand why you long to hear more from her. . . ."

Cornelia came over and wrapped her arm around Anna's waist. "Remind me to show you my latest drawings from last week's meeting," she whispered in Anna's ear.

"Let's start, shall we?" Mathilda's voice sounded from the corner of the room. She extinguished her cigar in one of Hilma's water jars and then clapped her hands.

"Come now!" she instructed. "De Fem" began to form their circle, each of them grasping the hand of the woman beside her. Through the tall windows of the studio, the light shifted from dusk to darkness. Only one candle, placed in the circle's center, illuminated the room as they started to chant for the spirits to visit their circle and reveal their wisdom.

Soon Mathilda's body began to tremble. A dark, husky voice emerged from her lips.

"Stop asking for the voices of the angels!" she boomed in a loud masculine voice. Her hands struck against the table.

The others shuddered as a current of heightened energy passed through the circle.

"Do not seek to hear from those who have departed from this earth. Listen to your new guides. . . .

"Who are these new guides? Tell us. . . . Show us our new path." Mathilda pleaded with the spirit that inhabited her body.

"The spirits have not chosen their prophet yet." She sucked in her breath. "The one that will be chosen will be able to read the map within the stars."

· · · · ·

As they walked arm in arm out of the studio, Anna felt the thrill and heat rising off Hilma's skin. It penetrated even the thick layers of her wool jumper and coat.

"How strange that Mathilda's voice became a man's tonight," Hilma remarked as she pulled Anna closer to her side. "It is as if the spirits were answering my question. A masculine and feminine energy must live within all of us."

Anna mumbled in agreement, but her mind was elsewhere.

"And when they mentioned they would be selecting a prophet who could read the constellations . . . did you think of one of us in particular?" She was fishing, hoping Anna would say she thought they meant her.

But Anna didn't answer. Now that they were passing the same spot where she'd been confronted by Hellström, a wave of nausea came over her. It was strange how a scent could linger in one's nostrils, but she could still smell the stench of alcohol on his breath, long after they had left each other in the park.

"What's the matter, Anna?"

"Nothing. I'm just tired."

"We're both exhausted, but it's not that—it's something else. I know it!"

The dark sky was studded with stars, and long icicles lined the edges of rooftops. Anna's eyes wetted. She took a deep breath of the crisp night air.

"You know me too well, my friend."

Hilma squeezed her hand. "Did I do something to upset you?"

"Not at all." She shook her head. "It's Hellström."

"Lars?" Hilma pulled her arm quickly out from Anna's and stopped walking.

"For goodness' sake, what did that man do now?"

Anna stood motionless. "I don't want to upset you—not after all of tonight's excitement."

"Tell me!" Hilma's face reddened. "I want to know."

Anna hesitated. "It happened right before the séance. . . . That's why I was late. He approached me when I was walking through the park on my way to your studio." She paused. "He threatened me. He suggested he was going to report us."

Hilma's face blanched.

"Report us? For what?"

Anna lowered her eyes.

"For what he called our 'sapphic meetings.'"

Hilma's chest rose beneath her coat; her heart rate escalated.

"I despise him," Anna blurted. "Why does he continue to torment us?"

Hilma's face looked defiant. "We've done nothing wrong, Anna."

But Anna didn't meet her gaze. She was terrified to think Hellström would create a scandal, humiliate the group and their families. Or even worse, try to have them jailed.

Anna knew in her heart what his accusations were really about. It had nothing to do with De Fem and whatever witchcraft Lars and his drinking companions had conceived. It had to do with her and Hilma.

"I need to ask you something." She stopped under a streetlamp. "Do you still have the sketchbook from Venice?"

Hilma looked puzzled. "Why do you ask?"

"Please tell me you kept it in a safe place."

"Of course, Anna," she answered quickly. She believed that

to be the truth—it had to be in one of the piles in her studio. She wasn't ashamed of its contents. It was one of her many notebooks that simply contained sketches of beauty.

· · · · ·

Italy. They had made the three-month trip right after they graduated from the Royal Academy, their spirits yearning to see many of the artistic masterpieces they had studied in school. Leaving behind the graphite-colored skies of Stockholm, Anna and Hilma arrived in Florence, a city bathed in crisp, bright light.

For days, they walked arm in arm through the city, marveling at the splendor they encountered at every corner. In the Uffizi, they gazed at the sensual paintings of Botticelli, admiring the soft palette and delicate brushwork with which the artist had rendered the female form.

"How lovely she is," Anna said as she stood in front of his *Birth of Venus*. The figure of Venus floating on a seashell, her long hair wrapped around her body, was a sight to behold.

Hilma had touched a thread of Anna's hair that had fallen from her bun. "She reminds me a little of you during the summer, when you let your hair fall down over your shoulders like a mermaid."

Hilma pulled Anna's finger to her chest. "You paint pictures with your words as well as with your brush. How lucky I am to have you by my side."

Every day that unfolded brought a newfound exhilaration, a thawing of the Swedish cold. All of their senses were heightened. There was a ripeness and operatic love for flesh in this new country that felt liberating to them, and they welcomed it with open arms.

As they walked through the Accademia, the statues of women and men carved from marble provided a reminder of their own life-drawing classes back in Stockholm and the unfairness they had experienced being in the all-female wing. The male students were permitted to draw from completely nude models. The female students, however, were given only models draped with cloth.

Hilma paused in front of Michelangelo's *David*.

"He reminds me a bit of Fredrik." A knowing smile curled at her lips.

Anna blushed. The memory was still vivid to her. Hilma had set out to find her own male model to draw from when she learned she wouldn't have the same opportunity as her male peers. Days later, she opened up her personal sketchbook and showed Anna a charcoal drawing of one of the men at school, Fredrik Johansson, with his legs slightly apart.

"God gave us our bodies," Hilma announced without any shame, then added defiantly, "I don't want to be denied an opportunity just because I'm female. Knowledge is power, Anna. We shouldn't be refused because of our sex."

Over the unfolding weeks, as they traveled more extensively throughout Italy, Anna felt herself welcoming her new identity as a stranger in a foreign land. There was no one to gossip about their activities, nothing that could get back to her family and make them worry she had taken her role as an artist too far.

She accepted Hilma's dares to go out without a corset, to wear her hair down, and even to be sketched by Hilma in the nude. She welcomed the decadence of drinking wine every night at dinner, of indulging in plates laden with pasta and desserts rich with amaretto and cream.

In mid-February, they arrived in Venice, a city that would inspire them to paint and to dream. As Hilma stepped out from the railway station, Anna gasped at the sight of the palazzi in seashell pink and oyster blue emerging from the sea. The image of a city rising from green waters was almost too much to conceive.

"I had no idea a place so magical could exist," she said, breathing into Hilma's ear.

"Nor did I," Hilma agreed.

Wrapped in their coats, they walked through the hidden streets and over narrow bridges, mist enveloping them.

"We must get our costumes for the carnival," Hilma insisted after they had dropped their bags off at the pension where they were staying. It had been her idea to time their arrival to coincide with Venice's annual masquerade.

The city was alive with pre-festivities. Paper lanterns in jewellike colors lined the streets. Fabric stores and mask makers were busy selling last-minute items: sparklers and candles, hooded robes, and silk-satin slippers.

In the secluded quarter of Dorsoduro, they discovered a storefront full of intricately painted masks. While several of the shops carried masks from the Commedia dell'arte, this window display was full of ones plucked from the wild: red foxes with pointed little ears, oval masks in the guise of wise old owls. But what piqued Hilma's interest the most was one covered in white feathers, with a small orange beak. The mask of a swan.

When they entered, Hilma asked the owner if she might examine it more closely.

"Si, signorina," he replied as his hands withdrew from his apron pockets and he went to retrieve the mask.

As he came closer to her, Hilma changed her request. "May I see it on her?" she asked in broken Italian. She pointed to Anna.

The man went over to Anna and tied the purple satin ribbons behind her head.

Hilma smiled. *"Bellissima."*

"It comes with wings too," the owner added. He retreated behind a heavy dark curtain and came back with two large white, feather-covered wings.

"Oh, how exquisite! Try them on, Anna!" Hilma cried.

Anna slipped her arms into the leather bands sewn into the panels of white feathers and began moving them up and down, playfully mimicking a bird in flight.

"How marvelous," Hilma chimed. "Anna, you're a swan!"

At once, Hilma began negotiating, her hands moving like an Italian's. She wanted not one mask with feathered wings, but two.

"Una bianca, una nera," she ordered. "One white, one black . . ." They settled on a price, and he promised to have the second set ready before sunset.

Hilma reached into her purse, but Anna stepped in and stopped her. "No, you need to be more careful than I," she insisted. She withdrew several crisp bills and handed them over for the down payment.

"You always take care of me," Hilma offered, gently touching her friend's sleeve.

"It gives me great pleasure," replied Anna.

"We'll be two beautiful birds tonight," Hilma whispered back. "I can hardly wait."

That evening, they wandered the streets lined in torchlight and danced in ancient stone piazzas with other merrymakers, all of their faces hidden behind festive masks.

Intoxicated and unbridled, Anna and Hilma locked hands and drank from goblets of rich red wine.

Beneath the layers of feathers, they found themselves transformed.

"In ancient Greece, the swan was a symbol of the sun. In other places, of the moon," Hilma mused to Anna as they lifted their glasses. The sensation of their wrists briefly touching felt like a butterfly's caress.

They returned to their room well past midnight, a Murano glass chandelier casting soft light from above as they removed each other's feathered mask and wings.

Undressed, Hilma looked more beautiful than ever. With her regal neck, slender arms, the curve of her backside, she was resplendent as she stood against the carved scrollwork of their wooden bed.

Anna reached for her sketchbook to record her, but Hilma took her hand instead.

"There is so much I want to know." Her voice lowered to a whisper. "Are we not put on this world to learn, to explore?"

She lifted Anna's wings from the velvet chair where they rested and placed them next to her own dark plumes on the bed. Without another word uttered between them, she guided Anna to lie down with her on the pile of feathers, their bodies entwining against the gossamer nest.

. . . . .

CHAPTER SEVEN

EBEN

Present Day
New York City

On November 10, I headed to Asphalt Green for a quick swim before my flight out of JFK that evening. Once again, I saw Willa and her dad, and this time I was even more impressed with her speed and skill. She was with a coach that morning. Not wanting to intrude, I didn't stop to say my usual hello.

I was heading to Stockholm to spend a few days at the Hilma af Klint Foundation, going through the archives, and to meet with Marie Cassel, the great-niece of one of the women of De Fem.

The Guggenheim exhibition was now less than a year away. We were on track, despite the hurried pace. Four months before, in July, Dr. Perlstein and I had traveled to Stockholm together to choose the paintings and most of the drawings we'd be featuring in the show.

This new trip was related to the catalog, one of my two major unfinished efforts. The other was securing funding. We were still looking for a sponsor to put up the last half million dollars.

As associate curator, I was invited to write one of the essays for the catalog. I had decided to focus on Hilma's decision to hide her work away. I hoped her notebooks would offer up some clues and had hired a translator to work with me at the foundation.

I arrived early Sunday morning and went from the airport to the Grand Hôtel and spent the day getting over my jet lag and going over my notes. I'd read everything written in English about Hilma af Klint by that point, and yet she remained an elusive and enigmatic woman. Why was she so secretive? Why did she destroy all of her correspondence ten years before she died? Why had she never married? How did "De Fem" aid her with her work? What was her relationship with Anna Cassel, who by all accounts had financially supported her, paying for her art supplies and covering her rent? Why did Hilma never show her work after one exhibition in 1916? Why were there no records of any critic seeing her work or commenting on it during her lifetime?

In my notebook, I had copied down a quote of Hilma's.

I had no idea what the paintings were supposed to depict, nevertheless I worked swiftly and surely without changing a single brushstroke.

It was no wonder I was having such a hard time getting to the heart of this furtive painter—there was so much even she didn't seem to know about her own work.

On Monday morning, I took a taxi to the foundation office to meet with Hilma's great-nephew, Johan af Klint, before my foray into the archives.

The receptionist informed me that Mr. af Klint wouldn't be meeting with me but instead I'd be seeing his associate Ebba Olsson. A few moments later, a soft-spoken woman in her mid-sixties came out, introduced herself, and led me into her office. She gestured to a side table with a carafe of water, a thermos of coffee, and a bowl of fruit and asked if I'd care for anything. I told her I was okay for now.

Without any more preamble, Ms. Olsson suggested I begin the interview.

"Well, some of my questions were specifically for Mr. af Klint."

"Why don't you ask me those? And if I don't know the answers, I'll do what I can to get them for you."

I nodded. "I'd like to know about his recollections of his great-aunt."

"Mr. af Klint was five when she died, so he often says that he doesn't remember his aunt Hilma well, but his father always described her as unsentimental, high-minded, and resolute. Very determined from a young age. 'Life is a farce if a person does not serve truth,' she used to say."

I wrote down the quote along with her observations.

Ms. Olsson went on to tell me that while Hilma never married, there was a family story that she had planned to wed a doctor, but Mr. af Klint didn't know why the nuptials were canceled.

I asked about Hilma's relationship with spiritualism.

"She was raised in a religious family, but her real interest began when she was seventeen years old and lost her younger sister to pneumonia. She wanted to see if she could reach her in the spirit world and began attending séances. Hilma's involvement with mysticism led to her joining the Edelweiss Society and later studying Theosophy. Starting in 1896, Hilma and four of her friends, now known as De Fem, began automatic-writing sessions and séances in an effort to reach spirits to guide them in their artistic endeavors. These guides eventually asked Hilma to take on the task of creating the paintings now known as the temple paintings."

I took down what she said, but mostly to be polite. Ms. Olsson was going over ground that I was already familiar with.

"Considering the size of the temple paintings, I was surprised to read that Hilma was only five feet tall," I said. "Do you know much about how she executed these large canvases?"

"From a partial footprint on one of the temple paintings, we believe she had them on the floor of her studio," she told me. "The ten largest were not done on one big stretched canvas, but rather on several interlocking pieces of paper that were painted first, then, after they were dried, pasted meticulously onto the canvas."

"Do you think De Fem helped her at all? Anna Cassel was also an artist, as was Cornelia."

Ms. Olsson was quiet for a moment, as if gathering her thoughts, before responding. "Hilma and Anna were lifelong friends, and while Anna, who was financially secure, helped Hilma in many ways, there's nothing to suggest she helped her as an artist."

"What about Cornelia? Any possibility she helped?" I asked.

"Cornelia only studied technical drawing," Ms. Olsson said.

"But there are collaborative notebooks. If members of De Fem worked together on those drawings, perhaps there was collaboration on the paintings too. Especially the large ones?"

Her answer was short. "No. The paintings were not collaborations." Clearly, she didn't want to travel down this path.

I decided to back off that path and try another. "Some sources suggest she might have had a relationship of a romantic nature with Anna, and then later, after Hilma's mother died, with her mother's nurse, Thomasine. Can you tell me anything about those relationships? Do you think Mr. af Klint's father ever mentioned anything? Hilma was such a radical artist—do you think she was as radical in other realms of her life?"

Ms. Olsson was quick to answer. "Hilma had very close female friends. Companions who mattered to her a great deal. That's all they were, companions."

She was clearly becoming annoyed by my probing. I supposed she might not have known anything more. Given the era, if Hilma was a lesbian or bisexual, she would have gone to great lengths to keep that hidden. I thought, as other scholars did, her sexual preferences might have even been one reason she destroyed so much of her correspondence.

In many countries in the early twentieth century, it was illegal to engage in relations with a member of the same sex. Oscar Wilde was imprisoned in England in 1895 for sodomy. He died five years later at age forty-six, partly as a result of how he had been treated in jail. Hilma and anyone else in Europe who read of the case, which made headlines worldwide, would have seen it as a cautionary tale.

Maybe I shouldn't have been asking about Hilma's sexuality— it was her feminism that was a theme of the show. The idea of De Fem members supporting one another, helping one another, working together to reach out beyond their own time and place, was very much a part of the history of these paintings and one of the reasons Dr. Perlstein and the rest of the staff believed this show was going to have such an impact. It was why it seemed exactly the right time for Hilma to be introduced to the world on such a great stage. Women were standing up for their rights as never before. Fighting with renewed vigor to be seen and heard. Demanding that abusive men in power finally be held accountable.

"Back to De Fem," I continued. "We've been wondering if you had X-rays or other tests done on the paintings to see if there was the possibility of more than one artist working on them."

Ms. Olsson frowned. "We have absolutely no doubt the paintings came from Hilma af Klint's mind, heart, and hand. The tests we have done were to examine the paint she used."

"And did you find anything unusual in the paint?"

"Yes, we found that the tempera paint Hilma used was unusual, because the pigment came not from ground minerals but from leaves and flowers. It was how they made paint in medieval times."

"Did you find any information about why she didn't use minerals?"

She gave me another annoyed look. Clearly, she resented my

questions, and yet she'd welcomed me here knowing I would have them. I guess they weren't the questions she'd expected. Or wanted.

"Now . . ." She stood. "I believe you wanted to visit the archives? We can give you an hour."

"An hour? I thought I had scheduled the whole day," I said.

"That must have been a miscommunication," she said. "My assistant will show you the way."

There was no question I was being chastised. My translator, a young man who was also an art historian, was already there, going through the notebooks I'd requested in advance. I joined him at the table, and for the next hour—which I managed to stretch to ninety minutes—we perused the pages of Hilma's notebooks. I studied the drawings while my translator went through as many pages as he could, taking down notes. We didn't get through a quarter of what I'd wanted, and I left frustrated and annoyed. Why had my questions made Ms. Olsson uncomfortable? Was she hiding a truth, or trying to avoid examining it?

* * * * *

The next day, I met with Marie Cassel, the great-niece of Anna Cassel, Hilma's lifelong friend, patron, and companion.

I had invited Marie to have lunch with me at the hotel, and at noon I walked into the Veranda restaurant to find her already seated at a table by the window. She had short feathery gray hair and was wearing a black sweater and slacks with a brightly colored jacket. Her eyeglass frames were made of multicolored plastic.

We'd talked on the phone several times, so we were comfortable enough to start chatting companionably. She asked me how my trip had been and how my research was going. I told her about my experience at the Hilma af Klint Foundation, and she nodded as if she'd expected as much.

"History told in the present is slanted by the person doing the telling," she said. "The canonization of Hilma is almost complete, and those in charge, who have the most to gain, don't want it to be derailed. It is documented that Anna, Hilma, and Cornelia were all artists and started off at the same school. They were close friends who, with the addition of Mathilda and Sigrid, engaged in séances and automatic-drawing sessions for years. It is simply ridiculous to believe that Hilma did all the work on her own, without any collaboration, when everything else these women did was a collaboration. It would have been a natural extension for them. The Hilma af Klint Foundation doesn't want to go where you are going, but the fact is, there are gaps in the documentation. Drawings done during the period—some by Hilma, some by Anna—will illustrate what I mean."

A waiter arrived. We ordered, both of us choosing the herring with Västerbotten cheese as a starter, then the grilled salmon with roasted pepper crème as the main for Marie, and a sirloin steak with green pepper sauce for me.

"Would you like some wine?" I asked her.

"Yes, white, please."

I looked to the waiter. "And I'll have a beer."

Once he had gone, Marie and I returned to my many unanswered questions.

Why did Hilma burn her correspondence?

What secrets was she hiding?

How involved were the other women in the paintings for the temple?

Why wouldn't the foundation do the due diligence of x-raying the paintings?

"I don't have answers," Marie said. "But I do have feelings about what you ask. Many on the Cassel side of my family are sensitives. I've had some experiences myself."

The waiter brought our drinks. I raised my glass to hers, and we toasted. Marie took a sip and then continued.

"I grew up with my great-aunt's paintings and drawings hanging on our walls. They have always gripped me. Kept my interest. Made me curious about the woman who created them. My two unmarried aunts who lived just a block away from us knew Anna well and indulged my curiosity about her. So even though I never met her, I felt like I knew her. I hope you don't think I'm crazy, but I sensed Hilma as well."

"What is it that you sensed?" I was dreading her answer. I didn't want to get sidetracked into a conversation about psychic phenomena. She surprised me by refusing to answer.

"I don't want to make trouble. My family and Hilma's are too intertwined. I just know in my heart there is more that happened than is discussed, but at the same time, it was long ago and far in the past and probably best left there. But I am plagued by questions, beginning with the notebooks Hilma left. Meticulous notebooks. All numbered, so we know one is missing. Why? And then there is the issue about the drawing. . . ."

She told me about a book that had recently been published that contained a sketch attributed to Hilma but that Anna had done of her own sister. "We have the sketch in our house," she said. "We know Hilma did a deathbed drawing of Lotten, but Anna drew her many times as well, and the one in the book was definitely done by Anna."

Over coffee, Marie told me there was a Danish art historian she wanted to introduce me to by email. "She is as interested in these questions as you are. We don't want to make trouble, but we want to find the truth. If Anna or any of the other women deserve credit for the paintings, we want them to have it."

"I'd be very interested in hearing what she has to say."

"And the rest of your trip? What do you have planned?"

"I'm leaving tomorrow, so I'd like to visit Hilma's resting place this afternoon."

"You should go now, before it is too dark."

She was right. Though it was only one fifteen in the afternoon, darkness would descend soon.

"It's terrible. We are heading into our darkest phase of the year. The sun doesn't come up until nine in the morning and during the worst period sets around two thirty. Once we are in the deepest of our dark days, when we part, we don't just say goodbye; we say, 'It is turning.' Meaning that each day the earth is turning a little bit more toward the sun. 'Yes, it is turning,' your friend will say. And you cheer the other person up just by mentioning this, reminding each other we are going toward the sun again."

Once I'd said goodbye to Marie Cassel, I took a taxi to

Galärvarvskyrkogården, the former navy graveyard where Hilma was buried. According to the guidebook I had consulted, this cemetery was established in 1742 and was one of several used by the navy.

From a florist at the gate I bought a bunch of simple, delicate flowers like those Hilma had drawn and painted. I'd noticed them both in her early, representational work and abstracted in her non-objective work.

Given the size of the cemetery, with over thirteen hundred graves and tombs, needing a map wasn't surprising, but even with one I still managed to get lost. Using the chapel and the bell tower as my North Star, I tried to reorient myself. But only when a woman who was also visiting came to my aid did I finally find what I was looking for.

I'd seen Michelangelo's elaborate tomb in the Basilica of Santa Croce in Florence and Raphael's tomb in the Pantheon in Rome. I'd visited Rodin's final resting place in Meudon and studied the bronze copy of his famous *Thinker* that sits outside his tomb. The abstract artist Barnett Newman is buried in Queens with a large black monolith marking his burial site. Alexander Archipenko, the Ukrainian cubist painter and sculptor, is memorialized with a large stylized angel. In the Green River Cemetery in East Hampton, a bronze plaque inscribed with Jackson Pollock's signature is embedded in a huge rock to mark where the artist is buried.

But Hilma af Klint's grave was invisible. I found the small gray stone flat in the ground, but there was only one name on it, *Viktor af Klint*. I knew that Hilma had been buried with her father, but seeing just how hidden she was stunned me. Just as she was invisible to the art world in life, she was invisible in death.

I pulled out my Moleskine and my pen and drew a sketch of the Guggenheim Museum. Done, I ripped it out and then, looking around, found a rock.

In the Jewish religion, we have a custom of placing rocks on graves. Eastern European Jewish lore teaches that the stones create a barrier between life and death, keeping the souls of the departed from coming back to haunt us.

The less esoteric reason is simply that the stones are markers of a loved one's visit. Flowers fade and wither, but a stone remains, solid and permanent.

For me there was yet another reason to carry on the tradition at my mother's gravesite. She was a sculptor—stone was her medium. Her gravesite bears one of her own rough slabs of marble with her name, birth date, and death date engraved upon it.

I took the drawing of the museum, placed it on Hilma's father's granite slab, and affixed it with the small stone I'd found. Then I laid the poppies beside it.

"Well," I said, out loud, surprising myself, "you aren't going to be invisible anymore."

• • • • •

Stockholm, December 1, 1904

Dear Diary,

How heavy my heart has been since last week's meeting at Sigrid's home. She made such an effort to make it perfect for all of us. You can see that even with most of her children having left the home, the two who remain are still so well loved. Their household maintains such an abundance of love! I was so touched to see her husband, Ernst, sharing stories with their youngest over a cup of warm cider as Sigrid busied herself in preparing the room for our meeting. He seems well aware of what we do in our weekly gatherings, and yet he does not condemn them as so many of the middle-class gentlemen in Stockholm might. Rather, he calls Sigrid his "little rainbow" and seems to fully embrace all her spiritual abilities.

Before we began, Sigrid offered us each a cup of tea that had been brewed with dried flowers, a recipe she said her grandmother had handed down. We all felt so blissfully calm after we finished our cups!

Afterward, perhaps because she was so relaxed by the tea, Mathilda offered Sigrid the chance to be the medium that evening. What a surprise turn that was for all of us! And I do wonder if we can ever go back to the way things used to be, as Sigrid was so triumphant in her channeling! She made contact with two guides, Amaliel and Georg, who spoke freely and at great length through her. These spirits seem to have much in store for De Fem and spoke of our performing a great task in the future. I could not stop drawing. I must have filled an entire notebook with my automatic sketches. I saw Saturn-like rings and golden halos form in my mind. Amber rays of light and other warm hues filled my vision and made me think that these two new spirits inhabited us all. Even Mathilda said she felt she saw similar images when we walked home that night.

But after I returned to my bedroom and slipped beneath my covers, all I could think about was my own love, Kristian. The others noticed I was wearing a new necklace, an expensive blue stone with small diamonds around the border, and I lied, telling them it was a family heirloom. Mathilda could have killed me with her glare when I fabricated my explanation. But I could hardly share the truth with them! I know Kristian bought it as a gift to show his devotion; he even said the color wasn't only to match my eyes but to remind me that our love was "like the water," in that it could "fill more than one shape," but now it only makes me sad. How little it means after seeing what a truly loving household Sigrid shares with her husband and children.

Mathilda and I have been fighting ever since the last séance. She tells me that I will bring shame on our family if I continue down this dangerous path with Kristian. But I cannot stop myself. Can an artist continue to paint without the fire of love?

She closed the door of her bedroom when we came home, and it remained shut the following morning. She hurts me so much.

I know it makes me a terrible sister to say this, but Sigrid showed us all how powerful she is as a medium. I believe my sister was not happy about this at all.

CHAPTER EIGHT

· · · · ·

Friday Night, No. 352
December 2, 1904
Stockholm

Cornelia touched the pale blue pendant around her neck and closed her eyes. It brought her comfort, a secret talisman to bring her closer to Kristian. She stretched herself across the white linen of her bed and felt the memory of his hands return to her.

It was an unexpected gift to fall in love at her age, when the prospects of marriage and motherhood had all but dissolved. It filled her with a youthful confidence that had ironically eluded her when she was an adolescent. Her creative energy had never been as strong as it was now.

She pulled down her notebook from last week's meeting and began leafing through its pages. Although Mathilda wouldn't admit it, everyone had noticed a palpable change in the room's energy when Sigrid was the one leading them in the séance. Cornelia's hands couldn't work quickly enough to sketch out all of the images that had flashed through her mind that night. Coil after coil filled the paper, large amoeba-like shapes and spirals that resembled seashells and snails.

Afterward, it was Hilma who first noticed the recurring pattern within these drawings.

"The spiral shape is significant," she remarked as she traced her finger around one of the rings. "It's a symbol for the constant evolution of the universe and our persistent quest for knowledge."

Mathilda raised an eyebrow. Not having led the meeting, she had been silent for the entire séance. But now her voice emerged with confidence and power. "It actually has another, even deeper meaning," she interjected.

Hilma looked puzzled. "What's that?"

"Remember I told you all how the universe comprised five elements: earth, water, wind, fire, and the quintessence, meaning the spirit?"

"Yes."

"Well, the spiral is the symbol of quintessence."

Cornelia had looked down at her drawings again, and her heart pumped with adrenaline. She had never felt so much energy run through her. Her hand felt like it had a life of its own.

Spiral upon spiral. Ring within ring. The images floated from the page like a constellation of planets and stars. With the women arriving later for their weekly gathering, Cornelia studied the drawings now and felt compelled to paint them larger and in color. She scanned her room for bigger sheets of paper but could find none.

It had been days since she had worked on any sewing. From

the corner, a wooden mannequin pinned with pieces of muslin leaped out at her. She reached to touch the coarse cotton fabric that Kristian had given her from his warehouse.

"It's hardly expensive, *älskling*," he had said affectionately as his finger gently moved one of the stray hairs that fell across her face. "So please take it . . . if it makes you happy."

"Yes, it will be perfect for creating a new dress pattern." She threw her arms around his neck and kissed him. Now, alone in her room, she looked at the squares of canvas and saw entirely new potential use for the material.

She reached into the corner for her palette and paints. Then, without removing the canvas from the mannequin, she touched her brush to the fabric and applied the first stroke. Soon it was covered in its entirety in brightly colored vortices and swirls.

· · · · ·

In Mathilda's study, the women of De Fem assembled. The altar was arranged with candles, the white crucifix, the golden triangle, and a vase of winter roses.

Cornelia entered a few minutes late, a smudge of blue paint streaked across her forehead. Mathilda pulled her sister aside and quickly took a wet finger to rub the skin clean.

"I brought some of my grandmother's tea," Sigrid shared. "I thought it really helped bring a sense of serenity to us last time before we began."

Anna held up her hand. "It gave me a terrible headache, I have to admit. I think I'm going to pass."

But when the maid entered and offered a tray of steaming cups, Hilma took hers *and* Anna's. "I'm sure no one minds," she said as she lifted the painted porcelain of one cup to her lips. "I did feel it increased my connection to the spirits when we were at Sigrid's."

"Me too," Cornelia agreed as she reached for her own serving.

Mathilda shook her head. "None for me, thank you. I'll need my full focus for channeling tonight." She folded her hands in her lap, waiting for them to finish.

"Let us join hands and embrace the circle, a symbol we have recognized as the spiral of knowledge," Mathilda soon began. "We yearn to seek more wisdom from those from beyond. Amaliel . . . Georg . . ." She chanted the names of the two new spirits that Sigrid had connected with during the last séance.

"Amaliel . . . Georg . . ." Mathilda slowly intoned the names, trying to invite them to speak through her. But only silence answered her.

After several minutes, Hilma pulled her hand away from Anna's and Cornelia's.

"I think Sigrid should try. She had a breakthrough last week, and the spirits connected with her profoundly."

An uncomfortable silence swept through the room. Mathilda's eyelids flashed open.

"Do you not want me to lead?" Her gaze fell hard upon Hilma's.

"I just want to hear more from Amaliel and Georg," Hilma answered, refusing to be intimidated.

"I feel the colors are starting to swirl around me," Cornelia added. Her empty teacup was pushed to the side, and her notebook was opened to a fresh page.

"Perhaps it's just a natural progression," Anna noted softly. "You've been our medium since the beginning. . . . Perhaps Sigrid should now be the one to lead us into the next ring of our journey." She purposely alluded to the spiral, to emphasize the importance of the pursuit of knowledge. Anna hoped it would soften the blow for Mathilda.

Mathilda's face tightened.

"I will not stand in the way if you think the spirits might prefer another leader."

"That's most generous of you," Anna offered. "I think we all must be open to change."

Hilma's eyes fell on Sigrid. The others watched as her focus lowered and her head bowed, as if she were newly anointed.

"Let us try to find harmony again." Sigrid spoke solemnly. She offered her hands to the others. Mathilda was the last to take Sigrid's fingers. But her reluctance was ignored by everyone.

"Amaliel . . . Georg," Sigrid soon began beseeching, "tell us more what you envision for us. . . . Guide us to reach our highest selves." Her head thrust back and eyes rolled inward, Sigrid's body jerked forth, and the loud masculine voice she had channeled last week returned.

"Cast away your need to hear voices from the dead. Your guides have a mission for the present.

"A temple must be built. With a circle in the center, a path that spirals toward the sun. Adorning its walls will be paintings as high and mighty as pillars. Flowers will sprout on the walls. . . ."

Cornelia reached for her pencil and began sketching the

descriptions that flowed from the spirits through Sigrid's tongue.

Anna glanced over and thought the flower that Cornelia was drawing resembled a dogwood blossom, a flower that symbolized purity.

"A gardener of the purist heart must build this great temple. Her hands must be capable of capturing the mysteries of creation. The power that makes the form change must always come from within, from the life that hides within the shape. . . . She must possess the ability to bring light out of darkness, reason out of chaos . . . ," Sigrid channeled. Her eyes remained closed, and she had not seen what Cornelia had drawn. Yet they remained eerily in sync. "The power of change must always come from within," she continued.

"One of you is chosen. Look inside yourself for the answer." Sigrid's voice roared even more loudly.

Hilma's heart leaped wildly inside her chest. As she glanced at Cornelia's drawing, she could see exactly the spirit Georg was describing: a church made from concentric circles, its spiraling walls decorated with paintings, every surface, line, and shape embodying the splendor and cycles of life.

· · · · ·

Stockholm, December 3, 1904

My dearest Anna,

What a meeting we had last night! I returned home and could hardly sleep a wink. Again, my head seemed to dance with a thousand swirls of colors, and I feel that even though I have no skills as a medium, I am becoming closer and closer to the spirits now that Sigrid has taken charge.

How brave you were to step in and smooth things over with Mathilda. I could hardly contain myself as we sat there, all waiting for her to make contact with Amaliel and Georg. I couldn't possibly endure another night of her pontificating about her vast spiritual knowledge. Yes, we all know that she's read the many books on her shelves and that every little relic in her office has some fascinating story of how her husband brought it back from his exotic travels. But I feel an urgency to start on the temple paintings the spirits mentioned. I believe I am the chosen one to lead the task they've set forth.

Of course, I know I can't do this alone. You, my cherished friend, must be there by my side! We should consider performing together the purification rituals that the spirits mentioned. Surely we both can forgo eating meat? It will give us an even deeper appreciation of nature if we only draw sustenance from that which flowers and bursts with God's splendor. I truly believe the spirits have a reason for wanting us to find nourishment only through the plants and vegetables that grow in the earth and on the vine. We will reproduce their vibrant colors through our paints and brushes.

*A circle within a circle of life, dear Anna. I can see it all so
clearly, like it's almost close enough to touch.*

Your loving,
Hilma

· · · · ·

Stockholm, January 12, 1905

Dear Hilma,

*It's been several weeks now since I made this pledge with you, and
all I can dream about is Mother's elk with cream sauce and
mushrooms! She had the cook prepare her famous recipe last night,
and the apartment was filled with the most succulent scents. There
isn't a vegetable in the world that smells as warm and inviting as
that dish. But do not worry; I remained loyal to my promise. My
mouth did not take a single bite, and I could tell how annoyed
Mother was that I refused even the smallest serving. "Lotten needs
it more than I." I laughed. But dear Josephine just shook her head
and told me that a woman my age needs to keep some weight on
her bones or the flesh will begin to sag!*

*I am eager for tomorrow's meeting at your studio, to learn more
about what the spirits envision for the temple and its paintings.
When I close my eyes, the great astronomer Tycho Brahe's
observatory on the island of Ven comes to mind! He, too, had a
vision to construct a castle to the stars. Wouldn't it be wonderful if*

we could find a piece of land on which we might construct this temple of paintings? I wish the five of us knew how to build, so we could create it with our own hands and hard work.

Until then, the least I can do is arrive early and help you move the furniture around the studio to make room for everyone. I hope the others don't mind that in all these years I've never hosted. But you know how Mother is about what she describes as "sheer foolishness, sitting around a table, waiting for spirits to arrive." I feel more uncomfortable with Lotten being excluded than with what Mother thinks, but still, it's so generous of you to offer the studio.

In the meantime, I keep my bedchamber as my secret room. That's where I store my cherished letters from you and my sketchbook from Italy. By the way, you never told me if you found yours. Please do keep it safe; you know how I worry.

Much love,
Anna

CHAPTER NINE

. . . . .

Friday Night, No. 356
January 15, 1905
Stockholm

Purity. Who was pure and who was not? Cornelia stood in front of the mirror and let her clothes drop to the floor. Her body looked gray in the dim winter light. She let her hands run over the curve of her breasts, the narrow of her waist, and the soft mound of her stomach. The sensation of her own touch felt like nothing compared to Kristian's. When he mapped her skin, she felt herself transform into something beautiful beneath his caress.

For so long, she had felt like a seedling beneath the soil, enveloped in darkness and unable to feel the warmth of the sun or the stardust of the night sky. But Kristian, whom she had loved when she was a young girl, this man she thought she would never see again, had unexpectedly returned to her late in life and brought her into full bloom.

Was that impure? Her eyes welled with tears.

She knew it was wrong to be with someone who was married. But Cornelia envisioned their love affair like her own private painting. She took her mental paintbrush and erased the image of his wife, Astrid, and their two teenage boys, their comfortable life in their apartment in the cozy district of Gamla Stan. Instead, she focused on the earlier years, when she and Kristian were adolescents and their lives first entwined.

It was a secret she kept from Hilma and Anna when they were at Slöjdskolan together. Seventeen-year-old Kristian, the boy who brought her colored pastels with a posy of matching blooms, had captured her heart almost immediately. They met in secret after her classes. They searched for secluded spaces where they could talk and slowly touch. He carried inside his jacket a small notebook in which he wrote down lines of poetry and he recited them into the air.

"Catch my words of love," he teased her. And she had reached into the sky, pretending to pull down every sonnet he spoke aloud, and pressed it into her heart. He made her feel liberated, freed from the weight of how—as a girl—she was supposed to behave. They were equals.

All the while she maintained her virtue. She never allowed Kristian's hands to wander too deeply beneath her dress. She held on to her modesty and waited to be his only under the bonds of marriage.

But then one day, he and his family simply vanished. She heard the gossip whispered by the neighbors, rumors that his father's debts had forced them to leave in the middle of the night. All Cornelia knew for certain was that she had returned home from school one afternoon with a canvas rolled beneath her arm that she was desperate to show Kristian, but he was not there. His house was dark and empty.

Her heart slipped into the shadows.

She could no longer paint. Her desire to attend classes waned. She could barely pull herself out of bed.

As Hilma and Anna flourished, their arms stretching upward toward the academy, Cornelia shrank. She became invisible.

· · · · ·

Improper. Impure. What did it even mean? Hadn't Anna once confessed she sometimes needed to see Hilma so badly that she woke up during the night and snuck across Stockholm to visit her in her studio? She justified her rash actions by claiming it calmed her nerves to watch Hilma paint. But was that the truth or just an explanation for something that was too difficult to explain? Cornelia didn't know, but she envied both women's boldness to do what was right for them.

The world was filled with rules made by others. But with her friend's influence, the artist inside her now felt confident enough to break some of them. The freedom that Hilma had spoken about when she attended the Edelweiss meeting in male clothes was something that Cornelia felt curious to explore. Hilma had told her, with such certainty in her voice, that in the near future, there would be no difference between female and male clothes.

"Why on earth should we wear corsets when they make us feel weak and uncomfortable?" she questioned in front of the others. Hilma was right. Society had kept women continually bound and constricted. Female fashion was yet another form of complicity.

Cornelia walked over to Mathilda and Anders's bedroom, completely nude and paying no attention to the maid's shocked face. She opened the closet and searched through Anders's clothes, her fingers gingerly caressing his dark wool jacket and matching vest. She pulled out a linen shirt and a pair of trousers and brought them back to her room.

The meeting at Hilma's studio was in just two hours. She hesitated for a moment, but then opened up Anders's shirt and slid her arms through the sleeves, then put on the trousers. The new sensation of the garments on her bare skin thrilled her. No corset, no brassiere. The feeling was so marvelous, she wished she could bottle it.

· · · · ·

Dressed in Anders's vestments, her long hair flowing over her shoulders, Cornelia strode into Mathilda's bedroom and sat down on the chair. She still couldn't believe the freedom the trousers afforded. Men could spread their legs in public, and no one would bat an eye! For the first time, she didn't need to keep her knees together, and a small giggle escaped her lips.

Just then Mathilda entered the room.

"Goodness, I thought Anders was back from the sea! You had me there for a second," she exclaimed as she marveled at the sight of Cornelia in her husband's clothes.

"You're not upset?"

"No, why should I be?" Mathilda shrugged. "Those clothes hardly get the use they should these days."

"But if you intend to go to the meeting like that, you'll have to hide your hair under this." She reached for a hat that was lying on the cabinet and gently placed it on her sister's head.

"I'm relieved you don't disapprove," Cornelia admitted.

Mathilda laughed out loud. "It was one of the things I liked about Hilma right away when I met her at the first Edelweiss meeting. In spiritual texts, it's written that everyone has male and female sides. It impressed me that she was brave enough to acknowledge that duality."

Cornelia patted her pant leg and smiled.

"It's the relief of not feeling bound by whale bone and laces that I love," Cornelia confessed. "I can only imagine how much better I'll be able to draw at tonight's meeting. . . ."

"Yes, and I think it will bring some cheer to the others too. I'll bring some brandy for us all to share. And maybe Hilma can even teach you how to ride a bike. I've heard gossip that she sometimes dresses up as a man to go for a ride."

Cornelia stood up and adjusted her outfit, tucking the shirttails into the waistband of the trousers.

"Male clothes are just so much more comfortable," she said as she walked toward the door. "I'll need a belt, though." She laughed.

"Just one more thing is essential for tonight," Mathilda remarked with a glint in her eye. "I'll be sure to pack us some cigars."

. . . . .

CHAPTER TEN

EBEN

Present Day
New York City

My first day back in New York after my trip to Stockholm, I found a message that Dr. Perlstein wanted to see me as soon as possible. After checking with her assistant, I received an appointment for eleven that morning.

Arriving at her office, I expected her to want to discuss my research in the archives and get an update on the catalog. Instead, she greeted me with a frown.

"Eben, do you have doubts about this exhibition?" she asked.

"Of course not. Why?"

"You aren't questioning our positioning Hilma af Klint as a revolutionary, years ahead of her time?"

I was concerned by Dr. Perlstein's questions and tone.

"No, of course not. Why are you asking?"

She didn't answer. Instead, she asked yet another question.

"So you are not under the misapprehension that you are researching an exposé of her."

"No."

"I've gotten a call about the questions you asked in Stockholm. You've ruffled feathers at the foundation. I had to do some serious damage control."

I guessed Ms. Olsson had complained. Certainly, Marie Cassel had not been upset by my questions—if anything, she'd made it clear she had even more of them than I did.

"Eben," Dr. Perlstein said, "your job isn't to be a detective. You're a curator. We are putting on a show that you suggested. You've had an important role in its creation. It wouldn't exist without you. But the questions that you asked in Stockholm have made the very people who are lending us the artwork very uncomfortable. Questioning the veracity of Hilma's paintings was, to put it frankly, stupid."

I knew I should accept the criticism, but I was angry. "No one has ever x-rayed a single one of those paintings. There was no actual will and testament. The message about keeping the paintings hidden for twenty years was in a notebook. Hilma was part of two groups of women artists—the first being De Fem; the second had at least seven members. There is an important scholar in Denmark who has identified approximately one hundred of the af Klint paintings as being painted by Anna Cassel. If there is a possibility that Hilma af Klint didn't work on the temple paintings alone but was helped by Anna Cassel and possibly Cornelia Cederberg or anyone else, we should at least address that."

Dr. Perlstein's phone rang. She ignored it. A moment later,

her assistant came to the door, told her who was on the phone, and said it was important. Before picking up the phone, Dr. Perlstein told me to stay, that our conversation wasn't finished.

While she was on the call, I rose and walked over to her wall of windows and looked down, watching the pedestrians below, umbrellas open to the rain I hadn't even realized had started. When she hung up, I turned back around.

"Eben, are you able to do the job that you were hired to do? Which is to create an exhibition of Hilma af Kint's work. Not question what these other women did or didn't contribute. We can mention them, of course, but this is about Hilma."

I didn't know why it mattered so much to me to find out about the secrets De Fem shared. To learn what was in the letters Hilma had burned. Or why one of her many notebooks had gone missing. Why did the foundation refuse to x-ray Hilma's paintings and do the kind of documentation that was considered basic in our field?

Dr. Perlstein didn't wait for me to answer. When she next spoke, her voice was tempered. She sounded concerned now, not angry.

"Eben, I know that one of your passions is learning the truth behind the work. I've read your thesis. For the last six years, I have applauded your industriousness and your curiosity. You wouldn't be here if I didn't. And yes, being a curator can mean solving puzzles. That is an aspect of what we do that I grant is not only challenging but exciting. Except this time, the direction you're taking is out of line. We are way past asking these questions. Can you see that?"

I had an irrational urge to quit on the spot, then go and do exactly what she was telling me not to—find out what really went on a hundred years ago in Stockholm.

"Will you allow me to say something personal, Eben?"

I was caught off guard by the question. "Sure."

"Mysteries," she said, "are like catnip to you. When you sense there's a secret in an artist's work or life, you have to solve it. Have you ever wondered if you think that by learning other artists' secrets, you'll be better able to understand your own mother's work?"

I looked away, back toward the window. I didn't quite know what to make of Dr. Perlstein's question. We'd never had such a personal conversation. In fact, no one, including my father, had ever said anything so deeply personal to me.

When for the second time in a very few minutes I didn't answer her, she continued. "Everyone who knew your mother said that like her sculpture, she was an enigma. How could someone so young create such sophisticated work? Barely out of art school, she had a master's sensibilities and vision. I can't imagine what it must have been like for you to grow up without her but with her pieces all around you, teasing you. Never being able to talk about her work with her."

This was definitely not a conversation I wanted to be having and I decided to bring it to a close.

"Dr. Perlstein, I'm sorry if I caused trouble in Stockholm. I'll stick to the job at hand."

"Good." She gave me a heartfelt smile, and the tension in the room began to lift. "Now, let's go over the catalog, okay? Where are we?"

For the next half hour, we pored over the layout of the book and the status of the essays.

"There's one we're missing," she said.

"I don't think so." I looked through the list again. "Everyone is on track to deliver by the end of the month."

"I'm not talking about one you've already assigned, but a new one I realized we should include while you were away."

"Oh?"

She reached behind her and pulled a book from the shelves. When she put it down in front of me, I felt my stomach churn.

"Have you read this?" she asked.

It was Blythe's book, based on her thesis: *Our Hecates: Spiritualism, Witchcraft, the Occult, and Women Painters 1890–1980.*

"I have."

"I know we're very concerned about how we are portraying Hilma. . . . How did you put it?"

"As a mystic instead of an artist?"

"Right. And you've done a great job collecting an impressive and fascinating array of essays that ensure her artistic stature. You've covered everything from her breakthroughs in non-objective painting to the difficulty of women artists of the period. The result is certain to ensure she's seen as a vital, interesting, revolutionary artist. I appreciate your sensitivity that she not be judged because of her occult leanings, but the fact is she was very much a spiritualist, and I think we've gone too far in the other direction."

"Hans Wertheim's essay covers that," I said, hoping I could cut Dr. Perlstein off at the pass.

"Only in short paragraphs of biographical fact. We need a

piece that will delve into how Hilma and De Fem used mediumship, mysticism, and channeling to find their artistic voices. I think we owe it to them to illuminate their faith and commitment to one another and how that created the environment necessary for Hilma to feel safe enough to accept the spirits' request. There are questions that, even if they cannot be answered, need to be explored. How secretive were De Fem's members about their experiments and ceremonies? How was spiritualism treated by the art establishment at the time? How influential were the spirits in Hilma's decision not to show the paintings? You love questions, Eben. There are dozens that need to be raised and discussed regarding this subject. And I think Blythe Larkin is the perfect writer to do it."

I wanted to argue, but I couldn't dispute what Dr. Perlstein had said. The truth was I'd felt from the very beginning that Blythe Larkin needed to write an essay for us. She'd devoted her thesis to the study of this phenomenon; she'd written one of the most important books on the subject.

I may not have had personal reasons for wanting to understand Hilma af Klint's secrets, but I certainly did for not asking Blythe to write an essay for us. Explaining them to Dr. Perlstein was out of the question.

"I'll do what I can," I said. "But it is short notice. She won't have more than a month to write it—even if I push the deadline."

"She's done all the research already." Dr. Perlstein patted the book. "And as a matter of fact, while you were gone, I ran into Miss Larkin and broached the subject. She seemed very interested."

I wasn't sure I understood. "You met with her last week?"

"Yes, we were both at the same gallery opening."

"She's in New York?"

Dr. Perlstein looked at me with open curiosity.

"Do you know her, Eben?"

I tried for nonchalance. "Yeah, we went to grad school together. I just thought she lived in London. Isn't that what it says . . . ?" I opened the book on the desk to the flap where there was a picture of Blythe standing at a lectern. I read out the information below the black-and-white shot.

"'Dr. Larkin teaches at the Courtauld and resides in London.'"

"Yes, she mentioned that London is her permanent base but that she's currently teaching at Columbia University while she researches a new book."

Blythe had been living in New York, and I didn't know? How long had she been here? Why hadn't she gotten in touch?

"I'll track her down," I said.

"No need," Dr. Perlstein said. "Here's her card." She opened her top desk drawer, rustled through some papers, and handed me a crisp white business card.

"And now to the funding," Dr. Perlstein said, moving to the next topic of business. "We're in great shape, but we still need one more sponsorship. Now that you're back, I need you to work on some ideas."

"Yes, I was working on that before I left. I might have some leads by the end of the day tomorrow or Wednesday."

"So I don't need to call in any favors yet?"

"Not yet. Give me another forty-eight hours."

Back in my office, I looked at the card that Dr. Perlstein had handed me. It listed a phone number as well as an email address. There was no question about which one I was going to use.

I typed out the message.

Hi, Blythe,

Dr. Perlstein just told me the two of you talked last week and you would potentially be interested in writing an essay for our Hilma af Klint catalog. Can we set up a time to talk about that?

If I had written it to any other colleague, I would have taken a minute to spell-check it and then just hit SEND. Not question my wording. Not look for any hidden meanings. Not deliberate over sending it at all. Not wonder if I should tell Dr. Perlstein that I'd contacted her but not send it and then blame lack of response on a lost email if it ever came up.

But if I did all those things, I would only wind up ashamed of myself. Why couldn't I just do what had to be done?

Because of the answers I didn't have. Again. Always.

Because Blythe had left me without telling me why.

Because of the ridiculous theme of my life, started by my mother.

I knew all that. But it didn't matter.

After graduating from Courtauld, I'd returned to New York. Depressed about Blythe, I was drinking and partying too much. My father recognized the signs and knew I needed help.

He told me he understood them all too well. That we Elliots were far better at avoiding and masking pain than we were at coping with it. He suggested I revisit Dr. Gleckle, a therapist who'd helped him when he'd been widowed and then helped me during my teenage years when my mother's death had finally hit home.

I didn't need a therapist to tell me why I was rereading my email to Blythe for the third time. I knew exactly what the problem was. I had known it in Stockholm during the conference. Had known it when I was putting together the potential catalog contributors and purposely left Blythe off my list.

But I was being ridiculous. She'd moved on. I'd moved on. Blythe's long-ago reasons for what she did no longer mattered. Neither did my long-ago bout of self-destruction.

My phone chirped. I looked at the caller ID, hit SEND on the email, and then answered the call.

"Daphne," I said. "I was hoping it was you."

"What a nice thing to say," she said, but her voice was all business. "I have some good news for you."

"Excellent."

"I have a client who is seriously interested in a Hilma sponsorship. She'd like to meet you and go over the details. Are you free for drinks tonight?"

"Yes, yes, that's fantastic. Who is it? Maybe I can—"

"I have another call," she interrupted. "See you at five at Cipriani's," she said, naming a chic Italian restaurant on Fifth Avenue where it could be impossible to get a table during dinner but was always relatively quiet for early cocktails.

I didn't get an email from Blythe that afternoon, and by the time I left to meet Daphne, I was torn between relief and annoyance.

• • • • •

As I walked through the door to the restaurant, I spotted Daphne seated next to a sixty-something woman at one of the round tables in the front room. The peach-toned lighting and the warm wood paneling flattered them both.

"Eben Elliot, meet Barbara Silverman." Daphne introduced us. Her client wore a perfectly fitted black jacket, one rope of large, lustrous—and, I was betting—natural pearls wrapped around her neck, and another rope around her wrist. Her helmet of black hair was impeccably styled and her makeup carefully applied. She whispered wealth in a way that many in society did.

I reached out and shook the woman's hand. She had a firm grip.

Almost as soon as I was seated, a waiter approached. I looked over at what my companions were drinking and nodded at their martini glasses.

"I'll have one of those but with extra olives and over ice," I said, and then returned my attention to Mrs. Silverman.

"It's a pleasure to meet you. I'm delighted that you're interested in sponsoring our show."

She smiled, and her eyes lit up as she said, "I have been visiting the Guggenheim since I was a little girl. My sister and I used to race down the rotunda. She usually won. There will be some vindication in having my name attached to this exhibit."

I liked her instantly.

"Eben, can you run through what the sponsorship will entail?" Daphne asked. "I've explained it to some extent, but it's always better to hear from you directly. You give it the panache it deserves."

I did as requested and had gotten through about a quarter of the perks when the waiter arrived with my drink and a bowl of the zucchini chips the restaurant was famous for.

I stopped explaining and raised my glass to the two women. "To little girls running down the rotunda ramp," I said.

Barbara Silverman smiled, raised her glass, and clinked mine. I took a satisfying sip and returned to my recitation. Both women were nodding when I finished.

"Quite honestly," Mrs. Silverman said, "it sounded perfect when Daphne told me about it. And now, hearing more from you, it's even more perfect. An unknown female artist rescued from obscurity. A woman who understood the present and had the foresight to see the future. I'm intrigued, Eben, and impressed."

"Let me show you some of the work."

I opened the folder I'd brought and guided Mrs. Silverman through two dozen eight-by-ten photos of Hilma af Klint's paintings, drawings, and notebooks. By that point, I'd given a similar presentation at least thirty times to other potential sponsors, as well as the contributors who were writing the catalog essays.

Mrs. Silverman's questions demonstrated her deep level of interest in and understanding of what she was looking at and its importance in the history of modern art. When I reached the photos of notebook pages, I explained that there was at least one notebook we knew of that was missing.

"A lost notebook? I find that really curious. Is there an investigation?"

"There is, but to no avail."

"Well, who doesn't love a good mystery? I have a friend who writes thrillers who would love to hear this story. If I go ahead and fund the exhibit, will you share some of the information with me? Maybe I could convince Steve Berry to write the search into one of his novels and get the show some more attention in a really interesting way."

"I'd be more than happy to share what I know with you, Mrs. Silverman."

"Please, call me Barbara. I do think it would be smart marketing."

"It would be," Daphne said.

"There's something here . . . ," Mrs. Silverman said as she pulled forward three of the photos—all of notebook pages—so that they were lined up in front of her. Leaning closer, she examined each of them carefully.

"I'm not an expert at all, but aren't these written by different hands?"

"Yes, another mystery for you," I told her.

Before I answered more fully, I thought about all of my own questions about this very subject and about Dr. Perlstein's warnings. "Hilma was part of a close-knit group of women who called themselves De Fem—'The Five.'" I explained about their spiritual quest. "There's evidence that from 1896 to 1906 there was some collaboration in the notebooks." I pointed to a section. "We know that's Anna Cassel's writing." I pointed to another section. "And that is Cornelia Cederberg's."

"Really, a collaboration in the notebooks! What about the paintings? Did they collaborate on those as well?" Mrs. Silverman asked.

"The Hilma af Klint Foundation has identified about one hundred of the more than one thousand paintings attributed to Hilma as having been painted by one of her friends, Anna Cassel, but we are steering clear of those paintings for the show."

"Did Hilma sign her name to them?" Mrs. Silverman didn't want to abandon the subject.

"No, they are unsigned, but Anna's family has a sizable archive of her works, and the styles and methods clearly identify them."

"Tell me more about this Anna."

"She was Hilma's companion for many years, as well as her patron. She helped build an atelier for her on the island of Munsö so she could work surrounded by nature and draw inspiration from it. . . ."

Mrs. Silverman raised her eyebrows. "Companion? Was Hilma married?"

"No, she never did marry."

"And was Anna married?"

"No, she wasn't either."

"So there's some gossip to add to the mystery." She looked at Daphne. "You didn't tell me there was all this drama too. I love it."

I felt a frisson of anxiety. We were headed right into the muck and mire that Dr. Perlstein warned me to steer clear of.

The mysteries surrounding Hilma were as interesting as the mysteries in her canvases.

"But the show is a retrospective of Hilma's work. I want to make that evident," I said.

Before Mrs. Silverman responded, the waiter approached and asked if we wanted another round.

Mrs. Silverman looked at her watch. "I wish I could, but I have to get home and change—I have an engagement tonight. But the two of you, do go ahead."

"Actually, I should go as well," Daphne said. "Can I have the check?" she asked the waiter.

Inside my pocket, I felt my phone vibrate. I never liked to check calls during meetings and so ignored it.

The three of us wrapped up the conversation while Daphne paid the bill. Outside, Mrs. Silverman offered to have her driver drop us off if we were going her way. Daphne accepted her offer; I declined. It was a beautiful night. Though it was a little chilly, I felt like walking home through the park.

I shook Mrs. Silverman's hand and thanked her for her interest. She reached out and hugged me. "I'm so excited about this, Eben. You can count me in. I feel like this show is going to make waves. There's nothing more exciting than riding a wave."

As I crossed the street and entered the park at the Sixtieth Street entrance, the Scholar's Gate, I thought that although Dr. Perlstein had started off the day annoyed with me, this news would go far in restoring me to her good graces.

Central Park is called the lungs of New York. Designed in 1857 by Frederick Law Olmsted, it replaced a group of shantytowns, settlements, sheep meadows, and natural forest. He and his team worked for almost twenty years to create 843 acres of green. Like most city kids, I thought of the park as my backyard.

I turned right and within minutes was enveloped by a quiet that is otherwise hard to find in Manhattan. The trees were ablaze with fall leaves, and I felt as if I were walking through a landscape painting, seeing different color combinations at every turn. One vista reminded me of van Gogh's park scene of trees ablaze with burnt-orange leaves displayed at the Museum Boijmans van Beuningen in Rotterdam. When a breeze blew leaves onto the footpath, I saw Georgia O'Keeffe's *Autumn Leaves, Lake George* in the scarlet, topaz, amber, and green composition at my feet. At the boat pond, the cobalt evening sky reflected in the water and the golden trees reminded me of Kandinsky's *Autumn in Murnau*. Which brought my thinking back to the woman who had preceded his forays into modern art but had not gotten any of the credit for it.

It wasn't until I reached the park's Eighty-Ninth Street exit that I remembered the call that had come during drinks. I pulled out my phone and looked down at a number I didn't recognize. I hit my voice mail.

"Eben . . ."

I knew who it was instantly. No one said my name with the same lilt.

An image came to mind. One of Hilma's paintings—of course—of two swans, one black and one white, an alchemical symbol she'd used over and over, said to depict the male and the female.

"Eben, I got your message. I'd be happy to meet. I'm free tomorrow early evening—around five—if that works for you. I have a gallery opening to attend at Gagosian, but I could meet you at the bar in the Mark Hotel?" Then there was a pause. *"Oh, I forgot, this is Blythe."*

·····

It was said that I should start the work with
the temple. During thirty days in solitude, I
will be alone and imprisoned, only to then be
set free. Even Anna will work alone for thirty
days.

. . . . .

CHAPTER ELEVEN

Friday Night, No. 428
October 5, 1906
Stockholm

The first month of autumn had brought with it an unexpected period of calm for Sigrid. De Fem was now approaching its tenth year, and the spirits had been adamant in their instructions. Hilma and Anna had to sequester themselves for thirty days to purify their work ahead of them. Now that their time of seclusion had come to an end, Sigrid was looking forward to hosting all five women together again.

She spent the early part of the morning cleaning her house and arranging the furniture for their meeting. Life passed far more slowly now that she and Ernst no longer had any children at home. They enjoyed the birds that came and visited them during breakfast, pecking on the seeds that Ernst sprinkled on the grass. They now drank their coffee not as cozy lovers, as they had early on in their marriage, nor rushed, as they had when their house was filled with babies. But rather they savored the first morning sips together, slowly bathing in each other's presence. Ernst was more than her husband and the father of her children. He had become her cherished and stalwart companion.

"I'm excited to see them all again tonight," Sigrid said, squeezing his hand. "And I'm relieved the spirits didn't also ask me to barricade myself in the room for thirty days. I would have missed you."

"I'm happy that I finally had you for a few Friday nights to myself."

He leaned over and kissed her. She breathed him in, holding his warmth inside her.

"Try to enjoy yourself this weekend." Sigrid's eyes fell to a corner of the room. Ernst's rifle was propped against the wall, his overnight bag beside it.

The spirits had given her a gift by calling for a monthlong reprieve. Sigrid felt her energy restored. But now she couldn't wait to see her friends.

· · · · ·

"I've missed seeing everyone," Cornelia announced as she stepped into Sigrid's living room. "It feels like forever since we've all been together." She kissed Sigrid on both cheeks. "You've made everything here look so warm and inviting."

The house appeared different to her than the last time they had all met there. Ernst and Sigrid had bought new furniture. Birch wood crackled in the fireplace. Cornelia noticed above the mantel a winter-landscape painting, which looked like it had been done by Anna's hand. On the sofa, a bearskin blanket covered the pale gray Gustavian upholstery.

Mathilda settled into Ernst's deep chair and pulled out a cigar. "Has anyone heard from either of them since they secluded themselves?"

Cornelia shook her head. "I tried to reach Anna, but there was no reply. And I haven't heard from Hilma either. . . ."

Sigrid sighed. "Well, I did send both of them a letter reminding them to come at seven p.m. Things seem so serious now; I almost wish they'd come dressed up in male clothing just for a giggle." She smiled, remembering how Cornelia had arrived at one of their meetings wearing trousers and a shirt, much like Hilma had done at the first Edelweiss gathering.

"Gosh, that does seem like long ago," Cornelia said wistfully.

"Yes," Sigrid agreed. "But regardless, it will be good to be all together again. I'm hopeful that the spirits will join us tonight, and I'm sure Hilma and Anna will want to hear from them too."

Mathilda nodded and blew a puff of blue smoke to the ceiling.

"Well, I know I am hoping the spirits join us too." Cornelia adjusted her notebook and the tin of oil pastels on her lap, her full skirt spread out beneath her. When Sigrid poured her a cup of her special tea, Cornelia welcomed it happily. Cigars had always made her sick, but this special brew brought her a sense of calm and inspired her to see the most wonderful colors when she did her drawings.

As the hour neared, the maid brought Hilma and Anna into

the parlor. A small shock came over the others. Hilma's and Anna's physical and spiritual transformation was apparent.

While both women looked thinner, their faces more angled and their clothes hanging loosely on their frames, each otherwise manifested her monthlong trial completely differently from the other. Anna appeared far more fragile, while Hilma radiated strength, as if her energy had been repurposed.

"I am so happy to see you both," Sigrid said as she opened her arms to embrace them. "And, Hilma! Just look at you. We should call you 'Lilla Himmel,' Little Sky. You have taken the spirits' words to heart and aspired toward the heavens."

Hilma didn't soften under Sigrid's effort to make the atmosphere more lighthearted. Instead, she remained solemn and restrained.

Anna forced a smile, despite her fatigue. "It's been quite a hardship not being able to have our meetings." She sighed. "And this is the longest I've gone without seeing Hilma since we were in school together."

Hilma, unmoved by Anna's sentimentality, thrust her shoulders back.

"I found the purification to be extremely beneficial. It allowed me to eliminate all distractions and focus on the path ahead."

She took a deep breath and turned up her nose. "Mathilda, you should not be polluting the room with your cigar smoke. The stench is offensive to both the spirits and me."

Mathilda rose to her feet, inhaled from the cigar deeply, then puffed a thick cloud of smoke in Hilma's direction.

"Are you now channeling the spirits' thoughts directly?"

Hilma stepped closer. Her eyes glowed in the firelight. "I am the one they have chosen." She took her hand and reached for Mathilda's cigar as the others looked on, and then extinguished it in the ashtray.

"Anna and I have gone to great lengths to change our diet, to spend thirty days in reflection. The responsibility of accepting a task from the spirits does not come without great sacrifice and intention."

Cornelia shifted in her seat. "Come now, Hilma. We appreciate the lengths you two have gone to, but Mathilda has smoked a cigar before each séance." She tried to defuse the tension. "It's been her ritual since the very beginning of De Fem."

Hilma turned her head toward Cornelia.

"Is that a bearskin behind you?" Hilma's eyes flared at the sight of the animal skin draped on the back of the sofa. "Did you not hear what the spirits said as they spoke through you, Sigrid?" Her voice escalated. "Those who come together to create the temple must respect that animals are sacred beings too."

Sigrid looked around the room. They had always enjoyed a certain level of banter before they sat down for their séance. This levity—the little bits of gossip, the bursts of laughter—had always brought her tremendous joy. It was one of the things she had loved about their Friday Night meetings. Yes, she had always wanted to put her medium skills to good use, but she had also craved a sense of sisterhood that escaped her in her daily life. She had longed to come together again with her friends after their monthlong break, but Hilma's entry had introduced an unexpected fury upon all of them.

"The bearskin is from my husband's hunting expedition, Hilma. It does not concern you or De Fem. However, if it offends you, I will remove it for tonight." She was surprised by her tone. It was as harsh as the one she used when her children had been small and they teetered on the brink of a tantrum.

Sigrid walked over to the couch, took the skin, and left to take it into another room. When she returned, she walked to the front of the roaring fireplace.

"Friends, it has been thirty days since we last saw one another. In the weeks we have been separated, two of us have taken extreme measures to advance the vision that Amaliel and Georg have expressed in our séances." She inhaled a deep breath of air, still pungent from the remnants of Mathilda's cigar. "But division within the group will only make the spirits believe we are not strong enough for the task." She extended her hands. "Let's make peace and join one another at the table."

"Thank you," Cornelia said, letting out a sigh of relief.

"Yes," Anna agreed. Despite being tired, she tried to rouse herself into a robust mood. She'd always hated any sort of discontent.

Mathilda and Hilma exchanged glances, then nodded in agreement.

"Come." Sigrid beckoned again.

The women all rose and walked toward the chairs.

• • • • •

The night soon yielded renewed activity. Sigrid shuddered as she surrendered to the spirits' overtaking her body. Words that conjured up shapes, figures, and colors flew out of her mouth.

"She is talking about the paintings," said Hilma. "I understand now; I can see her vision. The temple should be adorned with paintings that echo the stages of life: from chaos to creation, from birth to old age."

Cornelia was lost in her own trance. Page after page she filled. Her hands worked furiously, her fingers gripping one pastel after another, in order to capture all of the colors that flashed through her mind. At one point, after she had used every sheet of paper in her sketchbook, she began drawing on the white tablecloth. There wasn't enough surface to contain the abundance of shapes and colors that now burst forth.

Mathilda's eyes widened as she looked on at her sister. For years, she had thought little of Cornelia, had been frustrated by her propensity for dreaming and not working hard enough to make something of her natural talent. But now, with Cornelia's hair falling over her face and her body moving like a dancer to put down on paper all that came through her, Mathilda felt enormous pride.

"You are ready to begin your work," Sigrid announced to Anna and Hilma.

"The path is cleared for creation."

Sigrid's body shook, and suddenly Cornelia's hand stopped. The others opened their eyes. In front of them, the entire white tablecloth was saturated with a galaxy of shapes and bright colors.

Hilma's eyes flashed with wonder and determination, as if she had been waiting for this moment all her life.

"It's exactly how I imagined it," she exclaimed. "It's a map of the universe." She took a deep breath. "And it begins with the stars."

. . . . .

Together they folded the tablecloth, all of them soaking in the vision that the spirits had laid out before them.

"We'll need more space to work," Hilma informed the group. "The paintings will need to be tall in order to properly evoke the magnitude of the heavens," she mused aloud. "There won't be enough room in my studio. Does anyone know where we could find a bigger space?"

Cornelia's heart rose in her chest.

"Yes," she uttered without an ounce of hesitation. "I think I know someone who can help."

. . . . .

She didn't bother to make an excuse to Mathilda when she left. "I'm sure Kristian will help us." She said his name freely. "I'll ask him if we can use one of his warehouses."

Cornelia looked wild in the night sky. Her hands and cheeks were stained with pastel dust. Her hair had come out of its bun.

"You were always so quiet when you were little," Mathilda remarked softly. "I had no idea you possessed such a tempest inside you."

Cornelia stepped closer to her sister. "Please don't be upset with me. I'm coming into my own after all these years. I'm an artist, Sister." Her heart soared as she expressed the words. "My life can no longer be confined to black and white."

Stockholm, October 12, 1906

Dear Hilma,

I write to you with an exuberant heart. The joy from our last
few meetings has swept me into its wake, and I am filled with
profound determination to do everything I can to ensure
that De Fem is able to accomplish all that the spirits wish
of us.

    It has become clear that we have outgrown your studio,
Sigrid's home, and certainly my sister's office. We must accept
that more space is needed for you to fully realize your vision
of the Greatest Paintings. Over the past few days, I've put
all of my efforts into finding us a new studio, and I am happy
to share with you that I have succeeded! We will now have
access to a large warehouse in Värtahamnen. It is owned by a
very special childhood friend of mine. I can't give you any more
details about him, but I assure you that he is a kind and
warmhearted person, and that he will not tell anyone about our
secret project.

    For this week's Friday night meeting, I invite you and
the others to meet me at building number twenty-five. Walk the
path closest to the water, and number twenty-five will be the
third warehouse with large wooden doors. It has only a small
stove for heating, so please wear your woolen underwear to keep
warm.

    I'm so excited to show the building to all of you. It is a huge *empty space, and it even has a skylight that will be perfect for painting under the stars and moonlight.*

With deep affection,
Cornelia

And one more thing! Can you tell Anna the new location for me? It saves my writing one more letter!

· · · · ·

CHAPTER TWELVE

Friday Night, No. 429
October 12, 1906
Stockholm

In the quiet of her bedroom, Anna studied her face in the mirror, cupping her cheeks between her palms. The past month on her new vegetarian diet had given her a new sense of vitality. She felt refreshed and more inspired. Just this morning, after eating her breakfast of dandelion and radish salad, she had excused herself from the table and returned directly to her room to immerse herself in her painting.

The image had come to her at night, a huge saffron-colored rose against a chalk-blue sky. Anna imagined the flower as an almost hieroglyphic symbol: five rows of concentric petals with a single bright yellow blossom in the center. She had never considered herself to be a particularly courageous artist like Hilma, but her mind had now begun to open in a way she had never experienced before. In the same way that Cornelia closed her eyes and let her hand surrender to her automatic drawings, Anna felt herself venturing into uncharted waters.

She turned from the mirror and now gazed at the painting on the easel. It appeared fresh and, did she dare say, bold? Wholly different from anything she had ever painted before. Since she was old enough to clasp a pencil in her hand, Anna's artistic style had been to create an accurate rendering of what she saw before her. While her landscape paintings had become more atmospheric over the years, a development she attributed to sharing the Impressionists' affinity for working outside in nature, she had never been one to directly draw from her imagination. Hilma could easily invent a particular face or other image in her mind. But for Anna, her subject had to be so close that she could almost touch it.

This image, however, had come to her so differently. It arrived like a moonbeam in a starless sky. Bright and beckoning, pulling her toward a new horizon. She couldn't wait to show her friends.

An hour before they were all to meet at the new studio that Cornelia had arranged, Hilma surprised Anna with a visit.

"I thought I'd stop by and we could go to the new location together," Hilma announced as she entered the room. "Your mother was in the parlor with Lotten and the doctor. . . . She assured me it was all right to come directly upstairs."

Anna smiled and stepped away from the easel, revealing her latest painting.

"Oh my, what have you been up to?" Hilma laid down the leather portfolio she was carrying and stepped closer to examine the painting. Her finger rose to trace the five rows within the rose. Around the border, the lowercase letters *u, a,* and *o* were written in paint.

"I have been waiting for you to become inspired like this . . . and you've even used the letters that Cornelia inscribed in the De Fem notebooks." She could hardly contain her elation. "I think our purification rituals have set us both in the right direction." She turned to embrace Anna.

With Hilma folded into her, her friend's familiar scent filled Anna's nostrils. Hilma always carried the faint trace of pine in her hair and on her skin, a fragrance that came from all the turpentine and linseed oil she used every day. Anna bathed her face and hands in a basin of fresh milk after she painted, but Hilma had no interest in removing a perfume she felt defined her.

"I'm so proud of you for surrendering to what cannot be seen but only felt."

"Thank you," Anna replied. "Nearly everyone in De Fem has experienced visions of their own. It was finally time for me also to put down what is in my heart."

Hilma beamed. "I have a few new temperas I've done on paper too." She gestured toward her portfolio. "I think the group will be excited by what we're about to share with them."

"Get yourself ready," Hilma urged. "I feel like you. Tonight, I don't want to be late."

· · · · ·

Dressed in a flowing sage green smock, Cornelia greeted De Fem at the door of the warehouse and eagerly led them inside. Small votive candles burned around the perimeter of the room, and the skylight above danced with stars and moonlight.

"How did you ever manage to find such a perfect space?" Sigrid walked in and appraised the enormous room.

"I have a friend who likes to support artists," Cornelia answered. She didn't want to lie to the group, and after all, that was the truth. When she had asked Kristian, he had been amused by her request. "Most women want a new fur stole or a piece of jewelry, but my little Cornelia wants the use of my warehouse to paint with her friends?" He gave a small laugh, then wrapped her in his arms. "I'm happy to oblige, *älskling*. Just be careful that no one sees you. We don't want people to gossip about five women gathering in a warehouse alone late at night."

She had been careful when she arrived and told the other women not to attract attention. Now the room was all set up and ready for them to begin.

Cornelia had placed a large square of cotton cloth in the center, a blank invitation to be filled with colorful brush-strokes. Hilma glanced at it and then opened her portfolio case.

"I've brought a few things I've been working on," she announced. Carefully, she began to withdraw her latest tempera paintings. One with a long gold wheatlike sheaf with a blue garland beside it. Another one that was filled with tadpole- and amoeba-like shapes.

"And I also love this one very much," Hilma remarked, a smile spread over her face as she lifted Anna's painting of the golden rose.

"That's beautiful," Cornelia said. "And the symbolism of the five rows of petals is particularly meaningful."

"Yes, I can't agree more."

Anna remained quiet as she waited for her friend to inform the rest of De Fem that it was in fact her painting, but Hilma continued to speak as if it had come from her hand.

"The flower looks like a sun," added Cornelia. "It fills the paper with light."

"I know, exactly." Hilma grinned.

Anna opened her mouth, but the words remained trapped inside her throat. But even more painfully, they were also caught inside her heart.

"That painting is actually mine," she finally forced herself to say.

Puzzled, Hilma looked at her. "Oh, of course it is. . . . Did I fail to mention that?"

Mathilda, who had been standing removed from the group, grumbled to herself. How typical it was for Hilma not to give Anna credit! It was something she had worried about with her own sister. She had started to suspect that Hilma, with her notions of grandeur and self-importance and her belief that she was chosen above the others, was really only riding on the backs of the other, equally talented artists in the group, Anna and Cornelia.

"I didn't hear you say it was Anna's . . . ," Mathilda spoke up.

"I'm sure I did." Hilma shrugged, before continuing on to what she believed were more essential matters.

"And does it even matter whose hand actually created it? It's important for us to work as a group, to share our ideas," Hilma insisted. "I believe everything we do is part of a collective whole.

Mathilda's and Sigrid's channeling, Cornelia's drawings . . . and this painting by Anna, all of our contributions must be seen as one."

Anna paused. It wasn't that she was looking for any formal recognition, but the painting had been a monumental step for her.

"I only wanted the group to know that I have also been affected by Amaliel's and Georg's words." Tears filled Anna's eyes. Her sensitive nature almost always got the best of her. She felt like she was torn between running away from conflict, which she abhorred, and remaining truthful to herself.

"The rose is also a powerful symbol of love," she uttered softly as she tried to soothe the obvious discomfort in the room.

"Perhaps it is the message we all need before we begin our work tonight," Sigrid suggested. She looked over at Anna and saw her like an angel, with a soft amber glow enveloping her.

"If we are making acknowledgments, then," Hilma continued, "I'd like to also thank Cornelia for finding this wonderful new space for us." She extended her arms in a gesture of solidarity.

"Please let us put any hurt feelings behind us. Let's come together and begin."

· · · · ·

Anna began to slowly unpack her basket of supplies. Over the last two summers, she had amassed a brilliant collection of brightly shaded powders made from the wildflowers and verdant greens that grew near her family's summerhouse on the

lake. The landscape there was rich with blue violets, sunflow-
ers, roses, and juniper leaves. From July through August, she'd
taken their bounty of botanicals and laid them out in the sun.
The fragile red poppies dried within a few days, while other,
hardier blooms took longer. Once all the moisture from the
petals was removed, Anna would pulverize them into a chalk-
like consistency and store them for later, when they could be
mixed with either flaxseed oil or egg yolks to create paints of
varying hues.

"I'll need some silver birch," Hilma muttered as she began to
imagine the work ahead. "Did you bring some with you, Anna?"

"Yes, and I have some mugwort and buckthorn berries, too,
just in case you need more green paint for tonight." Anna was
well aware of how quickly Hilma went through her supplies.

Hilma didn't want there to be any hard feeling between
them for her previous misstep. "How fortunate I am that you
know exactly what colors I'm imagining for this series. . . ."

While she understood her friend hadn't intentionally set out
to hurt her, Anna knew all too well how Hilma often ignored
her contributions. "Thank you," she answered. "It gives me
comfort to know that some of the flowers we collected together will go into the paintings."

Hilma's mind, however, had already moved on. She stepped
back and squinted at the large bare canvas in the middle of the
room. "I want to convey how life comes from water. . . ." Her
hands gestured in the air. "The ocean, the sky, the tall blades
of grass—we are but small parts of a larger, intricate universe."

Anna knew exactly what pigments Hilma needed. She
pulled out the jar of rose madder from her basket and studied

the rich hue. She was confident that if she mixed it with the blue violet it would make the color even deeper. There were so many different shades they could create. Anna reached for a fresh jar of linseed oil and one of the graphite mortar slabs necessary for mixing the emulsion. She felt excited, like an alchemist who could create something special from her own private collection of ingredients.

"We'll need at least five different colors to begin with . . . ," Hilma instructed as she eyed the powdered pigments that Anna had brought.

"Do you need me to help?" Cornelia asked.

"If you can begin emulsifying the yellow color . . ." Anna handed her a jar of saffron-colored powder. "There're some extra slabs and pestles in my basket."

Watching as the other women worked in silence, Mathilda and Sigrid were excited by the sight of them sprinkling the powder onto the stone, the deliberate precision with which they added drops of amber-colored oil in order to bring the paint to life.

For Anna, however, their efforts brought on a sense of exhilaration, a much-needed satisfaction that she was helping execute the spirits' wishes.

"This first series will show the chaos in which life begins," Hilma explained.

She went over to one of the granite slabs and examined the blob of rich marine blue oil paint that rested in the center. "The color is perfect, Cornelia." Hilma then began rummaging through Anna's basket to find the best brush.

"I'm ready," she announced as she walked toward the canvas.

Sigrid felt transfixed as Hilma's aura transformed from green to gold.

The white cotton darkened with the length of Hilma's shadow as she knelt down, brush in hand, and applied the first stroke.

For the next two hours, Anna and Cornelia worked like assistant priestesses, combining the colors that Hilma requested. Soon the canvas became filled with the same images that had saturated the group's notebooks. Snaillike coils that echoed evolution, amoeba-like forms that evoked life's first shapes.

Sigrid sat crossed-legged on the floor, her hands calmly folded in her lap. Mathilda started to write down some observations in her notebook, but then found herself unable to concentrate. She watched as her sister repeatedly scraped more pigments onto Hilma's palette.

Cornelia was completely engrossed in the work.

"I need more fabric," Hilma announced. The one on the floor was nearly covered with her brushwork. Anna quickly went over to the bolt of canvas and cut more for her.

Soaked in perspiration as she worked to bring her vision to life, Hilma had taken off her blouse and skirt and now painted in nothing but a thin cotton chemise.

Mathilda, tired of having nothing to do, had looked up at the skylight to try to glean a sense of how many hours of darkness they had left, when suddenly she heard something drop against the roof. A shadowy figure passed over the frosted glass.

"Did you hear that?" she quickly asked Sigrid.

"Yes . . . I did. . . ." She stood up and craned her neck to see if she could make any sense of the noise.

"Someone has followed us here," Mathilda announced sharply. Her eyes turned to Hilma, who was oblivious to the commotion.

The only other person who seemed to detect the danger was Anna.

She looked up to see if she could make out the shadow above. But she didn't need to see who it was. She already sensed it was Hellström.

· · · · ·

Later that night, when Anna arrived at Hilma's studio, she found her friend asleep on her daybed. Her blouse, which she had hastily buttoned as they left the warehouse, was stained with blue paint.

"Hilma." Anna reached down and touched her.

"Wake up." She nudged Hilma again. "I need to talk to you. . . ."

Hilma sat up and rubbed her eyes. "What's wrong? Are you still mad at me?"

"No, that's not it. . . ."

Anna looked around the studio and the chaos within it. She didn't know how Alma and Charlotta could ever work in the same space with Hilma. She had overtaken everything. The floor was littered with scientific magazines, along with piles of gouache studies lifted from the pages of Cornelia's notebook sketches. Three wooden canvas stretchers were propped up against a stool, and a fourth had fallen to the floor. On her easel sat a canvas with an image of a jellyfish-like shape floating in the center. She had roughly painted in the background in a seashell pink, with yellow flowers bordering the edge.

"Where's the sketchbook?" Anna's voice sounded urgent.

"What sketchbook are you talking about? I have hundreds. You know that."

"The one from Venice, Hilma. The one I've been pestering you to find for ages."

Hilma made a face. "That was from nearly twenty years ago, Anna. I have no idea where it could be. . . ." She glanced around the studio. "Maybe it's in that pile over there. . . ." She pointed to a teetering pile of leather sketchbooks carelessly placed on a filing cabinet. "Or maybe it's home somewhere with Mother. . . ." She sighed. "Why are you even asking about it now?"

"Because, as I've told you before, it would be very dangerous for us if it were to ever fall into the wrong hands."

Hilma straightened herself up and put her bare feet on the floor. "Anna, we are artists. We draw bodies in the nude to learn anatomy. No one can arrest us for that."

"Those were not just anatomical sketches, Hilma. You know that. I opened myself up to you in a way that some might think was immoral."

Hilma shook her head. "I refuse to believe this nonsense. Who is to judge us? You know I don't believe we can be just one sex. I've said it many times—there's a male and a female part that exists in all of us."

"I think Hellström was spying on us in the warehouse tonight. I cannot even begin to imagine what would happen if he had that book in his possession." Anna searched Hilma's face for a reaction.

"Please just tell me you know where that sketchbook is . . . and that there's no way it could have gotten into his hands."

Hilma rose and began to fidget with the buttons on her blouse. She then looked up at Anna. "I'm sorry I can't tell you that with any certainty. I just don't have a memory for that kind of thing."

* * * * *

Anna stepped out of Hilma's building and looked at the trees with their first stippling of leaves.

Her heart was heavy. She realized Hilma was not as concerned as she was about Hellström's causing a scandal. Her friend had never been prone to worrying. That stoic trait had worked well for Hilma over the years, as she possessed a fearlessness that was enviable. Anna, however, was filled with dread. She hated to imagine a scandal clouding her family's good name, especially as the health of her sister, Lotten, had deteriorated significantly over the past few months. The doctors weren't sure if she would make it through the year.

Anna tiptoed to her room and shut the door when she arrived home. With the house asleep, she cherished the ability to now be alone and gather her thoughts.

Underneath her bed, in a box with a Florentine paper lid, Anna kept her most cherished drawings. Not the ones she had created back in art school, but the ones she had done outside the classroom. Many were from the summers at her family's country home, and a few were portraits she had done of her mother and sister. She rarely signed her drawings, believing the lines and strokes on her page were evidence enough of her own hand, and those she gifted her artwork to would always know it was from her.

But the box also contained private pieces of her art that she would never share with anyone. Inside the box, most personal to her was the notebook she had brought with her to Italy. The one whose pages were filled with sketches from the Uffizi and of terraced hilltops in Umbria. And the ones that she drew of Hilma in the privacy of their bedroom at the pension. Sometimes her friend let her draw her in her linen nightdress, while other times it was just her bare skin illuminated by the moon.

She did not know what Hilma had done with her own sketchbook from that time in their lives, but Anna had been careful to keep hers protected and far from prying eyes.

Anna lifted the notebook and began to look through its pages. The last sketch inside was a pencil drawing she had done of Hilma on the train after they left Venice. She was staring straight at Anna, her eyes filled with images of all the art and experiences they had shared throughout their recent journey. But more important was the expression of determination in her gaze, as if she were already dreaming of how she was going to use all of her newfound wisdom, and she believed there was a clear and certain path for her ahead.

. . . . .

CHAPTER THIRTEEN

E<small>BEN</small>

Present Day
New York City

I arrived at the Mark bar before Blythe. It was early still, and with a choice of tables, I snagged one in a corner. The Manhattan-chic décor included kidney-shaped, mirror-topped tables, and chairs upholstered in a black-and-white animal print. While I waited, I watched the only other people in the room. Two women sat side by side on a couch, with a Pomeranian between them. The dog had his own tiny green plastic bowl of water. As the women talked, the one with strawberry blond hair pet the dog almost absentmindedly. Though they were not speaking loudly, I could make out much of their conversation, as the lounge was otherwise empty. It seemed they were having a serious conversation about the history of pearls, and I recognized some of the names they mentioned, like Cartier and Tiffany. Others I didn't know, like Belperron and Fouquet.

When the waiter arrived, I ordered my regular dirty martini and settled back with an eye on the door to wait for Blythe.

Over the years, I had tried not to think about her often, but despite my best efforts, she was never far from my mind. I'd see a painting or hear a song or taste something and still, even after so long, would want to tell her about it. Her memory was like the scar on my chin. Even though I'd had it since childhood when I fell off my bike, it was in such a prominent spot, I couldn't look in the mirror without noticing it.

I'd met Blythe in our first year of graduate school. She was standing outside my door, at dusk. I'd just returned home from buying takeout for dinner. But I'd seen her before I met her.

Four hours earlier, I'd gone to the Tate Modern to see a Rothko exhibition. The artist was known for large color blocks with blurry edges that he advised viewing from eighteen inches away so the observer could be immersed in the paintings.

I was standing in a room filled with eight Rothkos—all black, white, and gray compositions—doing what the artist had instructed, but I wasn't feeling like I was entering into the paintings at all. My art history professor had delivered a lecture on Rothko that morning and told us about his visit to the show, claiming he'd had a spiritual revelation. I'd winced at the word "spiritual." But since our next assignment was visiting and writing up the exhibit, there I was, trying to force myself to metaphorically disappear into one of the canvases.

I had never spent much time before with a Rothko. Our professor had described how the paintings had an internal rhythm that moved and pulsed even though they were, of course, static. I'd read some critics who said they radiated mysterious light. Art lovers had written instructions on how to give yourself up to the paintings and to allow them to take you on an otherworldly journey. I had read about the artist's technique of using boundaries of colors and blurring outlines in an effort to awaken our emotions. But I wasn't responding. The artwork depressed me. I wondered if that was because I had also read that Rothko had been depressed when he painted these particular canvases. He'd recently left his wife and children and become ill. Sequestered in his studio, he continued to work on the gray-and-black canvases until finally succumbing to suicide at age sixty-six in 1970.

Reproduced on a wall of the exhibit was a quote from the artist:

> *"I'm not an abstractionist. I'm not interested in the*
> *relationship of color or form or anything else.*
> *I'm interested only in expressing basic human emotions:*
> *tragedy, ecstasy, doom, and so on."*
>
> —MARK ROTHKO

I sat down, pulled out my notebook, and jotted it down. I'd just finished writing and re-capped my pen when I heard what sounded like bells and looked up. There against all the gray doom was a woman, with her back to me, in front of the painting closest to the door.

She was wearing an orange silk shawl embroidered with

scarlet flowers and green leaves, a long skirt in a deeper orange, and emerald green suede boots. Her almost-white blond curls were tied off her face with a purple scarf.

The woman stood in front of the canvas without moving, seemingly mesmerized. I was aware of a deep stillness coming from her and envied her ability to enter into the painting so completely and so quickly.

I have spent my whole life around art, and yet the ability to be absorbed into a piece the way she was continues to elude me. I never cease to approach it with a fully conscious mind and an active curiosity that I seem unable to let go.

The woman in the flowing clothes spent long moments studying that one canvas. I still hadn't seen her face, but she was tall and slender and had multiple silver bracelets on each wrist. They jangled pleasantly as she finally walked from the first painting and on to the second.

And I? I studied her without knowing why. Every time I looked away, I found myself turning back. I waited for her to continue to move around the room so that I could see her face. Finally, she turned and I held my breath as her profile came into view. Her skin was pale, her cheekbones were high, her nose was sharp, her chin was a bit pointy, and her neck was long.

I could have found a way to approach her. But I had some totally irrational desire to see if she would discover me. But before she did, before I ever saw her face from the front, another woman came hurrying into the room. This one looked at me as she walked by, sizing me up but not giving any of her thoughts away. Then she reached and hugged my silver girl. That's how I was thinking of her, because of the way the lights shone on her blond hair and the armfuls of silver bracelets. In my mind I was hearing Simon and Garfunkel lyrics over and over as if I'd put the song on repeat—"Sail on, silver girl. / Sail on by. / Your time has come to shine."

The interloper said something in hushed tones to the silver girl and then she laughed. It sounded like a glass bell. And while they stood there talking to each other, I got up and left.

Exiting the museum, I thought about what it is that draws us to one person or another. I've read that it is a chemical attraction—our pheromones dancing in space with theirs. Such a down-to-earth explanation for something that feels like it's orchestrated in the heavens.

I spent a couple of hours at the Courtauld's library and then headed home, which was a twenty-minute walk, since I lived in Bloomsbury. The area had been home to Virginia Woolf and her set and was still slightly bohemian.

I stopped at a restaurant near my apartment to order a curry takeaway. Once the food was ready, I paid and proceeded around the corner.

Two teenage boys were walking ahead of me, so I didn't see the doorway to my building until I was almost upon it. And there I was startled to see, of all people, silver girl, leaning against the side of the building, writing something down.

It wasn't possible, I thought. I couldn't have just seen her that very day and then run into her here. But there she was.

As I approached, she looked up.

"It's you," she said. "I'm so glad."

"You are?" I had no idea that she had noticed me and far less of an idea why she would be glad.

"Yes, I found this." She held out my black notebook. "You left it behind in the Rothko room."

I shifted the bag of food and reached for the notebook. I didn't realize I'd lost it.

"I didn't mean to look through it, but I had to find you." She smiled.

"Yes, yes. Don't worry about that." I was wondering even as I said it what she had read as she'd searched through it. Had she really noted only my address, or had she read some of the entries or looked at the drawings? "I can't believe I left it. I have never done that before—but how kind of you to come all the way here to return it."

There was something shy about the way she looked down for a moment before looking back up at me. "It seemed important. Too important not to."

We utter millions of words in our lives. We hear as many said to us. We experience millions of individual moments. And yet somehow, we know which words and which moments to remember and hold on to.

In that moment, standing in front of my building with silver girl, I wasn't thinking that the woman talking to me would ever be more important to me than any other stranger. Yes, I'd noticed her and been taken by her eccentric looks, and the way she'd been engaged with the Rothkos had impressed, even moved, me. But there was still no reason for my brain to take mental photo after photo of every second of our exchange on my doorstep.

"Would you like to come up and have a glass of wine so I

can thank you properly?" I gestured to the bag. "If you're hungry, I even have a curry."

Much to my surprise she said yes.

My friends tell me that I can be torturously inquisitive. I know it's true. But I met my match with the woman who introduced herself to me over our shared bottle of white wine.

"My name is Blythe Larkin," she said after she took a first sip. "And this is quite good. Not graduate student quality."

"And my name is—"

"Eben Elliot," she interrupted, smiling.

I was momentarily confused as to how she knew and then realized. "Right. The notebook. Thank you again for finding it. And for making this effort."

"I know how important notebooks can be."

"It looked like you enjoyed the Rothkos," I said without thinking, and then wanted to smack myself. I had just admitted I'd been watching her. Now she'd think I was some kind of stalker.

"'Enjoy' isn't the word I'd use. It was a very difficult show to spend time with. The artist's pain seeps from the canvas. It's my third time seeing that show. I just keep getting pulled back into it." She shrugged. "I've been trying to understand how it's possible that so many people react to it in such similar ways." She took another sip of her wine. "It's partly what my thesis is about. 'The Spiritual in Art: Defying Logic.'"

"Spiritual as in religious?"

"A bit, but really more mystical, esoteric, even touching on the occult."

I raised my eyebrows.

"Not a believer?" she asked.

"I believe in skepticism. I'm sorry."

"Don't be. I need to address the skeptics too."

I asked her more about her thesis.

"I'm focusing on a handful of artists who thought they were in touch with higher spirits and whose work brings out very deep reactions in viewers. Reactions that defy logic."

"Did Rothko say he was in touch with . . . higher spirits— is that what you called them?"

"I don't actually know yet. I'm in the midst of my research, but I found this. . . . Hold on. . . ."

Blythe reached for her woven leather bag, opened it, and pulled out a notebook that was in every way the opposite of mine. My plain black Moleskine fit in my jacket pocket. I never ripped out pages or folded them back. At first glance, it didn't even look used.

On the cover of hers was a collage of various artists' work in a cacophony of colors and designs. The notebook itself bulged with torn-out articles she had tucked between the pages. Ribbons were sticking out of it, marking important in-formation, I presumed. Three bits of paper fell out just when she opened the book. They fluttered to the floor.

I picked them up and placed them on the table while Blythe riffled through her notebook for a few moments.

"Here it is," she said, and read from her notes. "Rothko believed pictures must be miraculous. He said, 'The people who weep before my pictures are having the same religious experience I had when I painted them. And if you, as you say, are moved only by their color relationship, then you miss the point.'"

I felt frustrated, as I always did whenever I was reminded of the emotional disconnect that I felt all too often, that I'd felt that afternoon, when examining artwork I could appreciate but never get inside of.

Blythe didn't stay to share my curry with me. After about forty minutes, she said she had plans and was already going to be late. And then in a flurry of colors and sounds, she stood up, gathered her things, and left.

It wasn't until she was down the stairs and I was alone again that I realized she'd left something behind—the faint but discernible scent of a bouquet of flowers.

Over the next few days, I was surprised by how often I thought about her: The next night, upon going into my fridge to take out what was left of the curry and seeing the white wine I'd opened when she'd arrived. The first time I used my notebook to jot something down. Walking to class, crossing Russell Square, by the fountain, I saw a flash of pale blond hair and thought the woman up ahead might be Blythe—but it wasn't. Then in the Gallery Café, while reading a review of the Rothko show in the *Times*, I thought I smelled her perfume.

Courtauld isn't that large a school—approximately five hundred students, including postgraduates, attend. So I thought I'd run into Blythe again, but as the days passed, I didn't. And I had no idea how to find her. I tried the school registry, but they wouldn't give out contact information.

About a week later, Blythe found me. I was in the stacks in the library. I had the call number of an obscure journal that supposedly contained an interview with Henry Moore, but the book wasn't on the shelf where it was supposed to be.

When I heard what sounded like bells, I turned around to see Blythe walking toward me, her arms full of books. She was wearing another crazy-colored outfit—this one turquoise and purple with splashes of yellow.

"Hello," she said. "I saw you across the room and thought I'd come say hi. And check that you still have your notebook and haven't left it somewhere else."

I laughed and pulled it out of my pocket, showed it to her, and uncapped my pen.

"Since I have it opened . . . You left before I could ask for your phone number. Could I have it?"

"You'd write it in there? In with all your wonderful drawings and notes?" she said, and then blushed.

"So how much of it did you look through?" I asked.

"I'm sorry. I opened it just to get your name and information. And then I couldn't help myself. Besides, when you find a journal, you really have to read it."

"That's the law?"

"Yes." She laughed. "It is the law. I mean, what good is it stumbling on secrets if you don't investigate them? Isn't that what we are even doing here getting our degrees? Becoming art detectives?"

"Yes, and I like the concept so much, I can't even be angry."

"Of course you can't be angry—if it weren't for me, you wouldn't even have your journal back."

"True." I hesitated. "So even after reading it, you decided to return it in person. I'd think after reading it, you would have been a bit worried I was a madman."

She cocked her head and studied me. The light in her eyes danced. It was an expression that I would come to learn she favored. It reminded me of Rose-Marie Ormond, a model in many of John Singer Sargent's portraits. He'd called her "the most charming girl that ever lived," and standing there in the library, I thought it was true of Blythe as well.

"Honestly, after looking through your journal, I knew there was no way I couldn't meet you. Well, after seeing it, really."

"What do you mean?"

"The notes are interesting enough—smart, well fashioned. You're good at connecting disparate ideas and coming up with provocative questions. But it was the drawings that made me want to meet you."

"But they're just references to places and things I want to remember."

She raised her eyebrows.

"What is it?" I asked.

"Every drawing in the entire book is a view of something through a hole. I wanted to meet you just so I could ask you what it is you are looking through—a peephole? A keyhole? An emptied-out knothole in a piece of wood? A crack in a rock?"

I didn't know how to answer her question. I am not an artist. That was my mother's job. I'm an art historian devoted to understanding the work an artist does. I want to put it in perspective. To see what influenced it. To track what it led to. I am fascinated by those moments when a person steps over the threshold and goes from being a student to being an artist.

"What I draw are just doodles of my view at a particular moment, and the holes . . . I just like the edges. But no way am I an artist."

"Ah, therein lies the most venerable question of the ages—what makes an artist? But we certainly can't begin to solve it here."

"Are you actually suggesting we try to solve it?" I smiled at her, thoroughly enjoying talking to her.

"No, actually. I don't think it can be solved." She made a disappointed face.

I laughed.

"How about we ty to solve something else entirely?" I asked.

"What?"

"Which pub I should take you to right now."

"I'll leave that to you," she said.

On the walk over to the place I'd chosen, I told her that it troubled me that she was so trusting.

"But I'm not trusting at all, Eben. Why would you think so?"

"You came up to my apartment. A stranger's apartment."

"I'd read almost all of your notebook on the train. You weren't a stranger. Strange, perhaps, but not a stranger."

"I'm not strange," I said.

"What are you, then?"

"Maybe a little bit sad," I said, quite shocked to realize that was how I felt and even more shocked I'd just blurted it out.

"Why are you sad?" she asked as we continued down the block toward the One Aldwych Hotel.

The boutique hotel was close to Courtauld, but its bar was

fairly pricey and not a student hangout—which was why I had chosen it. When I wanted to read, have a pint and some quiet, it was where I went. Often enough that I was on speaking terms with the bartender.

As we approached, I saw Blythe's admiring glance. The elegant Edwardian building had curved corners, a coppered cupola dome, and a mansard roof. Its female-head keystones and balustrade balconies reminded me of Parisian buildings.

"I'm from London, but I don't know this building," she said.

"It used to be the home of the *Morning Post* newspaper," I said, steering her inside. "Over the years, it housed several newspapers and magazines as well as the Ministry of Defence at one point and a bank. It's recently been renovated."

We'd come into the building. I held the door open, and I showed her into the lobby bar. "This was the paper's Advertisement Hall, and some of the features, like the window paneling, go back to those early days."

"Spoken like a true historian," she said as we sat down at a table.

Over a glass of white wine for her and a pint for me, we did the dance that people who feel those first frissons of attraction do—when you are full of optimistic excitement and everything is before you and possible.

As we talked, I realized how unusual Blythe was and how different our conversation was from the kind I typically had with someone I'd basically just met. It had to be because of the notebook. She'd read my thoughts—things I didn't share with anyone, not even the people I was closest to. She'd seen the way

I looked at the world. Add to that her intuition—which I wasn't quite aware of yet—and she was insightful in a way that both intrigued and scared me, making me comfortable and uncomfortable at the same impossible time.

"What is your thesis on?" she asked.

I shrugged.

"I told you mine; you have to tell me yours."

"Okay. The use of holes in Brancusi's and Henry Moore's sculpture."

"Ah," she said.

"Ah?"

She took a sip of wine, then looked into the room as if she were searching for someone. Only then did she look back at me. "Eben, I should tell you: I know who your mother was."

This was fairly unusual. My mother, Marion Weiss, and I didn't have the same last name.

"How do you know that—" Then I realized. "The picture in my notebook?"

She nodded. I had stumbled on a gallery on Bond Street that had one of my mother's pieces for sale, and I'd done a sketch, labeled it *Mom in London*. Blythe must have recognized it or researched it.

"How old were you when she died?" Blythe asked.

"Two." I took a crisp out of the black lacquer bowl on the table and munched on it.

"So you didn't know her at all?"

I shook my head. Ate another crisp.

"Was her work around when you were growing up?"

"Yes, and around still."

"So your thesis is about trying to understand her too, then."

"Not at all."

"I'm sorry, it's just that given the subject, and the drawings in your notebook . . ."

Maybe I'd been wrong about being comfortable with her.

"I apologize," Blythe continued. "It's just that I like a challenge."

"A challenge?" I was angry now. "What's the challenge here?"

"I don't know how you can care so much about art, want to devote your life to it, and yet keep yourself always one step away from it."

"How . . . That's a little presumptuous, isn't it?" I said, thinking I should ask for the check.

"I really am sorry. I just—"

"Isn't everyone who isn't an artist but who works within the arts an observer? Aren't you one?"

"Technically, of course, but that's not what I mean. It's how you write about looking at art in your journal. I believe the job of the artist is to create a work that a viewer can enter into. If we, the observers, the students, can't slip inside—then the artist has failed. You've chosen artists to focus on who, more than most, make that transition easy. Brancusi and Henry Moore both create mostly representational art that invites us in. Almost literally. They offer up beauty as opposed to kitsch or anger or abstractions that confound us. Your mother did that too. So if you can't enter into their work, into her work, you must be holding yourself back. You need to have faith in your ability to walk inside knowing you will be able to come out."

At some point, I stopped really listening and just watched her. Blythe was one of the most animated people I'd ever met. She moved a bit like a dancer, graceful and rhythmic, and hypnotic. Her speaking voice was unusual. A particular accent that she'd explained was due to growing up with a mother who was British and a father who was French.

"I've upset you," she said after a few moments.

"Yes . . . well . . . one thing I still don't understand is why this particular challenge would call to you."

"You are a dreamer who doesn't seem to believe in possibilities. Idealistic but without any faith. I wouldn't have thought those contradictions could exist at the same time in the same person. I want to show you that it's okay to believe and have faith."

"I don't quite know how to even respond to that."

"Because I've insulted you?"

"As a matter of fact, yes."

"Good," she said. "If you weren't insulted, you'd be too far gone to help."

"You aren't exactly a missionary, and I'm not exactly a heathen who needs to be saved."

"Don't be so sure," she said, and put her hand out on my arm.

Something in her touch and the way she was looking at me dissolved my anger.

"How many others have you saved?" I asked, teasing.

I might have seemed to be taking the conversation lightly, but I was, in fact, shaken by it. Blythe had zeroed in on exactly what I struggled with. If she could see so clearly what was wrong with me, was it possible that she could show me the way out of the maze?

"Don't get me wrong," she said. "I don't want to save you."

"Good, because I don't need saving."

"I just want to see if I can prove to you that it's safe to have some faith."

"And what will that do for you?"

For a moment she didn't say anything. I could see her thinking. "I'm not sure."

"Well, maybe that's what I'll wind up doing for you . . . helping you find the answer to that question."

And then I brushed her curls away from her face, leaned in, and kissed her, softly on the lips, tasting wine and salt from the crisps and maybe even a hint of possibility.

Ten years later, I watched Blythe walk into another hotel bar. So much time had passed, and yet I still thought of her as my silver girl. A moving rainbow, she was wearing a pale green jacket, a robin's-egg blue blouse, a long skirt emblazoned with scarlet flowers. She was still making music with her armful of bracelets.

Once she'd given the waiter her order—a glass of white wine—and he'd left, I asked her what I had vowed to myself not to ask her. I'd planned on talking about the show, the catalog, what we hoped she could help with, and not delving into the personal, but I failed from the outset.

"So, you're living here? I was surprised when Dr. Perlstein handed me your card. Disappointed you hadn't gotten in touch. Seeing you in Stockholm was . . ." I shrugged, not sure what I wanted to say. I'd written off the encounter as a moment out of time, just two old lovers rekindling a spark that flared for a moment and then suffocated for lack of oxygen. Why was I bringing it up now?

Blythe, who was always so outspoken, looked down and played with her wineglass, moving it to the right and then to the left and then back again.

"I am living here, but just for a few more weeks, till the end of the semester. Then back to London." She picked up the glass, and her bracelets played a few bars of a melancholy tune.

"Are you here alone?" I asked.

She shook her head, and I felt something seize up inside of me. So she was married despite not wearing a ring.

"I have a daughter; she's here with me. We are living with my parents, who've been living here for a while now."

I took a breath, held it, let it out, then asked, "You're not married?"

"No, and my daughter's father isn't in the picture."

It seemed as if every word of what she was telling me was demanding a great deal of effort. I was surprised by how much pain she seemed to be in and how desperately I wanted to ease that pain.

Before I could think of the right thing to say, she sat up a little straighter and changed the subject. "So, what was it you wanted to ask me about your upcoming show?"

"Right. So, Dr. Perlstein thinks I've played down the esoteric angle."

"Hilma as a mystic?"

"Yes. It's a delicate balance to tell that part of the story and not present her as some crazy psychic or, worse, a witch. You did a great job of doing that in your book. I read both—they were really excellent, by the way."

"Thanks," Blythe said.

"I guess I always knew we couldn't do the show justice without dipping into the realm of the occult, but I've been worried about how to keep it in balance."

"I understand," she said. "Especially coming from you."

"Because of how much grief I gave you in school about your beliefs?"

"It was one thing that you didn't believe in psychic phenomena. What I had such a hard time with was that you didn't have enough belief in me to even be open-minded."

The old argument. My stubborn rationality versus her willingness to suspend disbelief. I didn't want to revisit that now.

"We need an essay that takes us back to Hilma's sister dying and her first séances and then shows how her interest in spiritualism grew and what it meant to her. But there are issues with this track beyond not making Hilma seem crazy. This leads us into De Fem territory. Hilma didn't do the channeling or the séances alone. She didn't build the altar and say the prayers by herself. She didn't go to the meetings at the Edelweiss Society and the Theosophy Society without her friends."

"Right, but why is that a problem?"

"Because once we get into De Fem and their spiritual collaboration, it raises the question of an artistic collaboration. And Dr. Perlstein has warned me away from that."

"You've lost me, Eben."

"On my last trip to Stockholm, I stumbled on some information that confused me, and I wound up doing some investigating—or tried to, anyway. When I came back, I explained to Dr. Perlstein that there are serious gaps in the Hilma af Klint research that raise complicated questions: Why has there been no scientific evaluation of Hilma's paintings? Why have there been no X-rays to determine authenticity? Why has so much documentation been destroyed? Recently the foundation admitted that one hundred of the paintings in their archive were painted by Anna Cassel, and we are steering clear of them, but how do we know that's all there are? If their styles are so similar that her paintings were confused with Hilma's all this time, could it mean that there are more than one hundred miscredited pieces? Why hasn't the foundation further investigated? Recently a book surfaced that includes a sketch attributed to Hilma that Marie Cassel knows was done by Anna of her own sister—her family owns it. I've discussed all this with Dr. Perlstein, but she's made it very clear that I'm a curator here, not a detective."

"With all due respect to her, sometimes they are the same thing."

"Well, not this time. For the sake of the show, she's bought into the whole canonization of poor, lonely Hilma."

"And you haven't?"

"No. Have you?"

"I've tried not to."

"Listen, I didn't mean to get us off track here. I am in awe of Hilma's work. Truly. It's just that I don't see how anyone can write about the mystical angle without bringing up the artistic collaborations that many people believe existed between her and Anna and possibly Cornelia as well."

Blythe picked up her glass and finished her wine.

"Would you like another?" I asked.

She checked her watch. "Sure."

Something in me soared. I gestured to the waiter and ordered another round.

"Writing this essay sounds like traversing a minefield."

"I didn't mean to make it sound difficult. This show is clearly about Hilma, without a doubt. Her vision. Her paintings. Everyone agrees a certain amount of attention must be paid to De Fem. To keep them in the picture, so to speak. These women were fighting society. They were creating their own reality because the one they found themselves in wasn't welcoming. We talk about artists who ignore convention. Who are brave. We put them up on pedestals. We venerate them. But rarely do they exist in a vacuum. They either have support or they strike out because of lack of support. Picasso would not have been Picasso without his muses, even if he did treat them so badly. Van Gogh's brother is as famous as he is—who doesn't know Theo's story? Michelangelo memorialized his patrons in his sculptures.

"Wives and lovers, muses, dealers, collectors, patrons—no, they aren't artists, but they are creative too. They see what the artist has to offer, and their passion props up, supports, helps, saves the artists—gives them time and space and food and succor."

"Eben, are you talking about De Fem? Or are you still looking for insights about your mother?" Blythe whispered.

"I want to investigate this because if we are going to showcase Hilma's work, I feel a huge ethical responsibility to make sure it's legitimately her work. Marie Cassel and the Danish art historian she introduced me to both have made serious suggestions that information is being hidden. Or at least being ignored. Even if there isn't anything off about Hilma's work, won't it make her that much more fascinating to the art world if we know the answers to all these questions?"

"You're right, of course. But . . . I'm sorry if what I said was out of line," she said.

I looked at her face. Her damn beauty. I couldn't hold back. "Why the hell did you walk out on me? We were together, Blythe. We were making plans for the future. What the hell happened that made you think I didn't deserve an explanation about why you left?"

She at least had the grace to look guilty.

"I was wrong," she said quietly.

"You were brutal."

"I know this isn't going to really make sense, but I was saving us."

"Right. It doesn't make sense."

"I knew you loved me. I loved you. But you weren't ready. You still had no faith. I thought the only way we were going to go on loving each other was if I left. Before we destroyed what we had."

"Leaving destroyed it."

"Did it?"

I was stunned. Now, for the first time in all the years we'd known each other, she had silenced me with her bluntness.

"In Stockholm . . . ," she started.

"Yes?"

"We both found out the answer to that question, didn't we? Nothing was destroyed. It was . . ." She searched for a word. "Paused."

"We weren't a damn song. Play it for a while. Stop it for a while, then start it up again."

She shrugged. "Maybe, maybe not. But at the time, I had absolutely no doubt that if I didn't leave, I would ruin any chance of our ever hearing that music again." She smiled. "To use your tiny bit clichéd metaphor."

I burst out laughing. And she joined me. Some of the tension broke. I took her hand, lifted it up and pressed my lips to it, and breathed in her scent. For a moment, just a moment, there were no questions.

"Eben?"

I looked up.

"I came here to tell you that I couldn't help with the essay. I was afraid that it would be too difficult to see you and work with you. But I think I want to try. If you do."

"Yes, I'd like to," I said, almost certain that we were both referring to more than the essay and the questions I'd raised.

· · · · ·

Stockholm, April 12, 1907

My dear Anders,

Thank you for sending me the beautiful feather in your last letter. How I wish I could accompany you on your latest expedition! To hear the songs of the rain forest with you, to smell the exotic perfumes of the flowers, and feel the rich soil beneath my feet.

    Life here has become rather complicated with my weekly gatherings with Cornelia and her friends. For the past few months, I have tried to surrender to the fact that I'm no longer needed by them, but my stubbornness and hurt still persist. I feel deeply removed from the new path they have set themselves upon. Hilma has become so inflated in her sense of importance. She believes that the spirits have chosen her alone to create their new temple and its paintings. Can you imagine? It sounds almost Byzantine in inspiration, a circular cathedral ornamented with paintings that chronicle the history of creation. They began last week, and I can hardly understand any of it. And even more disturbing, I sense a dark cloud circling around Hilma and Anna, an ominous shadow that makes me believe that they're in danger somehow. And then yesterday, strangely, out of nowhere, I received an anonymous letter from someone saying they possess materials I should publish that reveal Hilma's "inner fire." What does that even mean? I will have to ask her about it at the next meeting.

    On a more positive note, Cornelia has amazed me with her newfound ability to draw in such an inspired state, and you'd never recognize her now. She's lost all traces of her former meekness.

She's grown more emboldened, more confident in herself, and certainly is using her natural artistic gifts to the fullest. But I wonder how much of this can be attributed to the spirits' vision, and how much to her clandestine love affair. I still won't name him, Anders, because I don't want to bring scandal to our household. But I know now that the man is the individual I originally suspected. Her first love has returned to her after all these years, only this time he brings along with him a wife and two teenage boys! What good can ever come of this?

And yet she is changed for the better. She is bursting with more life than ever and seems like she has turned back the hands of time, while I find myself turning grayer with each passing day. Today I will write my latest Efteråt column, and perhaps that will restore me. I am still feeling a little pushed aside by the others in De Fem, since I'm not an artist and they no longer look to me as their medium. I must find comfort in my own writing, and I'm lucky that I have it to fall back upon when my frustrations get the better of me. Don't worry about me, dearest. I will continue to keep the faith and wait for your next letter.

My humidor is nearly empty, so make sure to send more cigars.

Your loving wife,
Mathilda

CHAPTER FOURTEEN

. . . . .

Friday Night, No. 454
April 19, 1907
Stockholm

The pile of papers had grown thick on Mathilda's desk. Scientific reports, stories from people whom she met during her office hours, notes from attending the most recent Theosophy Society meeting in Stockholm. She had so much to write, so much to do, she often felt there just wasn't enough time in the day to finish it all.

Reaching for the latest issue of *Efteråt*, Mathilda stared at the cover. The magazine's logotype, with all the beams radiating from a five-pointed star, brought her tremendous comfort. Each point symbolized one of the five elements: air, earth, water, fire, and spirit. She opened it, scrolled through the pages that she had written, skimming through the headlines. What was missing? What must be covered in the next issue?

She put her hand to her forehead. The clock signaled that it was nearly seven p.m. In only half an hour, she would have to leave the house for the Friday Night Club. It would not be possible; she didn't have the time.

The mysterious letter that had arrived last week peeked out from beneath her pile of mail. Mathilda pulled it out and looked at it once again. The handwriting was messy, the words menacing.

Ms. Nilsson,

I hear you like to publish stories about people who are spiritually gifted. Do you also publish stories about those individuals who are spiritually depraved? I have something in my possession that I think might show another side of two of the women in your inner circle, Anna Cassel and Hilma af Klint. I think you'd be especially interested in seeing how the deviant Ms. af Klint has gone about capturing her beloved friend Anna. Perhaps we can make a time to meet to discuss a potential publication of the materials? I suspect the public would be eager to learn of Ms. af Klint's clandestine "inner fire." I wait for your response.

Sincerely,
A most concerned citizen of Stockholm

Mathilda shook her head and slipped the letter back beneath the stack. It was just one more reason she felt inclined to withdraw from the group. She took it as a sign.

There was absolutely no reason to prolong her decision. She

would inform Cornelia that she wouldn't be going with her to tonight's meeting, or any more meetings in the near future.

Mathilda pushed herself away from her desk and went to search for her sister.

· · · · ·

She discovered Cornelia in her room, her body hunched over her drawing table. In front of her were two large sheets of paper placed next to each other. She was busy drawing something that connected them.

Mathilda stopped at the door. "Is that for tonight?" she queried.

Cornelia didn't look up. Her pen was still moving, creating one thin line after another. She was deep in concentration.

"Mm," she muttered, still in her own mind.

"I just wanted to give you this. Can you bring it to Hilma?" Mathilda stepped forward and laid down a small journal in which she had written some of her notes from their weekly meetings.

Cornelia glanced up from her work and gave her a puzzled look.

"Why do you need me for that? Can't you do it yourself?"

"I'm not coming tonight."

Cornelia put down her pen.

"Why are you saying that? You have to come—we're not De Fem without you. We need you; you know that."

"It's becoming more and more of an art project," Mathilda grumbled. "I no longer have a role in the group." She was terse, her words spoken in staccato. "I can't see what you all are seeing; I can't hear what you are hearing. And besides, it takes too much time and energy away from my paper and my own spiritual activity. I must focus on my writing. That's where I can best make my contribution to the world." She contemplated mentioning the recent mysterious letter but decided against it.

"But you can't just leave us like that!" Cornelia stood up; her tone was defiant.

Mathilda thrust her shoulders back. "Actually, Cornelia, I can."

* * * * *

Sadness weighed on Cornelia as she left the apartment alone. Her sister's departure meant "The Five," as they'd always known it, would cease to exist. She just couldn't understand Mathilda's decision, especially now that they had finally embraced the spirits' message and Hilma had begun painting.

Nearly her whole life, Mathilda had told Cornelia she was the selfish one, that she saw the world only through her own narrow lens. But her sister was clearly thinking solely of herself now, certainly not of the group. The hypocrisy of Mathilda's thinking made Cornelia's blood boil. How could she be blind to the fact that the paintings were not competing against her; they were just another way to connect to the spirits?

She loathed having to tell the others.

And yet, part of her felt that her own conviction to stay and contribute was only made stronger. Cornelia was no longer in her sister's shadow. She would continue to give everything she could to manifest Hilma's vision for the temple and its paintings.

· · · · ·

The warehouse was just in front of the water, steps away from the dock, and all of the buildings that bordered it were used to store material unloaded from all the ships arriving. Only Kristian's warehouse remained empty.

Cornelia looked around her before opening the door. Kristian had told them to be extremely careful, or else they would have to stop coming. Recently, a man had visited his office, claiming that he had evidence that something suspicious had been going on in the building, but Kristian smelled alcohol on the man's breath, and suggested that he had gotten his warehouse confused with another. Still, Kristian warned Cornelia, they'd have to be more cautious.

Cornelia pushed the heavy door open with one arm. Under the other, she held a large flat package wrapped in string.

Hilma greeted her without looking up from the canvas that was placed in the center of the floor.

"You're late," Hilma stated flatly. Her tone was terse, and Cornelia braced herself. She didn't have enough energy to get into a tiff with anyone else, and she knew that Hilma's moods were more mercurial now because of her not eating properly. She ate so little lately, and all she drank was water. There was no joy in what she did outside her painting.

"She's becoming far too much of an ascetic," Sigrid had warned the others. "I'm concerned. One cannot live by eating just root vegetables."

Anna agreed. She'd adhered to the strict vegetarian regime for only thirty days, but Hilma had continued with it, believing it improved her painting and her relationship with the spirits.

"I'm so sorry, I didn't want to be late . . . ," Cornelia insisted. "I had a problem with my sister. Mathilda didn't want to come tonight." She handed the notebook to Hilma. "She told me to give this to you. It's her notes from our first Friday night meetings."

Hilma didn't take the book. Her hands were covered in pink and yellow paint stains; her face was stained too. She nodded at a bag placed on the floor.

"Leave it there. I have my own notes. I never trusted Mathilda to cover everything. Her mind has always been with her paper," she snapped.

"She won't be returning, will she . . . ," Sigrid stated as though it were already a fact.

"Why do you say that?" Cornelia knew she hadn't let on about what had transpired between them.

"I sensed her departure the last time we met. This morning when I awakened, I could no longer feel Mathilda in my thoughts. When I tried to conjure up the energy of De Fem, I could only feel the four of us."

"She has lost her connection with us too," Cornelia said sadly. "I tried to tell her that we still needed her, but she has made up her mind."

"Oh, I hope you conveyed how much we want her here. . . ." Anna put down her paintbrush. A pained expression came over her. "I hate to imagine her feeling excluded just because we're no longer having the weekly séances. . . ."

"The truth is we don't need her," Hilma said without any emotion. "She served her purpose."

"Don't be cruel, Hilma," Anna admonished.

"I'm not being unkind. I'm being ruthlessly honest."

Sigrid interrupted the women's exchange.

"We must accept Mathilda's decision and maintain neutrality. The spirits will not want the task to be tainted with disharmony."

Cornelia glanced over to Sigrid and whispered a thank-you. It pained her the most to have her sister withdraw from the group. And while it might have slipped the others' minds, Cornelia was well aware it was because of Mathilda's agreeing to be their medium for their inaugural Friday Night Meeting that they had all come together in the first place.

"You are right," Anna agreed. "We will miss your sister, Cornelia, but we must respect her decision."

Hilma didn't look up. She had returned to her work, painting three canvases at the same time. Anna had been assisting her, but now she'd gone to clean some brushes.

"Have you been here all day?" Cornelia asked.

Anna put her arm up to her forehead, stroked away some loose hair, leaving streaks of color on her skin.

"All week," she said, exhausted. "Hilma doesn't want to stop. She's obsessed, as I knew she'd be once she committed herself to the work."

"The spirits knew the right person to choose for all of this," Cornelia agreed.

Anna took the brushes and began wiping them dry with a cotton rag.

"Yes, Hilma has more than just artistic talent. She has the tenacity to achieve her vision at any cost or risk to herself."

Cornelia had no interest in disturbing Hilma in her work any further. Quietly, she walked over to an empty corner and took out the drawings she had brought with her. She then placed eight paper sheets on the floor. Adjusted the patterns so that all the lines came in perfect balance. She'd learned how to make large patterns a long time ago, when she first began making dresses, and there was even a time when she had sewed sails for ships. Now she used a similar method to convert some of the automatic drawings from their last meeting to a larger scale.

When all the compositions were in perfect harmony, she took a step back and watched the charcoal lines float together over the separate pieces. As she watched the image appear, she could clearly see that it was composed of flowers that resembled roses and lilies. And then the reappearing circles, always joined together.

Minutes later, she was surprised to find Hilma staring over her shoulder. Her voice startled her.

"What are you up to, here?" Hilma got down on her knees and peered at the drawings on the floor.

"I have been trying to figure out how to do the paintings as large as possible. I think this is a way. We can paint them like this, and then glue them together," Cornelia explained.

Hilma nodded. She held up one piece of paper to the light, and followed two overlapping circles with her finger, without touching the surface.

"Is this the one from last Friday?" she asked, intrigued.

"Yes, actually. I combined three of the pages in my notebook, as I interpreted the message as one."

"One," Hilma mumbled. "The circle of life—our existence is intrinsically linked to something else from the moment of conception. It is so clear to me now, how life is part of a pattern. One cell, divided into two . . . then dividing again and again," she explained. "We must start with the colors for male and female, the circles yellow and blue."

"And the flowers?" Cornelia asked, and pointed at the lilies.

"Yes, you are right—roses and lilies and some smaller buds. We will use the right colors for them. White, pink, and yellow. I will paint them myself. But first, we must start with the background."

"The oil paint will be too thick; it will ruin the paper. I think we'll need to use tempera," Anna pointed out.

"We can use the Isatis root for the pigment. That will mix easily with the egg yolks and make the perfect color."

Hilma closed her eyes and imagined the shade of deep indigo. A smile formed at her lips.

"Yes, that will be just right."

· · · · ·

Anna and Cornelia were both busy with the background. They painted from opposite ends of the image, turning all white fields on the pieces of papers into the most beautiful blue shade.

Cornelia stretched her arms to reach the middle of her section, accidently touching the yellow flowers that Hilma had started to paint. Strokes of yellow followed her paintbrush into the blue.

"Oh, watch out! Look, the blue is turning green. You must be more careful," Anna admonished.

Cornelia got up and looked at it from above. Anna was right; the blue color had a greenish hue to it now. She turned around in haste to find a cloth to clean her paintbrush, but inadvertently stepped on the paper.

"You've just put a footprint on the painting!" Hilma could barely keep her temper under control. "You need to be more careful."

Anna took a closer look at the footprint. "We can paint over it, Hilma."

Hilma stepped back and studied the paper. The colors that they had created were exactly the colors she imagined for this first painting in the series. Anna and Cornelia had helped her immensely in the preparations. And although she was chiefly responsible for painting the shapes that were connected to the spirits' visions, she knew she depended on the other women.

"No, leave it," she insisted. "Perhaps a single footprint in a series that embodies the path we seek to understand the universe relays something meaningful."

Sigrid stepped closer. "This is so eerie, but I must tell you, what you have just painted resembles something that came to me in a dream last night.

"I could actually see the whole universe around me, the stars and the planets. The magnitude of the place we call home. A sense of serenity enveloped me."

"Perhaps the spirits are letting us know they are happy with what we've created so far," Hilma mused.

"Yes, I think so." Sigrid nodded.

"We have been working so hard with the first set of paintings; we have twenty-six now . . . ," Hilma acknowledged. "We have become storytellers, communicating with our brushstrokes how the world started, how the elements came to life. But it doesn't end here. It is only the beginning. I think your vision, Sigrid, was also intended to tell us to keep going. . . ."

Hilma stood up and walked over to the wet pieces of paper. Assembled on the floor, the colorful sheets created one enormous composition.

"This new series will be about human life. This first one is about the genesis." She took a deep breath, and her tired body inflated with a newfound vigor. "No time for chatter; we must keep working. Are you with me? Can you stay a little longer?"

"We'll stay as long as you need us," Anna promised.

"Yes," Cornelia agreed.

Hilma went over to Sigrid's basket and withdrew several eggs. "We'll work until we have no more paint," she stated with conviction. "The spirits have entrusted me with making a powerful statement with these paintings." She wiped her hands on her apron. "And I will not disappoint them."

CHAPTER FIFTEEN

......

Friday Night, No. 455
April 26, 1907
Stockholm

In the notebooks, the plans for *The Ten Largest* paintings were like secret maps guiding to them to a higher understanding.

Hilma had decoded the automatic drawings, believing the circles and coils were a metaphor for the eternal stages of life. She thought of nothing else but achieving what the spirits had asked of her, and she threw herself body and mind into the task. She had no appetite for anything except seeing the paintings actualized.

It was Sigrid who always made sure to tuck a few hard-boiled eggs into her basket, along with the fresh ones she brought for the tempera paint.

"You must eat," Sigrid insisted to Hilma. She was compelled to mother and look out for her. As she was unable to assist the other women with painting, Sigrid's care for Hilma was her contribution.

"I'm not hungry." Hilma waved the food away.

"Please . . . the nourishment will help you paint longer."

Hilma reluctantly took the egg Sigrid offered and ate it without any enjoyment. "Is the paint ready?"

"How's this?" Cornelia asked. The glass jar with the bright blue color was lifted to the lantern for appraisal. The skylight brought in the moonlight from above.

"You need more emulsifier," Anna remarked. She reached back into her basket and handed the emulsifier to Cornelia to add into the paint.

For nearly twenty minutes, Anna had been working on creating the perfect shade of yellow. She wanted the shade to evoke the color of daffodils.

"The blue still isn't quite right," Hilma huffed after more emulsifier was added to Cornelia's blue. "It's far too strong. It needs to be a color found in nature."

Sigrid, content with having gotten some food into Hilma, was now on the floor with the notebook sketches from their past séances, an abundance of themes from marine life, spread out before her.

She closed her eyes and meditated. Hilma had been the strongest one to accept the formidable task of creating the temple paintings, but her mind worked almost too quickly, like a candle burning from both ends. Sigrid felt compelled to slow her down. She wanted to preserve her fire so it didn't extinguish before the work was completed.

"Drink some water, Hilma." Sigrid poured some liquid from the flask and offered it to her. "Remember, you need not just fire to create, but air and water too. . . ."

Hilma took a sip. "The blue should be the shade found in a mussel shell."

"Yes," Anna agreed. "Perhaps a Prussian blue, Hilma . . . We need to add some orange and a little black to it to get it just right."

Hilma watched as Anna added a pinch of brick-colored powder to the paint and blended it with a spatula. Then she added a dab of charcoal dust. Finding the exact shade was a special kind of alchemy that delighted every artist.

Anna held the glass jar to Hilma for final inspection.

"Yes, that's perfect," Hilma declared. She was finally content.

Anna nodded. She already knew she had gotten it just right.

. . . . .

Months later, they had completed eight of the ten paintings. Cornelia had just mounted the last paper square onto the canvas and Hilma stood behind her, ensuring that all the pieces were matched perfectly.

Sigrid stood to the side, appraising the beautiful lavender and pink colors, the sprouting of an enormous bulb shape in vibrant yellow.

The *Adulthood* paintings remained her favorite in the series. But perhaps that was natural. Wasn't adulthood the peak of life? The discovery of one's self, one's inner passions? She was the only one in the group who was a mother, and so much of her adult life had been spent bringing life into this world, nurturing it to ensure its survival and full development. Hilma's vision of the paintings was still anchored in the same tenets, but rather from a spiritual perspective. Life for her extended like an infinite ribbon. Along the way, she believed the soul was building and learning from every realm around her. Nature, physics, the guidance of the spirits—these were all ingredients that went into creating her art. It wasn't the same as a child, of course, but it was still very much a unique and lasting testament of creation.

"I need to see them hanging," Anna insisted. "Before the last two are painted . . . before we begin working on the ones that will be called *Old Age*." She walked over to Hilma and placed a hand on her shoulder. "Can we not display them as they're meant to be seen? We've only seen them horizontal on the floor. I want to see them vertical and in their full glory!"

Cornelia clapped her hands together. "Oh, absolutely! I think it's only right that we have the wisdom from the *Adulthood* paintings before we commence with the final two."

Hilma stayed silent for a moment, pondering Anna's request.

"How would we even hang them?" she asked. The warehouse had vast ceilings, so the height of the room wasn't a problem. But they didn't have the necessary hooks and wire or even a ladder.

"We don't need to hang them," Sigrid interrupted. "We could just prop the canvases up against the wall. We'd still be able to get a sense of them if we did it that way."

"A perfect and simple solution." Anna beamed.

"Yes," Hilma agreed. "The four of us should be able to manage that without too much fuss."

The paintings filled nearly the entire perimeter of the ware-house. The sheer enormity of the canvases, measuring nearly ten feet by eight, rich with color and symbolism, was breath-taking.

"It looks like a glimpse into the heavens." Sigrid's voice broke with emotion. She had spent her whole life seeing colors around her, but Hilma and the others had managed to create their own language, with so many varying shades that she could never have even imagined. And they all could be found in nature: seashell pink, whale blue, buttercup yellow.

The symbols and shapes in the paintings added even more meaning to the experience. There was the five-petaled symbol of purity in the dogwood blossoms, the eternal quest for wis-dom in the snaillike coils, and the recurring union of male and female in the appearance of blue and yellow circles in each canvas.

"What you've created is magnificent." Sigrid placed a hand on her heart.

"Yes, a constellation of stars and planets." Anna forced back her tears. "Oh, Hilma, you accomplished everything you set out to do! It's a map of deeper understanding beseeching us to contemplate the wisdom in the universe."

Hilma's hand began to shake. For several days now she had tried to hide her tremor. The exhaustion resulting from the work had finally overtaken her.

"The spirits gave us each one of those symbols," she in-sisted. "But thank you for insisting that we pause for a moment and take this all in." She looked around and soaked in the pigments they had created by hand, the rich pinks and violets, the deep blues, and the bright yellows. She could read each one like musical notes on the page.

"The end is so close, I can taste it," Hilma whispered. She reached down for her brush. "By next week's meeting, I want to stand in the room and see the vision completed. I want to breathe it all in."

. . . . .

That evening, the night sky stretched out above Cornelia like a canopy of black velvet as she began her walk home. She had never felt so light on her feet. The vision of the paintings mounted on the warehouse walls had created a sense of euphoria among the women, and now that she was outside, the happiness continued to follow her, filling her whole body and making her feel alive.

How lucky she was to be invited to Hilma's creative world, where the mind, the spirit, and the brush could create something new. Together they had made something so large, so revolutionary with its use of color, that it would challenge even the most established male painters. Hilma would never accept that she couldn't do something a man could do. She did not believe her sex limited her in any way. Mathilda might have grown weary of Hilma's strong personality, but Cornelia was inspired by her.

The streets were empty, and the windows in the buildings had grown dark. They had all stayed at the warehouse far longer than was prudent. She feared what her sister would say when she came home. She would probably torture her with the words she always spoke. "Hilma uses you, as she does Anna," she would rant. "Hilma takes hours away from your own art," Mathilda had warned her more than once, pointing out also that the sessions were no longer spiritual and that Hilma was just taking advantage of the two women for her own gain. "She is the queen bee, while you break your back constructing the hive. It makes no sense to me that you continue to help her." But it didn't matter to Cornelia. She fed on the inspiration and the creative energy that flowed between all of them. It gave her sustenance, just as her love for Kristian did. She did not condemn Hilma for taking charge and delegating responsibilities to her and the others. It was an efficient way to work, and she was happy to be included.

As she turned the corner where Kristian had his office, she couldn't help but look up at his window. Behind the thick glass, a faint light flickered. Could he really be there at this late hour? She knew she wouldn't be able to sleep if she didn't at least try to see him.

Cornelia rushed to the door, but it was locked. As she took a step back, a dark silhouette moved behind the glass pane. Someone was definitely there. She reached for some gravel on the street and threw a handful of tiny stones against the window, but there was no answer. She gathered a few more and tossed them again. Suddenly, Kristian's head appeared. She waved at him and smiled.

Minutes later he was at the door, holding it open for her and waving her inside. But when Cornelia saw Kristian's face, she was horrified. His left eye was bruised shut; his lip was swollen and purple. Dribbles of bloodstains ran down his shirt.

"*Älskling*, what has happened to you? You're hurt!"

Kristian's face sagged in the shadowy light.

"I got into a fight."

Cornelia took out a napkin from her pocket. She gently wiped the blood away from his jaw.

"I never thought of you as a person who would get into a brawl, Kristian." She had known him to be nothing but gentle. "This is so unlike you."

"I wouldn't typically, but this time I was given no choice."

"What do you mean?" Cornelia was puzzled.

Kristian reached for something on his desk. It was a notebook with a beautiful marbleized paper cover in red and blue. He gave it to Cornelia.

"What's this?"

She opened it, and all air escaped her when she saw what was inside. It was Anna; it was so clear to her. Naked, legs spread. The images were so shocking. It felt like a violation to look at them a second longer. She snapped the book closed.

"Where did you find this?" she stammered. "Who made these drawings?"

"I assume your friend Hilma did them. At least, that was what the men at the pub said. A whole group, standing in line to see. There was even a particularly drunken man who claimed he was August Strindberg! But he was so out of his mind, I could hardly believe it." Kristian sighed. "But all of this is so outrageous to me. Cornelia, what exactly are you doing at your meetings?"

Cornelia cupped her hand over her mouth and shook her head, refusing to entertain what Kristian suggested.

"No, no, don't think that. We are not doing anything inappropriate. You must believe me. We are working on the most beautiful paintings. . . . A whole new universe created out of colors and symbols, the way an astronomer looks at stars. Hilma is searching for deeper meaning and putting that down on paper and canvas."

"There's talk, Cornelia—terrible, dangerous gossip about your group of friends." He looked at her sternly. "You know they could be jailed for doing drawings like that. It's a good thing there isn't a signature on the sketches."

Cornelia's eyes welled with tears. "Hilma is so thirsty for knowledge; I think she only wanted to study—"

"Stop." Kristian raised his palm to interrupt her. "You and I both know this was not a scientific study. You saw what's inside."

She moved a hand over the cover. How fortunate they all were that Kristian had retrieved it.

"Who had this notebook in their possession? Who was showing it?"

"I believe it was the same man who told me he suspected something was going on at the warehouse, the one who had alcohol on his breath, but he was doing more than just showing the sketchbook. He charged money for it." Kristian swallowed hard. "He told stories about filthy gatherings in the harbor. I heard Hilma's name mentioned more than once."

"I hope you stopped him, darling!"

"What do you think? I defended you and wrestled the book from his hands." Kristian shook his head. "Then he attacked me. He did a lot of damage to my face, as you can see."

Cornelia reached out and placed a gentle finger on his swollen lip. "I'm so sorry you got hurt protecting us." She stroked Kristian's hair; it was as soft as corn silk.

"You must leave the warehouse, Cornelia."

She wasn't sure she was hearing him correctly. "We can't do that."

"For your own safety. I heard the man talk about your meetings at the harbor. He knows where you are. The last thing I need is the police coming to the warehouse when you're there."

"Hilma is an artist. The sketches are just anatomy sketches— I'm certain of it. All artists do them. Please let us stay, just a little bit longer."

Kristian lifted his hand, interrupting her. "Please stop insisting they are something harmless when they are not. They are dangerous and can get all of you in a lot of trouble." His voice rose. "Look at them again. These are not anatomical sketches; they are different."

Cornelia turned the pages. Anna was everywhere; the beauty of her gentle face could not be confused with that of another woman. The shape of her body was sensually captured, curled up in a bed, in a chair, standing tall with her hand on her own breast. Kristian was right. These were not scientific drawings. They were sketches of love.

Cornelia closed the notebook again.

"I will bring it to Hilma. She will be glad that it is in her safe possession again."

"And then you must pack up your things and leave, find a new place. Promise me you will do that straightaway."

"We will . . . but can you at least try to find out who this awful man was? I need to tell Anna and Hilma."

"I believe he was some kind of doctor. He had a leather satchel next to him that looked like a medical bag."

"A doctor?" Cornelia was incredulous. "How could a respected man behave like that? How terrible and cruel. I will warn Hilma, I promise."

Kristian reached for her arm and pulled her closer to him. "At least stay with me this evening. We can curl up on the sofa together, sleep together. I want to feel your heart against my skin."

She stood there, looking at him. He spoke of danger, not wanting her to get into trouble, yet their affair was full of peril; the threat of a scandal lurked every time they met.

"I don't want to bring any more trouble. . . ."

"You won't."

Cornelia let her coat fall to the floor. She kissed him gently, careful to avoid his bruised mouth, tenderly caressed him. She inhaled his breath into her own lungs. Tears rose in her eyes. "I love you so much," she whispered.

It was worth taking the risk. She folded into him and let him lead her to the couch.

·····

Lars,

Imagine my disgust when your letter was slipped underneath the door of my studio. I almost wish I had never opened it. It is hard to believe that you were once that young medical student whom I looked at with great admiration for your knowledge of the human body, your passion for science, your curiosity about how the latest treatments could cure those who suffer. And yet now, you have become a person who seeks to inspire suffering.

How does one transform from something beautiful into something so ugly and wretched? The spiritual laws suggest that we grow as we age, blossoming into something wiser as we understand that we are just one leaf in a vast and endless forest of trees.

I was far too young to know what type of man you truly were, but I was certainly wise enough to refuse your marriage proposals. The few times I saw you over the years were a mistake, and I see that now. I was misguided to think I could learn from you.

Do not threaten me. Do not dare to harm my friend Anna, or you will regret it until your last breath.

I never loved you, not for a moment. Your heart is as black as coal.

With disgust,
Hilma

CHAPTER SIXTEEN

· · · · ·

Friday Night, No. 456
May 3, 1907
Stockholm

Hilma leaned on the polished mahogany bar with one arm, exhausted. Her hand was open, as if she were waiting for the waiter to put a glass there. Only hours before, she'd posted her angry letter to Lars, and her nerves were still tangled in a knot. She knew alcohol wasn't something she should have, especially on her strict diet, but now she craved something to soothe her agitation. Lars had written that he would destroy Anna, blaming her for the reason she had refused to marry him all those years ago. Could someone really maintain such an unhealthy obsession for nearly two decades? Hilma shook her head. How could he still keep his medical license when he was clearly not mentally well?

"Sorry, we don't serve liquor at this early hour," the waiter apologized. "How about some coffee?"

"No. Please, I just need a small glass of a spirit. . . . I will drink it fast; no one will even see it," Hilma assured him. "You'll be helping out an artist."

"Very well, then," he said, pouring her a small glass. "Theodor Blanch is known to enjoy breaking the rules, so I guess I can too."

Hilma closed her eyes and drank it down in one swallow, grimacing as the strong taste hit the pit of her stomach.

"I haven't seen you here in quite a while," the waiter remarked. "Are you still painting?"

"I'm actually painting more than I ever have," Hilma boasted. "I just no longer do my work in my studio, because my canvases have grown in size; you would be amazed if you saw them." She looked behind her at the artwork displayed on the walls. "They're so large, they could never be displayed here."

"A shame." The waiter smiled. "It will be Theodor's loss."

The liquor had emboldened Hilma. "Let him suffer. Do you know how many times I asked him to let me have a show? He exhibited so many of my peers from the academy and never had time for my work." She glanced at the bar shelf, hopeful he'd offer her another glass.

"Maybe I have to dress up in a suit and tie to get my paintings hung on the walls," Hilma huffed.

She turned around and looked at the tables and chairs in the expansive room of the café.

The seats were all filled with people. Women in elegant hats, men in suits. The small talk that floated through the room sounded like music washing over her. She hadn't been around people in public for weeks.

"Ms. af Klint?"

The sound of the familiar voice caught her off guard.

She twirled around and there, behind her, stood Theodor Blanch, the art dealer who founded the café. Next to him was a man with dark black hair streaked with silver. His eyes, framed by metal glasses, stared at her intensely.

"It seems you keep different time than the public," Theodor said, amused, as he looked over at the small shot glass in front of her.

"I've never been one to run with the masses." She smiled and glanced in the direction of Theodor's two guests.

"Forgive me," he apologized. "This is Mr. Wassily Kandinsky, former lawyer turned painter." Theodor stepped back and introduced a forlorn-looking woman in a drab brown dress, her eyes fixed not on the art-filled walls or those in her company. Her eyes fell oddly at the ground. "And this is his traveling companion, Ms. Münter."

Hilma stretched out her hand to greet the morose-looking woman, but Ms. Münter didn't take it.

"They speak German and French, no Swedish yet. Which language do you prefer, Ms. af Klint?"

Hilma switched to German. She had learned the language as a girl but seldom spoke it. The woman responded flatly, which made Hilma feel even more tired.

"Who are they?" she asked in Swedish. "The woman's clearly a bore."

Theodor laughed. "They're travelers in the arts. . . . I'm thinking of inviting Kandinsky here to hold an exhibition. He paints landscapes, just like you do."

"I'm hardly painting landscapes anymore," she sniffed. "I'm

doing far more interesting things these days." She narrowed her eyes at Blanch. "And who exactly is she? She hardly looks like an artist or a muse."

"She is his student. They travel together for inspiration," Theodor said with a wink.

"So what does she paint?" Hilma asked.

"I didn't even ask." Theodor laughed. I'm more interested in him. He's already had quite a few paintings exhibited in Paris."

Turning to Kandinsky, Theodor said in German, "You know, Mademoiselle af Klint is an artist, just like you. She has even been chosen to have a prestigious studio in this building."

Kandinsky stared at her but asked her nothing about her art.

"Since you live in this building, might you have some art supplies I could borrow?" he said, finally breaking his silence. "I'm in desperate need of charcoal, and I couldn't find any today. Do you have some to spare? To sell?"

Hilma hesitated. She was always short on supplies herself. Anna was constantly treating her to new materials and had recently given her a new box of vine charcoal. She paused, contemplating whether she should share it with him.

"Can I come with you? Maybe you can show me some of your work?" he asked, his voice suddenly quite charming.

Theodor waved toward the stairs.

"You go," he urged in Swedish. "I'll enjoy myself with Ms. Münter in the meantime."

Hilma couldn't find a way to refuse Kandinsky.

"Come along, then." She gestured for him to follow her.

"It's just up the stairs. . . ." As they entered the studio, she saw him eye the mess.

"I see that you like a bit of chaos," he said, smirking, and lifted a magazine that was in his path.

Hilma ignored him and went to retrieve the box of charcoal on the table. She lifted the cover and removed two grapevine twigs.

"Here you are," she said. As she turned around to give them to him, he was no longer beside her, but rather in a corner of the studio, studying several of her canvases.

He had a few of them propped up against his leg as he peered over several more. Hilma held her breath for a second. At the bottom of the pile, she had hidden a few of the smaller paintings from the warehouse. They were not yet ready to meet the eyes of the world.

"Here you are," she said firmly. She gestured for him to follow her to the door, but he stayed planted, his focus completely absorbed by her paintings.

"This is so very interesting . . . ," he mumbled. He took a finger and traced the explosive lines of colors in front of him.

"I'm not finished with those pieces yet." She quickly stepped over to him and began to peel the canvases from his hands. "I was just testing colors. . . ."

Her annoyance at his brazen lack of manners was palpable. She disliked him immensely and now wished she had never offered to bring him into her private space.

"You'd probably enjoy some of my older pieces, or perhaps some of my colleague Alma's." She lifted one of her studio mate's canvases off an easel. "Here is a lovely landscape, just as you do, I'm sure. . . ."

But the strange man didn't move at all. Nothing could peel his eyes away from the paintings she had done in the warehouse.

"Well, you've surely seen enough, and now you have your charcoal." She slipped the fragile vines into an envelope and handed it to him. "We should return to the café. Theodor and your lady friend will wonder where you've vanished to," Hilma insisted.

"I'm very intrigued by what you've done. It's extraordinarily different," he mumbled, and reached for a small notebook in his pocket and made some entries.

"Thank you for this," he said as he waved the envelope containing the vine charcoal. "How much do you want for it?"

Hilma shook her head. "Never mind. It is always a pleasure to meet another artist."

Kandinsky didn't respond; his eyes had found something else in the studio to fixate on. Tacked to one of the walls was a black-and-white portrait of De Fem. Alma had been learning to take photographs and had asked the women if they would pose only a few weeks before, prior to Mathilda's departure.

"Is that you?" Kandinsky now pointed to the photograph, his finger hovering just above Hilma with her black hat and suit. Cornelia was in trousers. Beside her was a narrow-eyed Mathilda with a cigar between her fingers. "Are you one of those women?" His voice was soaked with disapproval.

"I'm not sure what you mean," answered Hilma tersely.

"A woman cannot behave as a man." He threw his shoulders back and shook his head in disgust.

"I am an artist," she answered defiantly. "I can be whatever I choose."

They did not part amicably. Kandinsky gripped the envelope with the charcoal and exited the studio abruptly, claiming he had to get back to Ms. Münter. Hilma couldn't get away from him fast enough.

Needing to clear her head and rid herself of thoughts of him, Hilma chose to walk toward Värta harbor. Several trams slowed down as they approached, but Hilma just waved them on. She craved solitude. Whenever her mind became too crowded with thoughts, she contemplated what she would do to rectify a muddy canvas. The prescription was the same. She'd take her palette knife and carve out some white spaces to let the light breathe in. The same remedy applied to her now as she inhaled the cold, fresh air.

The words that had infuriated her moments before, when Blanch referred to this dilettante painter Kandinsky as a "genius of color," began to fade away, as did Kandinsky's judgment against what *sort of women* she and the others in De Fem were. If she was going to be an artist who had confidence with every brushstroke she applied, she needed to not become so annoyed by what other people thought. It was easy to bestow generous praise upon others if one was in the business of selling paintings. But those who were in the rarefied circle of creating them needed to tune out meaningless noise. Hilma felt a confidence envelop her as she continued on her walk, a protective layer that now felt like a shield.

As the warehouse became visible, her pace quickened. She couldn't wait to enter that sacred space again. How amazing it had been to see eight of the paintings leaned against the walls. It felt as though she were seeing through a keyhole what the complete ten would look like in the temple space. No one could deny the magnitude of their accomplishment. What that Kandinsky man had seen in her studio was just a fragment of the big picture. Everything was coming into place as she had first imagined it when she heard the words Sigrid had channeled.

· · · · ·

Hilma pushed open the door with her hip and entered; she couldn't get to the space fast enough to see the paintings again. She knew it would fortify her even more, inspire her to finish the remaining two paintings. But as soon as she walked into the interior, her heart sank. The walls were empty. The room was stripped of any traces of the paintings. Where were they? She held her hand over her mouth.

A loud groan escaped her, a sound that resembled one made by a dying animal.

"Hilma!" Cornelia emerged from a corner. In her arms was a huge roll of canvas. She placed it on the floor, with other bolts of fabric.

"I'm so sorry," she apologized as she approached Hilma, "but we can no longer use this warehouse. We have to pack everything up tonight and move out."

"What are you talking about? We cannot do that; we need a space large enough to work in, and this is the only place we can do that." Hilma's eyes flared. "You know just as well as I do, we are not finished here yet; we still have work to do."

Cornelia opened her arms to Hilma. "Come here."

Hilma shook her head. "No. I feel like someone has betrayed me here. Is it you? Is it your friend Kristian?" Her voice was acrid and biting.

"Please," Cornelia begged. "You must let me explain."

She guided Hilma to one of the chairs in the middle of the room. On the seat, she had placed the notebook. Hilma knew exactly which one it was. Anna and she had bought matching notebooks in a small shop near the Ponte Vecchio, one that specialized in marbleized Florentine paper. She let go of Cornelia's hand, reached for the book, and clutched it to her chest.

"Did you look inside?"

Cornelia nodded.

"I can explain. These are studies, anatomy studies. We made them a long time ago . . . when we were young art students."

"Yes, I understand that. I know male artists do similar sketches all the time." She lowered her eyes. "It's just that this book got into the wrong hands. . . ."

"Who had it in their possession? Who stole it from me?" She suspected, of course, it was Lars. But perhaps he had passed it on to one of his friends. Hilma's heart was in her throat.

Cornelia knelt beside Hilma and took her hand again.

"My friend Kristian, the man who so generously lent us this warehouse, saw a group of men going through it at a pub. Another man was taking coins for each of them to take a peek at the pages."

"You mean to tell me he was charging money to look at my private drawings?"

Hilma's anger rose as she imagined the tawdry scene. She had spent her entire career trying to create art that contributed meaningful value to the world, and now her most intimate sketches were being sullied and cheapened—shown to a crowd of brutes who saw them merely as a form of crude titillation.

"Not only that, I'm afraid," Cornelia continued. "The man who had the sketchbook in his possession was talking loudly about us and the group, and what we were doing here late at night. He was spreading shameful lies.

"Kristian got into a fight with him over it. He was badly hurt, but he did manage to retrieve the book." Cornelia's voice softened. "He defended us and our reputation."

Hilma turned pale. "I don't understand how it got into his hands. I have not looked at it in many years. . . . I didn't even know it was missing from my studio, to be honest. Only recently, Anna asked me if I knew where it was."

"Well, because of Kristian, we have it back now."

"I will burn it, today."

"No, you mustn't do that. It's too beautiful for you to destroy. You just need to be more careful and keep it safe."

Hilma's mind was exploding in a thousand directions. Not only was there the embarrassment that her sketches had been ogled by Hellström and his friends, but more painfully, she felt her privacy had been violated. And to make matters worse, now Cornelia's friend was saying that because of the potentially dangerous gossip, the group could no longer use the warehouse.

"Do we really need to leave in such a hurry?"

Cornelia lowered her eyes. "I'm afraid we do. Kristian has been so generous to us, for such a long time. But he can't risk his business; we must understand that. And we must protect our work. What if someone broke in, destroyed all we've done? That loss would be too terrible to imagine."

Hilma nodded and then rose from the chair. She walked over to the two paintings that Cornelia had already rolled up. The beautiful colors and shapes were now hidden from view.

"We have no place to keep them if we have to leave this . . . ," she mumbled with sadness in her voice, her forehead leaning against the tips of the rolled canvases. "I just don't understand how any of this could happen." Hilma shut her eyes tight. "I must believe this is just one setback, that these paintings will eventually reach the temple walls they deserve."

· · · · ·

The door to the warehouse creaked open. Sigrid and Anna stood at the threshold with two baskets full of supplies. Sigrid had brought more eggs for the tempera paint at Hilma's request, and Anna was carrying additional jars of dried pigment. Fear struck them both when they saw Hilma curled up on the floor with her head in her hand.

"Oh my goodness, what has happened?" Anna rushed over to comfort her friend. "Did someone break in and steal the paintings?"

Hilma let go of the sketchbook and gave it to Anna.

"Lars must have had it all this time. . . . You were right to be concerned. . . ."

Anna took the book from Hilma and ran her hand over the cover. Although so many years had passed since she had posed for those private sketches, the memory of what she and Hilma shared was still pressed into its pages. A great sense of relief washed over her now that she knew it was in Hilma's possession.

"I'm glad it's back safely with you. . . ."

Hilma shook her head.

"Kristian saw him showing it to people at a bar, talking about us in the most terrible, salacious way. He will never leave us in peace, and he wants to destroy us."

Anna lifted her hand and began to smooth her hair. "He is a bitter old man full of threats . . . but he cannot destroy us. I won't let him."

This was one of the things she loved about Anna. A powerful inner strength always emerged from Anna when Hilma was at her weakest. She might look like a quiet mouse on the outside, but inside she was a lion.

"Cornelia says we must leave the warehouse today. Before we finish the remaining two paintings."

Sigrid stood quietly next to the group. "I think I saw this man you're speaking about lurking around the warehouse a few weeks ago. I had a terrible feeling about him; his aura was broken. All I saw around him were black patches. I should have said something to the group."

"How could you have known?" Anna answered sympathetically. "He has maintained this vendetta against Hilma for far too long."

"I was distracted already by the disharmony of our circle being broken, with Mathilda leaving. But still . . . I should have sensed that he was a threat to us."

"The paintings we've done so far are safe. We must be grateful for at least that," Cornelia said, trying to add something positive to the conversation.

Sigrid agreed. "Yes, and now we must come up with a plan for what to do with them." Her voice was solemn. "We could divide them between us."

Hilma shook her head.

"No, the paintings must never be separated. They must stay together, always."

She stood up and tried to regain her composure. Cornelia had carefully rolled up the eight paintings. The smaller paintings of the first series were stacked neatly beside them.

"I also have some of the earlier paintings still in my studio. And I realize now that is not the wisest place to keep them."

Hilma's agitation increased when she thought about how Kandinsky had been so bold as to start rifling through her canvases. That, too, had felt like a violation.

"A Russian painter came by yesterday and, without my permission, started looking through some of the early temple paintings."

"He must have thought they looked like madness," said Anna. "I'm sure he thought they were so crazy, he's not even thinking about them another second."

Hilma furrowed her brow. "I'm not so sure. It was hard to gauge his reaction. He did comment on the colors, praising how bold they were."

Sigrid nodded. "And he was right. The colors are beautiful. The meaning behind all of the shapes and the melding of the art and scientific discovery is unprecedented. Only you could help us obtain the spirits' vision, Hilma."

Hilma glanced at her hands. She had given up trying to remove the paint from underneath her fingernails. They would only become stained again.

"I have a sinking feeling that the world is not ready for these paintings just yet." She took a deep breath. "But one day it will be exactly as the spirits predicted. They will be shown in their full glory, transporting those who gaze upon the images and filling them with awe."

Cornelia's heart lifted at Hilma's words. "I believe that too, Hilma."

"But in the meantime, we must keep the paintings in a safe place. I have a barn on the island of Munsö where I spend my summers. It is not suitable to paint in, but we could certainly store *The Ten Largest* inside until we find a new place."

Anna contemplated the idea. She had visited the property several times with Hilma and knew the barn well.

"If they are put into storage indefinitely, perhaps you should sign them first."

Hilma paused and looked at the faces of her friends. "I don't think it would be right to do that. These paintings have been created by all of us in the room."

"I haven't painted anything at all," Sigrid said.

Hilma turned to Cornelia and Anna.

"We have just been assisting your visions, Hilma. You should sign them yourself," Anna insisted.

Hilma sighed. She was physically and emotionally exhausted from devoting every part of herself to ensuring the spirits' vision was achieved. When she had looked at the paintings propped up around the warehouse, she felt the way she imagined a mother felt seeing her child outside the womb for the first time. But she also knew that the paintings could never have been conceived without the help of the other women.

She paused for a moment to contemplate her honest feelings. Could such a monumental undertaking even be credited to De Fem? Its origins came from beyond. They could not ask the spirits to sign the canvases.

"No, that wouldn't be right," she answered. "These canvases are part of something far bigger than any of us. . . . The first seeds of inspiration came from the spirits, their words channeled by Sigrid. We, like the brushstrokes on the canvases, are just a part of a larger universe. The paintings will be part of a conversation in the future; that much I am sure of. We cannot own them; we can only safeguard them."

"The idea to store them on Munsö is a good one, Hilma," Anna said, placing a hand on her shoulder.

"We will do whatever you decide, Hilma," agreed Cornelia. "But please, let us finish the two last paintings tonight, before we pack things up. I feel that we must complete them here together, or else our work will not be done. As you've said before, it's essential that we show the circle of human life in its entirety. I can go to Kristian later, beg him to give us one more week to clear out this space."

"If you could manage that, it would give us enough time for the paintings to dry. And you are correct. Who knows when we will find a place large enough to finish? Do you have all of the paper, so we can begin mounting it to the canvas?"

The background had been painted in light pink on the eight pieces of paper days before, and Cornelia had already stacked them in anticipation of their having to leave.

"Yes, I have them here, and they are dry."

"Perhaps you can begin affixing them to new canvas, then . . . ," Hilma suggested. "Anna, can you start mixing the paint?"

Anna began pulling jars from her basket.

A new energy came over Hilma. The woman who only an hour before had lain crumpled in a ball now radiated a restored sense of purpose.

Cornelia began working at once on the arduous task of assembling the pieces of paper into a larger working surface. So much had to be done with care—the mixing of the glue and the application over the fabric, making sure it was evenly applied so bubbles wouldn't push through.

As Cornelia gently placed the pieces on the canvas, Mathilda's words came back to her, echoing inside her head: "She uses you; she has you working like an indentured servant, with no credit, with not a word of thanks."

The truth was, Mathilda was wrong. Hilma didn't want the credit all to herself; she wanted only to ensure the spirits' vision was achieved. She wholly believed the paintings were an embodiment of knowledge; she yearned for them to represent the wonders of the universe. She did not see this as something she possessed but rather as wisdom she wanted to share.

Still, it bereaved Cornelia that this might be the last time she would be in the presence of these large, beautiful paintings. When she'd placed the final square of paper, she pushed her hand to it, causing the glue to wet the paper under her fingers. The impression of her hand would always be there, just like her footprint in the earlier painting. Her role in their creation would exist in those imprints, like a fossil preserved over time.

· · · · ·

Hilma now stood over the assembled canvas like an empress.

She had wanted the last two paintings to come together in a powerful sense of closure. *The Ten Largest* began with *Birth* and would end with *Old Age*. She sighed deeply. What a metaphor. She would paint death just as they were leaving this sacred space.

The assembly of blue, yellow, and terra-cotta painted squares that Cornelia had created was in the profound shape of a cross. Flanking either side were flowerlike pinwheels with a rainbow of colors, floating on the paper to show that even in old age, the spirit can transcend and maintain its own vitality.

She took out an oil pastel and started to draw a thread along the huge picture on the floor. Not a straight one, for life isn't always straight and easy, but rather filled with unexpected and beautiful detours. The curling, roping line reminded her of the vines in nature. She continued to draw the twisting line down and around until it closed. For De Fem had reached the end, for now.

CHAPTER SEVENTEEN

. . . . .

EBEN

Present Day
New York City

In early December, we were ten months away from the opening of the Hilma af Klint exhibition. It was starting to look as if we were actually going to pull off getting the show and catalog in shape in time.

I had all the essays in hand, other than Blythe's, which she had said she would get to me by the December 30 deadline I'd given her. All the funding was in place as well, and the public relations department was busy doing its job, getting us advance buzz.

I hadn't seen Blythe again. I'd felt we both wanted to start seeing each other again, and I longed to reach out, but at the same time, I thought it would be smarter to let her finish the essay. That had to come first. And there was Daphne for me to figure out.

We had never seen each other often, because Daphne split her time between Los Angeles and New York. She usually spent more time on the West Coast. That fall was no different. But what was different was that I was suddenly aware that I didn't seem to miss her when she was away, and I probably should have if the relationship had been an important one.

On Thursday, December 14, she flew back into town for a close friend's weekend wedding. On Friday, I met Daphne at the rehearsal dinner at Majorelle, a French restaurant tucked inside a lovely boutique hotel, the Lowell, on East Sixty-Third Street. The private dining room was filled with glorious red and white roses with a nod to the upcoming Christmas season. Tiny pine trees decorated with satin bows sat on each table.

The bride and Daphne had grown up together, and during the dinner, Daphne was often out of her seat, chatting with all the people she knew there. During the break between the main course and dessert, Daphne returned to our table to tell me she'd just checked her phone and had a message from Barbara Silverman, who wanted to set up a meeting the following week.

"She said she wants to talk about the sponsorship identification," Daphne said.

"Is there a problem?" I asked.

"Not a problem, just a change. She decided she wanted the sponsorship to be in her family's company name."

"We haven't gone to press with any of the literature or signage, so we should have time. What's the company?"

Before she could answer, the bride-to-be came over and pulled Daphne away. Since the woman who'd been seated on my left was out of her seat, I didn't worry about being rude and got up. Out in the lobby, I pulled out my phone and typed "Barbara Silverman" and "board of directors" into Google.

I scanned the first hit, read the name of her family's company, and felt sick. The Delong Corporation was a conglomerate. They owned a cosmetics company, a clothing company, and a pharmaceutical company that was at the heart of a huge scandal. I wasn't completely sure of the particulars, so I went back to my Google search and clicked on a recent article detailing the situation.

The previous year, Delong had raised the prices of their most popular diabetes medicine. It hadn't been a normal increase. The callous indifference the company's president, Gregory Silverman, my donor's son, had shown in raising the price of the lifesaving drug by more than three hundred percent without reason had led to an investigation that uncovered a crime. Gregory Silverman had used corporate funds to conceal his defrauding of investors in a fledgling company.

During dessert I didn't discuss with Daphne what I'd read. I waited until we were back at her apartment on West Seventy-First. She'd moved into it shortly before we met. A year later, it was still being decorated—by a top firm, of course. Every time I visited, I noticed a bit more progress, but it was still not complete. It felt cold to me. While tasteful, the décor was impersonal and put me on edge. It seemed the only perk was the twenty-eighth-floor view over the city.

"Do you want anything to drink?" Daphne asked as she stepped out of her heels.

"A brandy, please," I said.

She fussed at the bar, a chrome-and-glass cart that fit the décor perfectly.

Above the couch was a new piece of art that hadn't been there last time—a framed print of Jeff Koons's *Balloon Dog*. The status piece left me as uncomfortable as the rest of the apartment.

"What was it about this print that made you choose it?" I asked.

"I didn't choose it; the decorator did."

"Because you like the artist?"

Daphne handed me the drink. "Because the artist is important," she said. "I buy art the way I tell my clients to buy it. Every purchase is a chance to invest smartly and grow your capital or risk it."

I took a sip of the brandy. It wasn't anything I hadn't heard her say before. And while I understood her credo when it came to managing a client's portfolio, that she adhered to it with what she hung in her own home struck me as mercenary.

I looked around at the other, equally "important" artwork and status furniture.

"What's your favorite piece here?"

Daphne looked at me as if I were speaking a foreign language.

"It's not about favorites. I entertain here; you know that. Every item was chosen to reflect my investment philosophy."

This was also nothing I hadn't heard before, but it struck me differently that night. Because I was seeing it through the lens of the funding she had brought me. Looking at the world she operated in versus the kind of world that Hilma and Anna had inhabited.

True, Anna had been very wealthy, her family owning coal mines, but she was a true patron of the arts. She supported Hilma for her entire life because she believed in her art, not because she saw it as an investment opportunity.

I wasn't so naive as to think that in the twenty-first century we could operate without corporate funding any more than Hilma could have created what she did without Anna's help. Nor did I think there was untold glory in denial or poverty. I didn't even fault Mrs. Silverman for wanting to sponsor a show, regardless of her reason. Nor could I argue that art wasn't an investment. Of course it was. But to buy art only because of its investment value, even if it didn't move you? To fill your apartment with pieces that spoke about you but not to you?

It was an affront to everything I had done with my life.

"Daphne, the museum isn't going to be able to take Mrs. Silverman's funding if in fact it is for a corporate sponsorship."

"Why?"

"You know about what her son did?"

"Stepson, but yes, and he is in prison serving his time."

"For fraud, yes, but I'm talking about the price gouging."

"It's not my job or yours to sit in judgment."

"Daphne, what they did was inhumane. It was pure, unadulterated greed."

"That's not up to us to determine. My client wants to pursue positive investments and believes funding the show of Hilma af Klint will raise the company's profile."

"Have you seen what is happening with the Forrests?" I

asked. "Our museum is being challenged to remove their name from the wing they endowed. As is every other institution in the country that they gave money to."

"I can't believe you are being so holier-than-thou about this. It's not easy to get funding for a virtually unknown nutjob who held séances in order to figure out what to paint. From Sweden, no less. What artists come from Sweden?"

I knew Daphne had drunk a bit of wine at dinner. And our after-dinner brandy probably hadn't been a good idea. She wasn't drunk, but she was less controlled, and I rarely saw her that way.

"It's an ethical issue," I said.

"Oh, Eben, please. Ethics?"

"Yes, ethics."

She burst out laughing. "I can't believe we're even having this conversation. My client is willing to give you one point three million dollars, and you are turning it down?"

"I'm not, but I believe once I tell Dr. Perlstein about this, on behalf of the museum, she absolutely will."

"I didn't ever think you'd turn Boy Scout on me."

"I'm not turning anything. It's tainted money. How can you not see that?"

I had other questions to ask her. How could she hang a print on her wall because it was by an important artist without even knowing if she liked it? Had she even decided if she really liked me, or had I just checked off enough boxes on some checklist she kept?

But I didn't ask her anything else. I was too surprised. Not at her, but at myself. How had I gotten caught up with her? What did it say about me that I had missed the clues?

I put my glass down. "I'm going to go home, Daphne."

"I think that's best. And—" She hesitated. "About the wedding tomorrow . . ."

"Yes?"

"I know it's not something you were looking forward to anyway, so don't feel obligated. It's not a sit-down dinner—I'll be fine on my own."

Her words echoed in my head during my walk home. She *was* fine on her own. That was what had attracted me to her, wasn't it? And the more I thought about it, that was what had attracted me to every woman I'd dated over the last eight years. They were always fine on their own. Independence was one thing, but I'd found a string of women who ultimately didn't want to be responsible for a relationship. And probably neither did I.

Upstairs in my apartment, I made a pot of coffee and sat down at the desk in a corner of the living room and started making notes about potential sources for new funding. Finding one was going to be virtually impossible at this late date.

At midnight, I stared down at the almost-empty yellow pad. Ripping off the top page, I crumpled it up and threw it across the room. Oddly, it went right through the hole in my mother's sculpture, landing on the windowsill.

I rose and walked over to retrieve it. At the window, I looked up. Despite New York's light pollution, there was a profusion of stars in the dark sky. When Hilma af Klint looked up at the nighttime sky on Munsö, how many more stars had she seen? The show was always on my mind now. *Paintings for the Future* was taking up all my time.

I hadn't abandoned my curiosity about all the members of De Fem. I had determined that while I could not include their story in the show to the level I wanted, I was going to pursue it at a later date. Maybe I'd go to back to Sweden and do more research there. Work with the Danish art historian. Leave no stone unturned.

But for now, it was Hilma I was focused on. And the longer I worked with the paintings themselves, the more I found myself caught up in their mystery.

So many people whom I'd met and spoken to in Sweden, at the museum and the foundation, so many of the scholars I'd enlisted to write essays for the catalog, so many of the curators at the Guggenheim who were involved, had told me the same thing. There was something intangible about working with Hilma's paintings that changed them in some way. That moved them more than they'd expected.

I felt as if I'd been changed in the last months by a force outside of myself. The paintings and the story spoke to me. Hilma's lifelong effort to translate her spirit's language spoke to me. I was in awe of her unending effort to understand the gift she had been given—even when, as suggested in the early notebooks, she herself didn't always know what it meant. I responded to the joy and beauty of the work itself and to the magic of Hilma's defying time's odds. To be so maligned in life and then decades and decades later to be discovered for the first time. And discovered as one of the first of her kind. To be put on a step higher than Kandinsky and Mondrian?

For a moment I almost wished that I had the psychic ability of any one of De Fem, or Marie Cassel's ability to close her eyes and reach out into the cosmos and commune with spirits.

But I couldn't do that, so instead, I impulsively called Blythe. I knew it was late, but I remembered her insomnia, and unless she'd found some miracle cure, she'd be up.

"Eben? Is something wrong?"

"No, I wanted to talk to you. You weren't sleeping, were you?"

She laughed. "You knew I wasn't sleeping, or you wouldn't have called."

"Can I come over there?"

Her no was immediate. "But let me come to you."

"If you're sure," I said. "It's just that I have been thinking about Hilma all night and realizing things. And you're the only person who might understand."

I could hear a smile in her voice when she said, "Really? How curious."

"Let me send a car. And text me when you turn onto the block. I'll come down to let you in."

I was waiting for her on the sidewalk. "I really hope it's not too late."

"I was still grading papers. I didn't even realize what time it was until after you got off the phone with me. I thought it was only ten. I hadn't even gotten into my robe—" She gestured at her ensemble. Under her coat I could see a long turquoise and green skirt, a pink shirt, and at least a dozen crazy beaded necklaces around her neck.

Upstairs, I opened the door, and she walked into the foyer and through to the living room. She headed right to one of my mother's marble sculptures. She stood as if transfixed for almost a full minute before speaking. And even then, she didn't take her eyes off the piece.

"I can't believe I didn't realize it," she said.

"What?"

"Before I met you, I was aware of your mother's work."

"Yes, you told me."

"I'd seen a few photos in the catalogs and read an article about her, but I never saw any of her pieces in person. There weren't any in museums in London."

"No, there aren't."

"Is there more of her work here?"

"Yes." I gestured. "Two more pieces in the living room. One in the dining area."

Following the direction of my arm, she walked into the living room and inspected both of the pieces in there.

"I hadn't seen any of Hilma's paintings in person when we were at school. My thesis was more heavily weighted to Georgina anyway. So I didn't make the connection."

"What connection? What are you talking about?"

"You don't see it, do you?" She nodded. "No, you wouldn't. You have lived with these your whole life. These shapes are imprinted on your soul."

I looked at the sculpture we were standing in front of. I

tried to see it the way a stranger would. I looked across the room at the other piece. Then I walked back to the foyer. And then into the dining area.

Finally, I saw it. And was astonished that I'd missed it.

The shapes that my mother sculpted out of marble were so similar to many of the shapes that Hilma af Klint featured in her temple paintings. The infinity symbol, the concentric circles, the double pyramids, the specific womblike ovals. Almost as if my mother had been a student of Hilma's.

"When were these done?" Blythe asked.

"The bulk were done between 1976 and 1987, the year she died."

"The first af Klint show was in 1986. So your mother couldn't have been influenced by her. Had she ever visited Stockholm?"

"I wouldn't know. But maybe we're making too much out of this. Is it really such a coincidence? My mother used many natural forms in her work. So did Hilma. So do many artists."

She frowned. "I suppose . . . you're right. . . . It just struck me. . . ."

"What's wrong?" I asked.

"Your first instinct is still to deny the possibility of something beyond what you know. Our biggest arguments were over your inability to have faith in anything but cold, hard logic, and—" She broke off.

"What?"

"I've been waiting to find a time to tell you this. I told you why I left you. I realized that you were not ready to change and let in possibilities. That if an idea wasn't rational, you didn't believe it was legitimate. And I couldn't be with you and face what I had to face if you weren't at least open to the magic of the universe."

"What did you have to face?" I asked.

"Why did you call me tonight, Eben?" she asked without answering my question.

"I had a conversation about the show's funding that made me aware that I feel differently about Hilma and her work than I do about other artists. And I wanted to tell you about it. I didn't think there was anyone I could tell about it other than you who would understand even half of what I had to say."

"And what is that?"

"Let's go sit down."

She crossed the room, and we went into the living room. She sat in one of the two chairs facing each other across from the couch. I sat in the other.

"I realized tonight that when we were together at Courtauld," I said, "I was frightened of your search. That if you were right, if some artists are able to connect to the energy and spirit of the cosmos, like Hilma, like Rothko, perhaps even like my mother, that if there are messages and meanings in some of their work that is beyond our understanding, I would fail at ever deciphering what I so desperately wanted to know."

"And the reason for telling me now?"

I shrugged. "Maybe because I finally saw that my stubbornness was in the way of us working. I should have realized that years ago. I should have gone after you."

"Yes, maybe."

"But I've never known how to do that. Once someone leaves me . . . I suppose I shut down."

She was nodding, and in her face there was something that I couldn't read.

"I shouldn't have left the way I did, Eben. I should have explained, but I . . . I was so sure that if I stayed, this thing that we had would be destroyed, and that if there was any hope of keeping it alive, I needed to be away from you. To protect what was us. And then . . ."

She had started to cry. I rose and went to her and pulled her up. I put my arms around her and held her. All of my senses came alive as I was holding this woman again. I smelled her hair and her skin and felt the way she still fit into me. It was as if my body, independent of my mind, had a memory of her, and I responded the way that I always had to her—no, I responded in a way I never quite had, because all the years of missing her had changed me. Time and revelations had changed me. Hilma's paintings had changed me. Opening myself up to believing in something—in anything—that I couldn't explain rationally was the biggest change of all.

When she pulled her head back and looked at my face, I could see she felt it too. There were silver tracks of tears on her cheeks, and her eyes were brighter and bluer from the crying, but there was understanding in them that I hadn't seen there before.

"There is something else I need to tell you. I want to say it the right way. But first, I want to apologize," she said, and then she leaned forward and kissed me. It was gentle and a little unsure for a moment. For both of us. And then it wasn't anymore. We weren't the same as we had been at Courtauld or in Stockholm. This kiss was a little sadder for what we had missed and the time we had lost. But as it continued, it became something new. This kiss was more deliberate. Harder. Angry for a few moments and then full of a passion that was different from what I remembered.

When you make love with someone for the first time, it is usually awkward, for all its astonishing desire and wonderful newness. You don't know where to put your hands or your lips. You don't know what the other person likes or how to maneuver yourself. The smells and the tastes are unfamiliar. And for all the thrills, that first time can also be strange and make you feel self-conscious.

With Blythe that night, there was all that wonderful newness and wonderful desire without any of the awkwardness. We knew each other's smells and tastes. Our memories moved us, and as the night fell away, we found each other again . . . my silver girl who was different now and the same . . . and me.

We made love and fell asleep and then woke and made love again, and then as light was just dawning, Blythe said she had to go.

"But it's only five o'clock."

"I need to get back."

"Why so early?"

"My daughter."

I'd forgotten.

"My parents are there, but I didn't tell her I was going out, so I don't want her to wake up without me being home."

When she'd told me about her daughter at the Mark, I'd

been surprised. Of course, rationally I knew she'd moved on after me and had built a life. Of course she could have had a child. But the mention of her daughter now, while she was in my bed, felt like a curtain being drawn between us. I was disappointed in myself. I tried to tell myself that I shouldn't let it bother me. That I was being a narcissistic fool. We had just spent the night being so close. As close as I had ever been with anyone before. I should have been happy with that, grateful.

"We have more to talk about," she said, seeing my face, which I supposed revealed my feelings.

I nodded. "Yes."

"But I need to hurry now."

"I understand."

She dressed quickly while I watched her glorious body disappear under the layers of colors. Just before she was ready to go, I jumped up, pulled on my jogging pants and a sweatshirt, and walked her downstairs. I opened the front door. She put her hand out to keep it open.

"I've hoped for this," she said. "But I don't want to make any mistakes this time. So let me go slow, all right?"

Without waiting for my response, she kissed me goodbye quickly and then was gone, flying down the front steps and leaving me wondering exactly what she was referring to.

· · · · ·

Four hours later, I had the unpleasant task of telling Dr. Perlstein about the funding issue. Being exhausted didn't help me as I explained.

"How could this possibly happen now?" she asked.

"Until yesterday, the funding was coming from Mrs. Silverman's family's foundation—her father was a real estate magnate and a great philanthropist. We did our due diligence. There was not a single red flag about taking the sponsorship. But she changed her mind and decided she wanted the sponsorship to be in her husband's company's name. She thought the Delong Corporation's funding Hilma might help take some of the limelight off her stepson."

Dr. Perlstein picked up a glass miniature of the museum off her desk, looked at it, then put it back down.

"This is a disaster. I didn't want to have to go to the board for the funding, but I suppose it's my next step. I've asked them too many times in the last two years."

"I'm sorry."

She shook her head. "This isn't your fault. Everything is a political minefield these days."

We sat and brainstormed for a half hour, making lists of possible last-minute sponsors. At ten, she left for an appointment. I went back to my office and then, at eleven, took myself to the park to walk its serpentine pathways and try to clear my head.

I stumbled on a fashion photo shoot at the Bethesda Fountain. I stood and watched for a few minutes as the stylist draped the models in magnificent gossamer shawls and scarves in various shades of blue ranging from deep sapphire to pale powder blue. It was like watching someone paint with fabrics. The models looked as if they were made of the same stuff as the very blue sky and the clouds.

It gave me an idea. Taking a seat on a bench, I pulled out my Moleskine and jotted down some notes. When I looked up, the stylist was working on a new setup with a red color palette, and I watched her create another illusion.

Back at the office, I got an appointment with Dr. Perlstein, who had time to see me at five p.m. I was so excited to present my potential solution to the funding problem that I almost burst into her office.

"What if we sold the exclusive rights to photograph the show and excerpt the catalog to one of the major women's magazines? Do a whole issue focused on female empowerment. Tell a deeper version of the story that we can't tell in paintings alone about Hilma and De Fem. About their problems fitting into their male-dominated society and how they supported each other through their friendship.

"I realized this afternoon the question everyone has been asking is wrong—it's not, why aren't there more great women artists? There are. The question is, why don't we pay more attention to great women artists? And not just painters. Sculptors. Filmmakers. Photographers. Using Hilma as an example can shine light on the problem. Here's a brilliant woman creating astonishing work, yet she's unknown to all but those deeply familiar with the twentieth-century non-object art movement and—"

Dr. Perlstein held up her hand. "Stop. I'm sold. And you know what else? We have permission from the Hilma af Klint Foundation to do merchandising . . . so instead of just mugs and notebooks, we could work with the magazine to find some up-and-coming female designers to use some of Hilma's artwork to create a small line. . . ." She picked up a pencil and started sketching. "A tunic, a kimono, a scarf . . ."

We spent the next hour going over various publications that might be interested. Then I worked most of that night creating an elaborate presentation. Our time was short. The catalog was scheduled to go to the printers in a month; the sponsors had to be included in the acknowledgments.

By the end of the following day, Dr. Perlstein had identified three potential sponsors. We had meetings with two on Thursday and the last on Friday.

All three were interested and promised to take the idea to their editorial boards and advertisers and get back to us as soon as possible.

I had texted Blythe to let her know what we were attempting with potential funders and to get some quotes from her lecture to include in the presentation I was creating.

After my final meeting, on Friday, I found a text from her asking how the meetings had gone. I told her we'd know in a few days. And then, without overthinking it, asked her if we could see each other over the weekend. She wrote back almost immediately, saying she was going to be away, doing some research at a Yale library, but she did want to see me and was glad I'd reached out.

She'd ring me when she got back.

. . . . .

Saturday morning, as usual, I went swimming. The little girl whom I'd gotten used to seeing was at the pool again, already in the water, swimming steadily. Her father raised a hand in greeting and then returned to his reading material.

About a half hour into my forty-five minutes of laps, I realized there was a change in the movement next to me and I turned. The little girl was in distress. I didn't hesitate.

I dove under the water, swam into her lane, and picked her up. She sputtered as I lifted her out of the water and put her on the edge of the pool. Then I jumped up and knelt beside her. Her color was fine, but she was clutching her leg. Her face was contorted, but her breathing didn't seem affected.

I guessed what was wrong.

"Do you have a cramp?" I asked.

She nodded.

"You'll be okay. Can I try to work it out? I get them all the time."

"Yes," she whispered through the pain.

I could feel the calf muscle spasming under my fingers. I massaged it the way I massaged my own muscles when I got cramps. It took only a few seconds for the muscle to calm down.

"The pain is gone, right?" I asked.

"Willa?" her father was running over. "What happened? I was reading—what happened?"

"She's fine now," I told him. "A leg cramp."

"I never had one before," the little girl said to both of us. "My coach taught me what to do, but it hurt worse than anything I ever felt."

Her father bent down to scoop her up, but she shook her head. "I'm okay now. I want to finish swimming."

"I don't think you should," he said, and then looked at me for confirmation.

I hesitated, not wanting to interfere, but I knew what she needed.

"Actually, if she could get back in the water and swim a few laps, easy-peasy, it would be better for her leg."

Her father looked at me oddly for a moment. Then turned back to Willa. "Is that what you want to do?"

She nodded.

"Okay, but I'm standing right here."

She smiled. "I'm okay now, Pop." She turned, sat down on the edge of the pool, and slipped in.

Willa's father looked at me again. "I don't know how to thank you."

"She wasn't in danger, just scared. Next time she'll know what it is and not be surprised."

· · · · ·

Stockholm, April 17, 1908

Dearest Hilma,

Please come as soon as you can. I know how hard these past few months have been for you, but Lotten has taken a terrible turn for the worse. Her breathing has become so shallow, and she spends nearly all hours with her eyes closed. The doctor says that she no longer has weeks to live, only days.

Love,
Anna

. . . . .

CHAPTER EIGHTEEN

April 17–24, 1908
Stockholm

"The doctor says she's reaching the end." Anna burst into tears as Hilma stepped into the foyer. "My heart is breaking. I'm so grateful you came straightaway."

Hilma wrapped her arms around Anna. Her embrace provided a comfort that transcended words.

"I'm sorry I haven't visited in so long. . . . It pains me to learn Lotten is so fragile now."

Anna forced back tears. It felt so good to see Hilma after so many months. She knew her friend had suffered a period of depression after her exhausting trip to Switzerland to meet with Rudolf Steiner. Hilma had made the arduous journey to the mountains, believing the philosopher, reformer, and self-professed clairvoyant would be impressed by *The Ten Largest* paintings and the spiritual guidance she'd received to produce them.

"He'd be the perfect person to create a temple to house them," Hilma had gushed to Anna, knowing that Steiner was also a trained architect. But she soon realized that she had been terribly wrong about him. Steiner dismissed the paintings and expressed no interest in helping Hilma make a temple to display them. In fact, he chastised her for their very creation. "It's a deadly sin to make art from spiritual activity," he reprimanded.

Despite her insistence that he take her more seriously, Steiner wouldn't engage in any further conversation. Hilma had returned heartbroken and rejected. She hadn't been able to pick up a paintbrush or even a stub of charcoal ever since.

Anna hoped that the urgency of making a final sketch of Lotten for the family might help Hilma get her hands moving again and do both of them good. The sketch she had done back in February no longer resembled her sister.

"Is she asleep upstairs?" Hilma put down her sketchbook and pencil case on the small oak table.

"She's resting in the parlor. Mother had a new daybed brought in a few weeks ago, one with a deep velvet cushion that helps ensure Lotten's comfort."

Hilma reached for Anna's hands and squeezed them.

"Thank you for agreeing to capture her in these last moments, Hilma. I couldn't do it myself. My tears would destroy the paper."

"I'm happy to do it and will start working at once. As long as it does not upset Lotten."

"I think she'll most probably be asleep. . . ."

"Let's not waste any time, then, Anna." Hilma clutched her

sketch pad, and the two friends began to slowly walk toward the French doors leading to the parlor.

Sleeping on the velvet daybed, Lotten looked like an angel in repose. Josephine was sitting beside her; a piece of needle-point remained in her lap. The needle and thread lingered beside the fabric, untouched.

"Mother Cassel," Hilma said softly, and kissed her on both cheeks.

Josephine pulled Hilma's hands into her own. "We're so grateful that you've come to do Lotten's portrait."

"Of course . . . I would do anything for your family." Hilma's voice broke. She looked down again at Lotten and couldn't believe how pale she'd become. She resembled one of the carved alabaster statues she and Anna had been so fond of in their youth.

"Let me leave you so you can work without disturbance." Josephine stood up from her chair. "Please sit down and make yourself at home." She withdrew a handkerchief to dab her eyes. "Sonja will bring you some tea."

"I'll come back shortly to check on you," added Anna. Hilma's eyes were glassy. Her emotion made Anna's heart break even more.

"No," she said quietly. "Please stay. I want you here by my side."

The sound of Hilma's graphite pencil moving across the page soon filled the air. Hilma drew each line carefully, endeavoring to make a perfect rendering of Lotten.

She began by sketching Lotten's oval face, then added the

curls that draped over her shoulder and linen nightdress. Absent were the abstract shapes, the squiggles, and bright, bold colors she had relied on for the temple paintings. When she began to add her features, Lotten's eyes fluttered open.

"Hilma, you've come to visit. . . . Are you drawing me?"

"Yes," Hilma answered, her face brightening as Lotten managed to speak a few words. "But it's a challenge to render someone so beautiful and celestial on the page. . . ."

"You're too kind, dear Hilma. . . . It must be quite a task to draw someone who is one step away from being a ghost."

Her paper-white hand lifted from beneath the coverlet. The long fingers, which had always filled the parlor with piano music, trembled as Lotten moved some stray curls from her face.

"It is so good to see you. It's been far too long since you've come to visit Mother and me." Even the shortest sentences were exhausting for her to speak. Lotten closed her eyes again.

Hilma continued to fill in Lotten's features, her small delicate nose, her Cupid's bow mouth. Just like Anna, she appeared younger than her years. There was hardly a fine line or wrinkle on her face.

"Drawing you, I'm reminded of our summers together on the lake . . . how you always so generously agreed to be a muse for Anna or me. You were such a good sport to help us."

Lotten smiled. "Yes. It's lovely to think there are a few portraits of me that will remain after I'm gone."

Anna leaned forward in her chair. "Don't say that, Sister. You are here now, and we're not letting you go anywhere." She reached for Lotten's hand and gripped it tightly.

Hilma continued to work quickly. She was aware that each

minute she had in Lotten's presence was precious. Hilma had now nearly finished Lotten's likeness. In all of her time as an artist, she never tired of the satisfaction she felt from seeing how something in her subject's heart, mind, and eyes could be transferred onto the page.

"I'm nearly done, Lotten. Would you like to see it?" Hilma asked her, leaning in closer with her sketchbook so Lotten needn't strain to view it.

"Yes," Lotten replied, her voice barely a whisper. "Thanks to you, I'm no longer afraid I will vanish."

• • • • •

Lotten's funeral was planned for the following Friday at Oscar's Church, with its lovely stained-glass windows that overlooked the harbor. Afterward, the family held a small reception for relatives and friends at their home.

It was the first time in over a year that Anna had seen all of the women together. Even Mathilda came to the church to pay her respects. They shared the same pew, sitting shoulder to shoulder, their black mourning clothes in sharp contrast to their milk white faces.

At the reception following the service, Sigrid came over to Anna and embraced her.

"Your sister's light surrounds you," she observed. Her words comforted Anna.

"It's so good to see you and the others. I'm touched everyone came."

"It's not the same now that we don't meet every week," Cornelia said.

"Yes." Anna nodded. "It was a very sacred time. I must admit I haven't been able to do much painting since Lotten's health worsened."

Cornelia stepped closer and kissed both of Anna's cheeks. "I'm so sorry about your sister." Her words caught in her throat. "Mathilda and I . . ."

Mathilda's gaze lifted. She had aged considerably in the past year. Her hair, plaited at the back of her head, was now completely silver. The skin around her eyes and jawline sagged, making her once-vigorous demeanor sad and deflated.

"We are truly sorry," she said, filling in Cornelia's words. "Losing a sister changes one's heart forever."

According to a letter Cornelia had sent Anna, she had moved out the month before. The room in Mathilda's apartment had grown too small for her. They talked so little to each other, and even when they did manage to exchange a few words, it invariably resulted in an argument.

When Kristian told Cornelia he could no longer see her, that his wife had grown suspicious and he needed to make the painful decision to put his family first, Mathilda would not be the one to wipe away her tears.

"I told you nothing would come of this folly. And now you are fifty-four years old with nothing to show for yourself but a roomful of fabric and a few paintings in a barn somewhere in the north of Sweden that don't even bear your signature. . . ." Her voice trailed off with disdain.

But Cornelia would not let her sister have the last word. The next afternoon, she took the necklace with the beautiful blue stone that Kristian had bought her, the one that reminded him of her eyes and the sea, and sold it back to the jewelry shop where he had purchased it. "Our love is like water," he had once told her. "It can fill any shape."

Now she would let his love fill her in another way; she would let it buy her freedom.

She took the sum she received from the sale and applied it toward the first month's rent for a small studio apartment. The very next afternoon, she placed a classified advertisement in the newspaper offering affordable drawing lessons to women of all ages. Within a week, her first wave of students arrived at her door.

Every time Cornelia bent over one of her students' sketches and saw how she had brought to life something fresh on the page, it reaffirmed for her that her talents were not being wasted. As she worked with the women, building their confidence and artistic skill, the world became a better place.

During her time of heartbreak over losing Kristian, the one thing that had saved her was the knowledge that not only had she helped create *The Ten Largest* paintings, but she had also gained much wisdom in the process. She had learned that there are many parts that help make something whole. Her love affair with Kristian had been a necessary piece for her life's journey. Without his love the second time around, she might never have painted with the colors she had or found the patience to figure out how to assemble the small individual papers. De Fem would never have had the warehouse to create their last paintings together.

Kristian might not have been willing to leave his family for her, but he had helped her transform into a woman who would never again be without her paint and brushes. The tears on her pillow were the rainwater she needed to plant the seeds of her garden, her new life. And Cornelia was determined to see it bloom and grow.

· · · · ·

After nearly all of the guests had left the reception, Hilma sat alone on the daybed where Lotten had spent her final days. Anna, weary from making small talk for so many hours, her heart still grieving from the loss of her sister, finally sat down next to her. She was relieved she had someone she could be silent with. It felt like a balm to her soul.

Slowly she turned to Hilma. "The drawing you did of Lotten is now in Mother's bedroom. It gives her great comfort."

"I am glad for that."

"Did you notice the new oil painting I did in the living room?"

"Yes, of course. It caught my attention right away. Four pine trees in a circle. Another lone one in the center. The metaphor wasn't lost on me. I understood it at first glance."

"Nothing is ever lost on you, Hilma." Anna rested her hands in her lap. It felt good to speak about something other than illness and death. Just sitting next to Hilma, hearing her talking about a painting, breathed life into Anna.

"I needed to paint De Fem somehow in my own hand. During the last month of Lotten's life, we took her up to convalesce at our family's villa in Västmanland, and on one of my walks, I stumbled upon this eerie circle of trees. A large pine was in the center. It was sturdy and strong, with branches on its highest peak. It reminded me of Sigrid. Two other trees grew slightly apart, one lush with foliage, the other withered. That reminded me of Cornelia and Mathilda. But the two trees with the most greenery on them, the ones that mingled so close together that their branches touched . . . those two reminded me of us, Hilma."

Hilma's face softened. "I sensed that when I stood looking at it. You and I, we may have grown with different roots, but our flowering has always intensified because of each other."

"I feel so grateful that we're building the studio now in Munsö. It will be a special place to paint, and *The Ten Largest* will be so much safer there than in the old barn." Anna smiled.

"Yes, you've been so generous to help finance it," Hilma added. "When I sleep at night, I imagine the builder's sketches and how wondrous it will be to have a large vaulted ceiling. It's almost as if we were building our own church. But instead of a rose window, we will have the paintings to bring color and light into the one, vast room."

Anna reached for Hilma's hand. "The walls will be made of pine. De Fem will always keep a protective shield over the temple paintings."

·····

Stockholm, June 13, 1917

Dear Hilma,

How wonderful to hear that the atelier is finally finished. It feels like such an accomplishment to have seen this idea through. Now you will have the space and serenity you need to finish your life's work. I am excited to see what will come from your brush now that you will be living on the island. You will draw so much inspiration from the landscape we both love so deeply, and finally The Ten Largest will have a better, more hospitable home, instead of that musty barn!

I am making plans to come see it next week.

I can hardly wait.

Your loving,
Anna

CHAPTER NINETEEN

* * * * *

September 20, 1917
Island of Munsö

The studio was built on the grounds of the Baroness Giertta's property, on a deed Anna paid to rent the land for one hundred years. The wood the studio was built from was, as Anna promised, strong and fragrant pine.

When Anna first walked with Hilma through the finished structure, before the paintings were moved there for safekeeping, the two of them stood in the center of it and felt that the place was indeed as special and sacred as they intended it to be.

"I'm relieved I let go of my studio in Stockholm," admitted Hilma. "I had definitely outgrown it."

"You will see the snow fall, hear the rain patter, and gaze at the moon from the window above." She pointed to the window that the architect had placed within the roofline so that Hilma would never be far from the elements that inspired her.

Hilma blinked. "It was so thoughtful of you to ask him to do that."

"I remembered how wonderful that window was in the warehouse."

"Yes," Hilma agreed. "That space offered so much magic too."

That evening, they transferred nearly all the large canvases into the newly constructed space. They spread out a blanket on the wood floor and sat down to eat sandwiches.

"I will grow old here," Hilma said as she craned her neck to look at the stars.

"I'm comforted knowing you now have a safe and inspiring place to work," added Anna. She could never think of Hilma as growing old. She defied time. She pushed on when others idled. She was a garden of constant bloom.

· · · · ·

They uncrated boxes of art supplies and placed the materials on shelves. Hilma had brought with her just one suitcase packed with clothes and smocks. The building had only a small loft allotted for a living space, with the rest of the structure meant for her painting.

"Alma and Charlotta have already promised to come and work more on the smaller temple paintings. It's a shame Cornelia is so busy with her art school."

"It's for the best," reflected Anna. "She has found her own new temple where she can create."

Hilma shrugged. "But you still must come and visit me often. . . . There is still so much work to be done."

"I will come as much as I can and help as much as I am able," Anna said. "But you know how I prefer to work outside . . . to draw from nature. I find the answers to my spiritual questions through observing the birds in the reeds, the butterflies in flight. My mind has never worked exactly as yours."

Anna's heart opened as she spoke. Hilma had always worked toward crafting the future, whereas she preferred to work in the moment, to observe the simple pleasures of what surrounded her.

"But I will never stop supporting you. I hope you know that."

Anna had constructed the atelier as a way of showing her unwavering devotion, her belief that the paintings Hilma created were worthy of being housed properly. She wanted to reinforce for Hilma that she didn't need Steiner or any other man to continue her life's work.

"After Switzerland, it felt like you were the only person in this world who believed in me," Hilma confessed. "Steiner ridiculed me, told me that a woman should never have even attempted such a folly. To think how I admired him and believed he'd help us create our temple . . ."

"You will have a temple for the paintings one day," Anna assured. "But in the meantime, you have a sacred space to work."

"Come," Hilma said. "Your body must be as tired as mine from moving all of those enormous canvases."

She led Anna beneath the skylight. "I don't want to sleep in the loft on this first night. . . . I want to sleep beneath the stars with you."

Underneath the window, they let their bodies stretch out, their fingers grazing each other's, their toes touching, like children. Even though they were nearly sixty and their bodies no longer felt as vital as they once did, a restorative warmth flooded through Anna. She felt content, like a nesting swan.

· · · · ·

CHAPTER TWENTY

EBEN

Present Day
New York City

I saw Blythe several times when she returned from Yale. We were both moving slowly, tentative and worried about jumping back into a relationship too quickly. Her semester at Columbia would be finishing at the end of the month, and she was planning on going back to London to resume teaching at Courtauld in January. She'd said she'd be happy to help me with my detective work on De Fem then.

She turned in her essay the week before Christmas, and it was everything I'd hoped it was going to be, delving into the spiritual aspects of Hilma's work in a way that was historically rich, accessible, and fascinating. I took her out to celebrate at La Grenouille. I had planned on suggesting that I could come and visit her in London over the holidays.

She looked so beautiful that night, sitting among the profusion of flowers the restaurant was known for. In honor of the season, she was in a vintage red velvet dress with a white mink cuff and collar. She'd braided pearls in her hair. I ordered champagne for us both and made a toast.

"To our first collaboration," I said, and clinked her glass.

She clinked back, took a sip.

"Eben," she started, then stopped.

"What is it?" I knew something was wrong.

"It's not actually our first collaboration."

"It's not?" I was thinking back to Courtauld, trying desperately to remember what project we'd done together.

"No."

She was toying with the stem of her glass and looked nervous.

"What is it?"

"You know I have a child," she said.

"Of course."

Blythe's eyes were filling with tears. "I've been trying to figure out the best way to tell you this but . . . she's ours, Eben. She's ours."

I sat stunned, unsure I'd really heard right.

"There's never been the right time and—"

I was trying to count. To figure out when . . . what . . . "How old is she?"

"Eight."

"And you waited all these years?"

"I—"

"Did you know you were pregnant when you broke up with me? Was that why? Were you keeping it from me?"

"No, I didn't know until two and a half months after you went back to America."

"And you chose not to contact me, not to fill me in?"

"I didn't think you'd . . ." She stumbled on her words. "I didn't want you to come back to me just because of the accident of the pregnancy. And that's what it would have been. Maybe the right thing but for totally the wrong reason."

I did a horrible thing then. But she had done an even more horrible thing, hadn't she? I stood up, went over to the maître d', gave him a hundred-dollar bill, and then without saying a word, I walked out of the restaurant into the cold night, leaving Blythe sitting by herself on the banquette.

Avoidance had always been one of my survival techniques. I'm ashamed to say I readily employed it for ten solid months. As the fall date of the opening of the Hilma af Klint exhibit loomed, we endured the usual glitches in putting on a rotunda show. But nothing that derailed us.

October arrived with much fanfare. The designer and the magazine we'd partnered with were putting a lot of energy into promoting the show. The press had fallen in love with the originality and the theme of the show. Hilma af Klint and De Fem were very appealing in the #MeToo era, just as we had all hoped.

The guest list for opening night included Guggenheim VIPs, New York City elite, the crème de la crème of the art world, and all the contributors to the catalog.

Dr. Perlstein had also invited the people in Sweden who had helped us put the show together, including the directors of the

Hilma af Klint Foundation and the curators at the Moderna Museet.

The only person I had personally invited was Marie Cassel. I'd warned her that I hadn't been able to get Anna or any of the other members of De Fem the acknowledgment they deserved, but we'd introduced them and left the door open to further investigation. She was disappointed at first but then rallied, saying a start would have to be enough.

Opening night was a grand gala with all the glitz and glamour we had anticipated and then some. Hilma had captured everyone's imagination.

For me, it was a surreal evening. From that snowy day in Stockholm when I first saw a Hilma af Klint painting and noticed the snail shapes that were identical to the Guggenheim spiral, my life had gone through upheavals both professionally and personally.

I'd almost quit my job, almost lost my job, and in the end redeemed myself with Dr. Perlstein and learned quite a bit along the way. I'd stopped seeing Daphne and had remained unattached for the longest period in my life—no serial dating, no escaping. I'd reconnected with Blythe, learned that I had a child, and then walked out on any chance of meeting that child. I'd spent so much time trying to forgive and understand the decisions that this woman, to whom I was forever connected, had made in keeping our child a secret for so many years.

The evening slipped by in a haze of hands to shake, conversations to engage in, and champagne glasses to sip from, put down and lose, only to pick up another one a few rounds of the room later. The Guggenheim's entire esteemed board of directors was there, as well as friends of the museum and art aficionados from around the globe.

The art took second place to the event. Partially because almost no one could really see the paintings for the crowd. But also because openings were often like that. The serious viewings had happened earlier in the day for the art press and would continue the next day for the top-tier museum members. After that, and for the next six months, members of the public could come and spend time discovering Hilma's paintings for themselves.

I walked home at one a.m. I was exhausted and enormously pleased. It had probably been the best night of my career. Bar none. But there was a sliver of disappointment that shrouded the viewing. Like a splinter that hurts just enough so you can't forget about it. Blythe had not been there.

But I didn't allow myself to dwell on that. The next day was going to be an emotional one. I was going to be escorting Marie Cassel around the exhibit. I'd offered her a private showing before we opened to the public, but she'd declined. She wanted to be there when other people were viewing the exhibit, so she could witness their reactions.

I sat in my living room that night, with a glass of brandy, pulled out my phone, and stared at the screen. I wanted to tell someone what the night had been like. How amazing it was to watch the bedecked crowds catching glimpses of Hilma's stunning paintings as they made their way up the ramp. About the buzz of excitement that signaled the show was going to be huge.

But the only person whom I could think of calling, who

would understand, was Blythe. And we weren't speaking. I knew it was up to me to contact her. To apologize for abandoning her at La Grenouille—and, by extension, for abandoning our child. But something stopped me. Anger? Frustration? Powerlessness? How could she have lied to me for so many years—well, not lied, but hidden the truth from me? Kept me from something that was my right to know?

So I didn't call her. I sipped the drink and then forced myself to go to sleep.

After a dreamless six hours, I woke up to the first day of *Hilma af Klint, Paintings for the Future.*

At eleven a.m., I met Marie Cassel in the foyer of the museum, took her by the arm, and walked her inside. She stood in wonder as she looked at the interior of the building. I saw it through her eyes. The swirl rising up in a graceful arc, higher and higher, ending in a light-filled skylight echoing the building's snail form—the shape that had so captivated Hilma af Klint that she'd wanted to use it for her own temple, while across the ocean another great artist, Frank Lloyd Wright, had the same vision. Two strangers with no connection. Or had there been a connection? A cosmic connection that, like so many things about this show's coming together, about the coincidences that made it happen, about the power of the work, defied logic.

For the first time in my life, I was willing to entertain the idea of a synchronicity that seemed anything but arbitrary. I wanted to laugh at the irony of how Blythe would react to my almost-conversion.

"Shall we?" I asked Marie as I gestured upward.

"Yes," she said with awe and delight.

I took her arm again, and we walked up the ramp to the first landing, where I showed her the information painted on the wall describing Hilma and De Fem.

"'In 1896,'" I read out loud, "'af Klint began to hold regular séances with four other women. Collectively calling themselves "The Five" (De Fem), the group, like other spiritualists of the era, understood their endeavors as a way of obtaining direct access to a higher order of knowledge. All over Scandinavia, the rest of Europe, and America, spiritualism underwent a major revival during the second half of the nineteenth century. Fueled by the latest scientific discoveries being reported almost daily from x-ray technology to the discovery of atoms, all of these new wonders fueled the imagination of both the creative and intellectual communities.'"

After I finished reading, we proceeded walking up to *The Ten Largest*, the wall-filling temple paintings that were on exhibit for the first time in America.

Together, the abstracts told a symbolic story of the cycle of life: going from childhood, to youth, to adulthood, and finally old age. Ben Davis, reporting for Artnet.com, had written about why they were so right for our time.

They are also, to a contemporary eye at least, very feminine, in a way that stands as a pre-rebuttal of the machismo that later came to dominate abstract rhetoric as it rose to art-historical preeminence. The works of "The Ten Largest" are not figurative, but the forms they channel—the blossoms, lacy garlands, and curlicues; the looping, cursive lines of cryptic text that surge across the surface; the palette of pinks and lavenders, peaches and baby blues—draw freshness, to a contemporary eye, from their symbolic associations with feminine iconography.

At the same time, all this is splashed at such a brazen scale that it also undoes period stereotypes of feminine modesty and decorum—though this unleashed expressive freedom was probably itself made possible by the fact that af Klint hardly ever showed these works publicly.

Marie turned away from the paintings and stood, looking at the people walking by and watching their faces.

"Eben, do you remember how I told you once the seasons change, it seems as if the darkness pulls a big wool hat down over all of Stockholm? As it gets darker and darker, when you meet someone on the street, or speak on the phone, it's typical to mention the darkness. And talk about how hard it is to endure. Especially if we have snow and slush as well. But then December twenty-first comes, and the longest night passes. The earth has spun into the position that promises it will soon become lighter. And once that day is done, whenever we see our friends and acquaintances, we say, 'Now it is turning,' and finally we can smile again.

"I hoped this show would reveal not just the part my great-aunt played in Hilma's life, but the part all of De Fem played. I wanted all of those women to be lifted up. For the world to learn about five women who didn't know where they were going or what they could accomplish, who met with nothing but obstacles, but didn't ever give up. And now, here, I feel the darkness is coming to an end. The recognition is on its way. There is much more to do, but you helped take off the wool hat that has been covering De Fem. I can say now, Eben, it's turning! It's getting lighter."

She took my hands in hers. She had tears in her eyes. And to be honest, so did I, and I hugged her. And that was when, over her shoulder, I saw the most amazing sight.

Blythe was coming up the ramp, her blond hair illuminated in the sunshine pouring down from the skylight. And beside her, holding her hand, was a little girl, with that same pale blond hair. Willa was looking up, wonder on her face. But it didn't compare at all to the wonder I was feeling.

Pop must have been what the little swimmer called her grandfather. Not her father.

Blythe had noticed me, and she looked surprised. She probably hadn't thought I'd be on the floor. But she held my eyes as she and Willa climbed toward me and the suite of the cycle-of-life paintings.

I let go of Marie Cassel and raised my hand in greeting to Blythe and walked toward her. It truly was a Hecate moment, I thought, that somehow the child I'd met swimming, whom I'd talked to and admired and helped, was Blythe's daughter.

Was my daughter.

I knew then that I was ready to do what Blythe had told me I needed to do so long ago, to have some faith that if I walked through the hole, I'd find my heart, not lose it.

EPILOGUE

• • • • •

October 1933
Island of Munsö

Standing underneath the skylight of the atelier, bathed in the early-morning rays of the summer sun, Hilma felt the serenity of her decision wash over her. It was no small feat to have reached her seventy-first year and to have Anna again beside her. She had walked into this studio nearly two decades earlier, vowing not to leave until the vision she had received from the spirits was completed. Finally, she was able to say that her life's work was finished, and once it was sealed away, only then would she finally rest.

Hilma looked down at her hands. The paper-thin skin was no longer taut across her bones; it had slackened and creased like unstretched cloth. Yet her spirit still felt vital and strong.

When Anna arrived back at the studio weeks before, a small bag clasped in her age-spotted hand, Hilma had joked with her. "We can't really be this ancient, can we?"

Anna's blue eyes glinted, despite the fine webbing beneath them. Her hair had grown completely white. She had experienced her friend in nearly all of the seasons of her life, from adolescence to old age. She had shared the budding of countless springs with her and the crisp bittersweetness of fall. Now in their autumn years, they were united once again.

"Time has certainly brushed its strokes over us," answered Anna as she stepped inside. "We both knew we would not be immune to what happens to every creature, great and small."

Hilma nodded. "I'm sorry for the mess," she apologized.

The atelier, once filled with open space, was now overrun with finished canvases and stacks of drawings. From the ceiling, long metal hooks dangled from the rafters, and paintings floated like colorful kites in the air. Sketchbooks and towers of ragged-edged notebooks sat stacked on the main table. The floor was so cluttered, one could hardly see it. The only available space was where Hilma now stood, beneath the beautiful skylight window.

Anna remained motionless, breathing Hilma in. They had suffered through periods of hurt feelings, months when only a letter or two passed between them. Yet, Anna always kept her promise to maintain the atelier for Hilma and pay for all of its expenses. Even when she had broken Anna's heart and brought a woman named Thomasine, her mother's former nurse, to live in the studio with her.

Hilma took a step toward her. She wore a long navy smock. At its hem, a smear of white paint flashed across the cotton like a bolt of lightning.

"Thank you for coming . . . for agreeing to help me with all of this. The task of sealing away the paintings is too great for me to do alone."

Anna put down her bag. Hilma, despite the white hair, the wrinkles, and the thin, wiry frame beneath her flowing caftan, still radiated a penetrating light.

"It's good to finally see you again," she said softly. "At this point in our lives, we shouldn't waste any more time. We must do as much as we can to push forward."

"Yes," Hilma agreed. "I have been doing as much as I can to prepare, but I move as slow as a snail now." She smiled. "Who knew that shape would have yet another meaning?"

Anna nodded. "When you painted the *Old Age* series, we did not realize we would one day bend as we do." She touched her back.

"If I sit and ponder, dark clouds come over me. The rejections have been hard. . . . You know how much I worked to see these paintings properly displayed, to see them housed in a temple one day. Disappointment is a cloak that drapes me in shadow." Hilma sighed.

"And yet I refuse to stand still and let these paintings die. I prefer the path of the caterpillar." Her eyes brightened. "This studio is my chrysalis, and my paintings will remain protected in a silken cocoon. Only when the time is right will the doors unlock and my life's work will emerge as a butterfly that the world rejoices to see."

She let out an enormous laugh, delighted at her own words, and for a moment Anna didn't see the silver hair, the stained smock. She only heard Hilma's voice, and it was timeless and beautiful. Within seconds, the exhaustion from her journey and the ache in her bones dissolved, and being in the room again with her friend restored her.

"I must believe that all of this will be understood by those who come after me. . . ." Hilma gestured toward the amassed paintings that surrounded her. Anna's eyes fell on two of the paintings from *The Ten Largest*. It felt good to see them again after so long. She smiled, noting that Cornelia's tiny footprint was still fossilized in the paper.

"I've written down as much explanation as possible. Whoever finds all of this will have a lot to read." Hilma gestured toward the table. "There are thousands of pages explaining everything we did in the Friday Night Club, and what I continued in the years after. . . ."

"You have been tireless in your work," Anna acknowledged as she appraised the room. "But are you sure this is the only way? You're shutting away so much, Hilma. Who knows what will happen in twenty years? Europe is heading toward dark times; you read the papers. . . . This man Adolf Hitler, he is a madman, and I worry how the world will suffer. . . ."

Hilma nodded. "He is a terrible devil. I can hardly read the headlines anymore about what he's doing in Germany." Her voice was filled with disgust.

"So, you ask me if I worry; if this is the right thing to do?" Hilma shook her head.

"I think it's the only thing to do, Anna. If they are burning books in Germany, imprisoning the artists and intellectuals, who knows how safe any of us will be . . . ?"

Anna was quiet.

"I'm too old to worry about myself. It's the art, and *only* the art, that concerns me now."

* * * * *

The ladder to the loft was not easy to climb. Anna held her bag in one hand and slowly made her way up. On the top level were a bed for sleeping and a wooden desk, its entire surface covered with more papers. She pulled out the chair and sat down. The desk overlooked a small window. The view of the pine trees, the lake a strip of blue just beyond, was a welcome landscape that settled her. She had felt anxious during the long journey from Stockholm, but now a sense of peace and contentment came over her. She was happy to see the studio perhaps for the last time, and she would stay as long as it took to help Hilma get everything in order.

When Anna received Hilma's letter beseeching her for help, her first instinct was to decline the invitation. Anna's health had been fragile for some time. Her lungs were severely weakened from a lifetime of asthma, and packing up notebooks and storing away enormous canvases were not easy tasks for any woman, particularly a seventy-three-year-old one. And then there was the pain of being with Hilma once again, a woman who held her close and pushed her away for almost her entire adult life. It was a dance that she now thought she should sit out.

But the pull of Hilma was too strong. In the weeks before she answered the letter, Hilma began visiting her in her dreams. She always appeared in a white smock, her hair loosened from its bun. She hovered over Anna like a wraith, pleading with her to make the journey. Only when she finally sat down and wrote a letter saying yes, she'd come and help pack everything away, did the apparitions cease to appear.

Anna now looked at the bed. It had been years since she had slept in it. There had been others who had slept beneath the linen with Hilma, and she pushed the thoughts of them to another part of her mind.

"I will come if it's only us," she wrote. *"I'm too old to pretend it would be acceptable any other way."*

"Of course. You alone will always be my chou chou," Hilma answered.

As Anna now settled into the loft, she was confident she had made the right decision in coming. Her vow to always support Hilma was something she intended to honor until her last breath. She opened the window, happy to inhale the fresh air.

· · · · ·

They inhabited the space between them with respect and genuine care. Each morning, Anna awakened and tiptoed past a sleeping Hilma, the stack of paintings wrapped in brown paper, her body folded into a chair.

She walked slowly down the earthen path, breathing in the scents of juniper and pine. Sometimes she felt the breath of her sister on her neck, Lotten's voice reminding her to savor the beauty around her. Other times she gazed at the red roses and remembered how Hilma had once placed one behind her ear.

With each journey outside the studio, she felt her burdens

disappear, and when she returned to the atelier, she was ready to do whatever was asked of her.

In the final weeks, when nearly every canvas had been prepared as Hilma intended, she would receive her final task.

"The private notebooks that I've put upstairs, the letters, the diaries—all of that now needs to be burned," Hilma instructed. "Read whatever you'd like beforehand, but I do not want any of my personal details to remain."

· · · · ·

The letters and postcards had been amassed over five decades of friendship, a connection that transcended more than most could ever understand. For days, as Hilma worked tirelessly making the final preparations so that everything would withstand the cold and dampness of the Swedish winters, Anna read through all of the correspondence and diaries that Hilma intended to burn.

She knew Hilma believed this was a gift to Anna, to allow her to immerse herself in their unique story one last time. The diaries that had been put aside for her began with Hilma as a teenager. The first entry was dated September 1879, when Hilma mentioned meeting a new girl on the first day of art school.

"She is slender and bright with copper hair. . . . She isn't afraid of my bossy nature. On the contrary, she seems to grow in it, like it's nourishing water that feeds her soul. . . . I'm happy to have a new friend."

There were postcards they exchanged with each other during their travels with their families. Some were created on pieces of watercolor paper on which they had painted with their own hands images that inspired them. Anna recognized several she had sent to Hilma over the years, one with an impressionistic painting of the flowers outside her bedroom window on Lake Mälaren. Another was of the trees near the house in Åre.

As she continued to read through the written exchanges between them, Anna discovered within the pages of one of Hilma's diaries a card addressed to her but never sent. On the outside was a sketch of the Helsinki Cathedral, from a trip that Hilma had taken to visit her mother's Finnish relatives. On the inside, Hilma had written a note. *"I miss you, dear friend. The lakes shimmer like glass. When I see my reflection, I see a part of myself is missing. . . . How I wish you were here."*

When she finally came to the notebook from their trip to Italy, the one that contained the intimate drawings that had gotten them into so much trouble during the last year of the Friday Night Club, Anna felt that it was too private for her to read. She knew how she felt about that time they had shared, but she and Hilma had never spoken openly about it. It had always felt to Anna that if she had tried to put words to the experience, she would only sully it somehow.

"Are you certain you don't mind me looking through these pages?" She came down the stairs holding the notebook carefully between two hands, as though it were a piece of ceramic that could break.

Hilma's eyes lifted. She laid down the brown wrapping paper she held in her hands.

"Everything you are to me exceeds what is written on those pages, what is drawn in pencil, or colored in with paint." She stood up and brushed off the dust on her apron. "When I look around the room and I see this lifetime of work, I know it wouldn't have been possible without you. . . . But my private pages, from my time with you in Italy—I will not have them fall into the wrong hands again. It will only be my work that remains long after I am gone."

Anna stepped closer. In the past few days, more space had been created in the room as the wrapped paintings were stacked flat on top of one another with rolled newsprint cushioning in between.

Hilma moved toward her until the two of them met just beneath the skylight window. It was past midnight, and the moon was only now just emerging from the clouds.

Anna blinked away tears. "You used to say you needed to understand the universe, that painting allowed you to make sense of all the chaos. . . ."

"Yes, that's right," Hilma said as she reached to touch Anna's hand, the skin so transparent, her blue veins appeared to float just beneath the surface.

"I'm so grateful to have this time with you. Seeing you again has helped settle the unrest inside my heart." She pulled Hilma close and kissed her softly on the cheek.

· · · · ·

The last morning, she looked through all the papers one final time. She reread the pages that had moved her most deeply and glanced at images of her twenty-two-year-old self, naked and ripe, captured in the deft pencil strokes of Hilma's hand. On the back of the page, Hilma had written simply, *"My Anna."*

"All of it must be burned." Hilma's words floated in Anna's ears. Part of her was relieved that this chapter of their lives would remain private, particularly after the heartache that had happened when it had fallen into the wrong hands.

But when she came upon the black-and-white portrait of De Fem, she paused. The image took her back to when they posed for it. She smiled looking at Hilma in the black suit and hat, the mischievous grin alight on her face. Her finger touched the face of beautiful Cornelia, the intense stare of Sigrid, and even cranky Mathilda with her cigar. She missed all of these women. She could never allow the flames to engulf that one lasting relic of their time together.

Anna slipped the photograph into her pocket and placed a hand over it. She would protect their memory not with fire, but rather with her own warmth.

· · · · ·

The plume of smoke rose skyward as it feasted on the diary pages and the intimate drawings that were meant for no other eyes but theirs.

As Anna watched the fire rise, Hilma approached and touched her shoulder. "There is one last letter to be burned," she announced. "I wrote it late last night. I felt compelled to make everything in my heart clear, so I can finally be at peace." She handed the fresh envelope to Anna, leaving her alone to open it.

The paper was as thin as onionskin, the writing as delicate as silken thread.

My dear Anna,

The studio is almost fully enveloped in darkness except for a pale moonbeam that comes from the skylight above. You are asleep upstairs, and this beautiful space feels exquisitely whole now that you have briefly returned.

As you know, I have never been the sentimental type. But the weight of old age is heavy upon me now, and I am overcome with a sense of urgency to be clear with you. Who knows how long we will have together once the monumental task of packing everything away is done? So, to ensure I leave this world knowing you have heard my feelings through my own hand, I pick up my pen to write these words to you, a gesture to make certain there is never any doubt of how much you have always meant to me.

From the moment I first saw you walking toward me on the steps of our art school, I felt someone had thrown a golden lasso around my heart. Your bright, searching eyes. Your noble gait and, what I was soon to learn, your curious mind. Anna, I had never had a friend like you before that moment, nor after.

You were the one who stood beside me when I was criticized for being too arrogant, the friend who never once let me believe that I wasn't as talented as those artists whose work was displayed on Blanch's walls. You alone, Anna, gave me a space to paint; you helped purchase the supplies. When I was in a foul mood, you forgave. When I became entwined with others, you still continued to love.

The spirits showed us that the universe can be explained through color and line, words and shapes. But they did not dare give us the code to unlock the great mystery of love. And I wonder if that is because what makes love beautiful is that it can never actually be explained.

It is a twist of irony that we see our lives in hindsight, a story told backward, when we reach the age we are now. But finally, I must draw open the curtain and acknowledge all that you've done for me. So read these words, my cherished friend, my true beloved. And know that you will remain my eternal swan, who lives within my heart forever.

Always yours,
Hilma

Anna's hands trembled with emotion. After all these years, she finally felt seen.

She placed her hand on her pocket, wishing to put Hilma's letter with the photograph of De Fem.

But she could not betray her friend, despite wanting to hold on to those written words that she had waited a lifetime to hear.

Anna lifted the letter and dropped it into the flames.

• • • • •

"My work here is now done," Hilma said as she went outside to retrieve Anna. "We only need to shut the doors and go."

Anna walked over to her and handed her an envelope that contained some of the ash she'd collected. "I took some of the cinders from the fire," she explained. "Tuck it someplace safe so it can rest among all the other sacred things."

Hilma nodded. "I'll lay it on top, so it is like the hearts and organs they put inside the tombs of the pharaohs to keep their treasure secure."

• • • • •

The bonfire was now just dust and glowing embers. Anna accepted Hilma's hand, and they entered the studio one last time. Gone were the pinwheel drawings floating from the rafters, and the easels were now pushed into a corner. The enormous temple paintings were laid flat, carefully wrapped and covered with a blanket. The notebooks that set out to explain the symbols and thoughts behind the paintings were all packed away in boxes.

Anna had to close her eyes to bring it all back into color.

They locked the doors, and Hilma threaded her hand into Anna's. A gentle breeze rippled through the trees, and both women inhaled the crisp, restorative air.

Hilma stopped midstep and turned to her. Her lined face softened as she soaked in Anna's features.

"I meant what I said in my letter. You never left me . . . even when you were mad at me. You forgave. You continued to pay to maintain this place so I could work here freely." Her withered hand reached to touch Anna's face.

"I have always believed in you, Hilma."

"We never married; we didn't have children, but we're still leaving something beautiful behind, aren't we?"

Anna's hand gripped Hilma's tightly, using all of her strength. "I believe that for some people children are their legacy, while for others it is their music, their writing, their art . . .

but in all cases, we as human beings are compelled to leave something here on this earth that contributes to the future."

For the first time in her memory, Anna thought she saw tears form in Hilma's eyes, and the sheer emotion of it overwhelmed her.

"One thing, however, that I am certain of, my friend . . . is that the name Hilma af Klint will not be forgotten." Anna took a deep breath. "That is something I know with all my conviction. Your paintings will one day be unlocked and shared for all the world to see."

AUTHORS' NOTE

· · · · ·

The inspiration for our novel, *The Friday Night Club*, first came about after a visit to the Hilma af Klint exhibition *Paintings for the Future* at the Guggenheim Museum in New York in 2019.

At the museum, one of us noticed a small caption underneath a black-and-white photograph of Hilma that mentioned the artist had created a special group called the Friday Night Club, which consisted of her and four other women—Anna Cassel, Cornelia Cederberg, Mathilda Nilsson, and Sigrid Hedman—who gathered each week to provide one another artistic and spiritual sustenance and often performed séances in an attempt to channel spirits to guide them in their work. None of the other four were mentioned anywhere else in the exhibit, and, as we later learned, for all intents and purposes, they have since been relegated to being just a footnote in the now famous and celebrated Hilma's personal history. Immediately, the question of who these four women were began to simmer, and the idea of a novel started to unfold around our desire to discover more about them.

At the heart of any good novel are questions that propel the author on a quest for more information and insight to glean a better understanding of the chosen subject matter. We wanted to learn what drove them to come together to seek higher knowledge and to pursue an artistic endeavor like *The Paintings for the Temple* at a time when women had such few opportunities outside of their traditional roles as wives, mothers, and home-makers.

Once we began our preliminary research, we immediately sensed the basis of a historical novel in which the voices of Hilma and the other four women could be brought back to life more than one hundred years after their time together at the turn of the twentieth century. We were profoundly struck by the beauty and timeliness of what De Fem was founded upon: five women yearning for wisdom, creative independence, and a sense of purpose.

Many times, we felt that the "spirits" were indeed with us, guiding us in strange and unexpected directions as our project unfolded. It became a joke among ourselves that "Hilma" was helping us find the correct way to tell her story. There were chapters that somehow got "magically" erased on our Drop-box or for which the same plot idea came to each of us inde-pendently. When COVID–19 struck and we were all sheltered in place, on different continents and in different time zones, having a novel to work on together that was centered upon collaborative artistic energy lent even deeper meaning to the project. Those daily calls and brainstorming sessions became a lifeline for us.

· · · · ·

It is important to note that the present-day portion of this book was largely inspired by the show at the Guggenheim, which ran from October 12, 2018 to April 23, 2019, but that the museum personnel, the funding issues, the solutions, the legal ramifications, the protests, and even the merchandise we mention are all imagined by us. Only the paintings we refer to and the dates are the same. Also, our characters from these sections, including Eben Elliot and his boss, Dr. Perlstein, are not based on real people and instead were created entirely from our imaginations. Similarly, while the Hilma af Klint Foundation does exist in real life, our version is fictional, as are the people we portray working there.

Marie Cassel, whom we mention in the novel, is in fact Anna Cassel's great-niece, and we are eternally grateful for her support and for helping to bring Anna to life. It should be noted that Anna actually had four sisters, but we've focused our attention only on her relationship with Lotten in our novel. Bia Lamke also generously shared her family's memories of Cornelia, Mathilda, and Anders. We are also immensely grateful to our wonderful and dedicated agents, Julia Angelin and Sally Wofford-Girand, who placed this novel around the world, and to Kate Seaver and the Berkley team for their passion and support. Thank you to Hedvig Ersman for expressing an interest in this project from the very beginning and for answering any questions we sent her way. We are equally thankful for

Yvette Lee's and Marty Bax's help with our research, as well as for the Royal Library in Stockholm, which offered us the opportunity to read through existing copies of *Efteråt* magazine, allowing us to discover the written voices of Mathilda and Sigrid still preserved in time. The questions and doubts that Eben raises about Hilma and De Fem are in part questions and doubts that others have raised previously but none have ever answered definitively, as far as we can discern. So, while this book is our effort to use fiction to wonder and perhaps suggest what might have been, it is also a testament to our own artistic beliefs and values.

At its core, *The Friday Night Club* is rooted in what it means to be an artist and to have a circle of friends who support your desire to leave something of meaning behind in this world. It is about forcing yourself into uncharted territory, being brave, and having the conviction to stay true to your vision, despite the pressures and the skeptics of the outside world. Hilma af Klint created artwork that was revolutionary in her lifetime, yet until recently was universally dismissed, misunderstood, or ignored. Even the survival of the paintings was a miracle, for they existed for decades in an attic without any professional preservation, an example of the artwork's defiance against all odds. It is a shame she and De Fem were not alive in 2019 to see the six hundred thousand people who bought tickets to view the exhibit at the Guggenheim, the largest attendance of any Guggenheim exhibit ever. It seems she was right. She was painting for the future.

THE
FRIDAY
NIGHT
CLUB

. . . . .

Sofia Lundberg

Alyson Richman

M.J. Rose

READERS GUIDE

QUESTIONS FOR DISCUSSION

•••••

1. At its core, *The Friday Night Club* is about the artist's pursuit to search and understand the universe. Do you feel a connection with Hilma and De Fem's quest to find deeper meaning in the world around them? Do you admire their perseverance, since they had so little support from society and the artistic world?

2. Exploration of the atom, the X-ray, and other scientific discoveries contributed much to Hilma's artistic vision. Can you think of examples of how art and science inspire each other today?

3. To get funding for the exhibition, Eben navigates a very politicized art world. How museums must navigate getting such financial support from corporate sponsors has been in the news recently. Do you feel getting funding to promote the arts justifies ethical compromises?

4. Hilma and De Fem created a very modern and proto-feminist agenda that was ahead of its time. What do you think inspired them to be independent and forward-thinking when all around them women were being relegated to the roles of mothers and wives?

5. Eben describes himself as an art detective. Have you ever thought of museum curators as art detectives? What aspect of Eben's job did you find the most surprising or interesting?

6. Hilma and Anna had a lifelong friendship and possibly a love affair. Do you feel that their relationship influenced their art and the creation of the *Paintings for the Temple*?

7. Spiritualism and belief in paranormal activity are often met with cynicism and doubt. How do you feel these subjects were portrayed in the book? Do you feel these women were connected to a higher power?

8. Would it change your opinion of a piece of art if the attributed artist didn't work alone? Would it change your opinion of the artist?

Photo by Oskar Lundberg

Sofia Lundberg is a journalist and former magazine editor. Her debut novel, *The Red Address Book*, has been published in thirty-seven territories worldwide. Lauded by critics for her ability to sweep readers off their feet and take them on journeys through time and space, love and loss, Lundberg is the shining star of heartwarming— and heart-wrenching—Scandinavian fiction. She lives in Stockholm with her son.

SalomonssonAgency.se/Sofia-Lundberg

Alyson Richman is the *USA Today* and #1 international bestselling author of several historical novels, including *The Velvet Hours, The Garden of Letters,* and *The Lost Wife,* which is currently in development for a major motion picture. Alyson graduated from Wellesley College with a degree in art history and Japanese studies. She is an accomplished painter and her novels combine her deep love of art, historical research, and travel. Alyson's novels have been published in twenty-five languages and have reached the bestseller lists both in the United States and abroad. She lives with her husband and two children on Long Island, where she is currently at work on her next novel.

AlysonRichman.com

Photo by Doug Scofield

M.J. Rose is a *New York Times* and *USA Today* best-selling author who grew up in New York City exploring the labyrinthine galleries of the Metropolitan Museum of Art and the dark tunnels and lush gardens of Central Park. She is the author of more than a dozen novels published in more than thirty countries; the founder of the first marketing company for authors, AuthorBuzz.com; and cofounder of 1001DarkNights .com. The TV show *Past Life* was based on her Reincarnationist series.

MJRose.com

Ready to find
your next great read?

Let us help.

Visit prh.com/nextread

Penguin
Random
House